Silencing the Women:

The Witch Trials of Mary Bliss Parsons

Kathy-Ann Becker

'15

Published by BookLocker.com, Inc., Bradenton, Florida.

Printed in the United States of America.

This is a work of historical fiction, based on actual persons and events. The author has taken creative liberty with many details to enhance the reader's experience.

BookLocker.com, Inc.
2013

First Edition

Disclaimer

This story is biographical fiction. All the characters are real. All reflections upon persons who have lived are intentional by the author and are documented by town, county, and court records. Some of the events are fictionalized and are based upon historical evidence and/or upon perceptions translated by the family Muse.

Cover Painting Credit

The cover is a painting entitled "Halloween" by artist, Donna Horn.

Dedication

To my father, The Reverend Wells E. Behee, Masters of Divinity, for his doctrine of love and his hopeful wrestling with free will; and to my mother, Mary, for keeping our feet on the ground. This is the continuation of a project they started together.

Acknowledgements

This story is the brainchild of my parents. They nurtured this project from its infancy. As genealogists do, they drove hundreds of miles to remote libraries and graveyards to search out the threads of family history. They helped me discover my multiple great-grandmother and great-grandfather's stories. When my father's mind lost its way, my mother continued. She critiqued my earlier manuscripts diligently, and showed off the drafts to her friends at church and in the community. My parents were killed together in a car accident before she could see the completion of this book. May her pride be warranted.

A great deal of this book was written in Newfoundland, my seasonal home for the last thirty years. Hearing old English dialects enriched the language of this story.

Friends and family have contributed to this book. My friend and pretend-adopted son, Don Chapin, was the first person to encourage me at a timely moment. Most notable proofreaders, literary advisors, and editors were: Mary and Wells Behee, Myron Becker, David Brule, Louise Cochran, Kate Fiduccia, Jim Levinson, Carolyn Manley, Rosie Pearson, Chris Pollock, Alys Terrien Queen, Chris Queen, Karen Scotti Scannell, and Ann Wright. These people devoted a significant amount of time improving the book you hold in your hands. I am grateful to all of these people for their help in unburying the voice of Mary Bliss Parsons.

To my circle of family and friends, unnamed, who have been so special in sustaining me, thank you for your encouragement. I remember and hold dear what you have done. To my extended family, all the branches of you everywhere in the world, here is a piece of you. To everyone descended from the Puritan dream, here is what we are made of.

Prologue: Northampton, Massachusetts

Ancient memories welled out of the fragrant thawing ground.
An old sorrow stirred in the raw earth where it had been pressed.
Something had happened here long ago.
Someone had been here, grieving, looking over the town.

A disturbing event occurred during the early spring thaw of 1972. It was something that I could not explain and did not report. I was twenty-one years old, a recent arrival to Northampton. Drawn from Ohio by the love of my future husband, I had secured a new and ideal job at Forbes Library as Stack Supervisor. I had the responsibility of overseeing that books in the main collection were properly shelved with quiet orderliness and due care. When something unusual began to occur, I decided not to mention it in order to protect the decorum of my work-place persona.

The odd thing began on the first warmish Monday at the end of winter. That day the air was so fresh and the sun so bright that, on impulse, I left my homemade lunch behind in the stuffy break room. I walked right out through the high arched doors of the massive granite and sandstone building into the brilliant sunshine. The feeling of oncoming spring was elating. I decided to take a walk down the street. I had just turned out of the library yard and started the descent toward town when I was startled by a powerful sense that a person was in trouble. I looked around to see if someone might be in need of help. I could find no one showing any appearance of distress. I shrugged off the feeling of concern and went on, being a little more careful than usual in watching out for traffic as I crossed the intersection.

The next day I went out again. A bad feeling stopped me in exactly the same place. The sense of warning was very strong. Something was wrong, but I could not see it. On the third day, I left the library determined to walk fast and let nothing stop me. It was a plain, grey day with no wind and no hint of storm. Ugly heaps of filthy snow remained near the curb, pockmarked with melt holes and bits of trash. Trying not to see any of it, I stepped over the spot where I had been bothered without breaking stride. With my next footfall, instead of moving ahead, I stopped. An invisible sadness held me heavily. I could not push through it without denying that I cared.

I scanned the nearby buildings. I wondered if perhaps a person inside one of them was trying to get my attention. The sidewalk where I stood lay before an old house with slightly parted curtains. I furtively peeked toward its windows. I watched for a face or any flutter of response. There was no answering movement behind the curtains or any sense of relationship between the house and the pool of despair just beyond its dooryard. There was another nearby building in the square, a weathered brick church with a massive wooden bell tower that filled the sky with the cool calm grace of an aged church that has sheltered its members for many generations. I felt no comfort from its congregation for the one whose grief filled this place.

Any source of worry was unidentifiable. I decided simply to wait there once and for all to see what would happen, trying to look nonchalant under the eyes of anyone who might notice. I stood listening and watching. When awareness did come, it was of the salt-stained sidewalk, of the ground heaving below it.

Beneath the concrete, living soils were imperceptibly flexing in the thaw. In tiny crevices between the fines of fragmented rock crystals and the residues of ancient humus, breathless air was warming. Long frozen energies were waking. A subtle earth-bound rhythm emanated from the darkness. An old, faint echo seemed to be vibrating within the hillside. The pulse of blood beating in my feet and legs responded with a sensation of warmth. My mind filled with a slow chant: "A woman stood here in great pain."

Standing in that place, a waking dream opened to me. A long skirt brushed across coarse grasses. At the whispering sound, buildings disappeared. Without church spires to punctuate the encircling mountain ranges, the broad plains of the Connecticut River spread out below, vast and primeval. Thin wisps of smoke from the fires of Indians and white settlers rose up from a sparsely habited plantation. Areas of human activity showed as dark specks upon the immensity of meadowland. Although the open expanse was huge, it was dwarfed by the surrounding green forest of massive trees: elm, sycamore, maple, oak, beech, and chestnut. Only the sky held back the limitlessness of the reaching green canopy. Trees marched up and over the far horizons, covering chains of low mountains in dark greenery that turned black in the distance. Each shrouded range hid others behind it. The wall of infinity was penetrated only by the secret eyes of nature.

The vision that filled my eyes was vivid and bright. It lasted for only a moment. When it faded, I knew one thing. I was standing in the footsteps of a woman who had been here long before ground was broken for home or church. She was gone, but her story was not.

Retreating to the library, I began to search for facts, curious if the message in the land could be confirmed. Within faded books were bountiful histories of the early settlement of the Connecticut River Valley with descriptions of the great effort it had taken to travel overland across rivers, mountains, and swamps to penetrate this magnificent hidden paradise. Many great natural obstacles had barred the way. Then as now, the unusually oriented east west peaks of the Holyoke Range jutted in a long looming line across the valley. Before the face of these massive mountains, the southerly flowing river slowed and widened silently coiling into a huge oxbow. Not stopped in its way to the sea, the river's tongue licked a widening hole for itself through the mountains. Revenging bedrock ledges shredded the sluicing surge into a wild cataract. The river roared over rapids, dropping nearly sixty feet in a mist of tumbling foam.

Threading around these barriers of water and rock were narrow trails made by the feet of wild animals and the native people who followed them. Over these faint web-works of paths the white settlers had come; by horseback, oxcart, and by foot. For the woman whose skirts had rustled here in Northampton so long ago, the hard-attained view of this beautiful valley must have offered both promise and warning. The possibility of a ready escape from it had been left far behind. She had traveled to the brink of the absolute unknown with only a meadow to buffer her from the unrelenting heathen wilderness.

My curiosity brought me back to the hillside to revisit it with speculations. The soils had warmed under the weekend sun and become stable. The bright slapping beat of sneakers and sandals and the ticking of high heels had replaced antique subterranean reverberations. The women who walked around me were shoppers headed at a brisk clip for the Green Street boutiques or patrons intent upon a purpose at Forbes Library and Smith College co-eds grouped for forays into town. Rooftops hid the mountains. Church steeples made peace with the endlessness of the sky. As a balm and a farewell to the sad woman from another time, I offered a stamp of my own feet upon the sidewalk that entombed the place where I had experienced her mystery. There was something I needed to know about this place. I did not know what.

One night twenty years later, my father called excitedly to tell me about his genealogical research. He announced with relish that I had inadvertently returned to a place where ancestors had once made their lives, where descendants still lived unknown to us. He had discovered that our ancestors were early settlers of Northampton. One of them, his great-grandmother of nine generations, had been accused of witchcraft.

"That means" he said, "that your multiple great-grandmother is the Witch of Northampton." He paused for effect. As a minister, he knew how to deliver his points. The title of "witch" was unexpectedly unpleasant. Nothing my father said was familiar, yet his words rang intimately with my own uneasy thoughts about the unknown woman in pain upon the hillside. The earth at Northampton was indeed full of stories. Mary Bliss Parsons became a family research project. Images of her filled my mind. Sometimes I felt as if I were living two lives simultaneously.

She had been among the early Puritan planters at a time when the land at Nonotuck was the most northerly edge of settlement on the Connecticut River. Each man and family had been chosen for the skills they could contribute to the effort of building a peaceful, Godly, and profitable paradise. All the settlers labored with devotion in a land of new hope. Their survival depended upon wariness to the ever-present dangers. To them, the raw land was unredeemed of pagan sins and concealed a familiarity with evil. If disturbed, malignant spirits and old savage demons moved in disguise to visit inexplicable punishments of accident and ailment, affliction and torment. There were signs that the

Devil hid his cloven hoof prints among the deer tracks in the morning dew of the meadows. Overly familiar mice squeezed into the settlers' homes, skittering along the rafters to spy upon the God-fearing with little black knowing eyes, looking for openings to Satan-prick a soul. Incautious speech, an uncomfortable look, a suspicious action, the rancor of jealousy were all intolerable to the necessary vigilance. Every breach in the fragile balances holding people together broke bonds and let in fear.

When things began to go wrong in the young community, the cause had to be found. Fingers began to point at Mary Bliss Parsons. Because of her husband's uncanny successes, she was too rich. Her beauty was too distracting. The challenge of her intelligent outspokenness was too uncomfortably provocative. Eyes followed her. Festering in the insinuations of gossip, an ugly taint of doubt tightened inextricably around her. It is suspected, even today, that because of her pride, she caused and deserved her fate.

Court records spanning a time of eighteen years reveal the minds of those who sought evidence upon which to judge Mary Bliss Parsons as innocent or guilty. The testimony reveals an unholy alliance created by the elite and self-selected brotherhood of men who controlled government, religion, and the marketplace. To this, Mary Bliss Parsons, like all women, was expected to contribute only her contrition. Her accusers' words drip familiarly with the poisons injected by that which feeds greedily in webs spun of fear. Like all public tragedies, time has dimmed recollection. The effects still run in the veins of people living. In the echoes of the pulse of her blood are warnings that can still be heard.

It is said that the themes of time repeat rhythmically until the lessons are learned. We can meet the soft echoes of those whose blood we sustain. Muse upon the mind of Mary Bliss Parsons, who is gone three hundred years. Her struggle to reach grace is now in your hands.

Chapter 1

Suffer a Witch

Boston Jail, Massachusetts, March 1674

My accuser told the Judge,
"I know she is of the Devil,
for I cannot have my mind
from her."

From this prison cell where I am kept, all my life seems so long ago. This time is like not living. The grip of the damp and cold shrinks my insides against my bones in shivering cramps and burning numbness. My neck and shoulders and all my joints pain. My empty arms ache to hold my babies; my hands to grasp a spoon, a broom, or any common thing from home. I must not think of my body except to keep it alive, but not to feel its hurt.

A week ago, I stood before the court to answer accusations of being a witch. I was clean, warm, and confident. I expected that the judges would never believe the petty accusations against me. I presented myself before the court as a sign of respect. I thought I would be going home with my husband that very day.

Instead, the Judges questioned whether I have the fear of God before my eyes. I realized that their first duty was to preserve the Massachusetts Bay Company, not to protect me. Suddenly it became apparent that my troubles were not about to end. The judges ordered that I appear before the next session of court. The next session of the court will not be held until May. That is almost three months from now. Worse than anything I could have imagined, they ordered that I be held in prison until then.

The world has seemingly gone mad. It is my enemies who cause me to be judged by man and by the deceits of the Devil. I have done no wrong.

I have my mind and my beliefs. That is all I have. Somehow, I must protect my mind from the fear and grief that threatens to overwhelm me here in the unspeakable horror of this jail. When the judges call me, I must be ready. By the time I come before the court in May to answer to the charge of witchcraft, I must know how to convince them of my innocence. I am innocent.

I pace this dark stinking cell in tight circles. I try to warm myself. I try to hold back the cold walls from smothering me. When I walk, I remember. I am a wife, a mother, an honest woman of forty-six years. I have nine good children living. The youngest is only two years old. My children, how I ache to be with them. My father would be shocked to see me here. How my mother must be suffering that she cannot save me. My parents fled England to escape imprisonment such as this.

I am not alone here. Eleven other women prisoners surround me. Their crowding presence is unpleasant and gives no comfort. None is behaving better than a trapped animal. Some have gone silent, but others clamor incessant moaning rants or prayers that are swallowed up by the hissing darkness that surrounds us.

Without day or night to guide me, I have begun to swirl into blackness without landmarks. Do not let me fall toward the death that threatens to consume me, nor to the darkness and cold, nor to this filth, nor to the jealousies of lies, nor succumb to shame. Do not let me slip away as an unrecognizable corruption to my husband, my children, and my mother. Help me to find a way.

Today, Lord, I declare to You my commitment to live. I have begun to create a discipline for myself. I have noticed that a feeling of light comes when I think back upon my life. I must refuse to see the walls, the floor, or the blank eyes of those around me, or anything that holds me here. Beginning this day, I will close out the ugly things around me that beckon me to lose my truth and trust. I will turn toward the brightness and color that once lit my days. I will practice recalling everything. Until the calamities are past, I will discipline myself to cry unto You through my memories that You may enlighten my darkness.

16

Try me, O God, and know my heart: Prove me and know my thoughts; and consider if there be any wickedness in me,and lead me in the way forever. (Psalm 140: 23-24)

Chapter 2

Instructive Stories of Evil and Resistance

Recalling England

I can trust my thoughts only to You, my Creator. Here is my story. I pray that You will accept it as my offering. It is all that I have to bring to You.

Do not take my withdrawal from the ponderous pomposity of earthly ministers who use Your name to crown themselves as pulpit princes to be a sign that I have forsaken You. No, my Father, for the sake of my family, accept me as Yours. Return to my soul the strength of those who came before me.

You know that my family was among those faithful saints elected by You to purify Your church of papist pomp. I am raised as one of those elected by You, Lord, to seek salvation, to worship in the pure simple ways You desire of us. We are the worshipful, whose work is to purify society and ourselves. It is difficult for us because the Devil has many devious ways to trick people into believing that they work in Your name.

From the first, when I was just a child, I remember becoming aware that many around us laughed at the way our brethren stubbornly honored the holy Sabbath. We were derided and called Puritans for living simply in the essence of Your Scripture.

The urgency of Your commands to resist evil is a necessity I suckled from my mother's milk. Mother insisted that I learn to hold fast to my faith even when all else was taken from us. I learned early that the earth is full of cruelty and dark places. Obedience to Your laws has been my only certain sustenance since I left my mother's arms.

Father told me stories about who we are and the promises we keep in trust with our bond of love for You. He told each of my brothers and sisters the same stories, as they reached the right age to hear. Father's stories were given as a warning that even though we gather before You as Your faithful congregation, quiet avoidance of trouble offers no promise of protection.

The stories of my father were about the Bliss family and the reigns of wicked kings and queens who had tried to turn us from You. Long before I was born, generations of Blisses lived as farmers in the west country of England. Because of Your generosity, my family had prospered. They lived worshipfully and simply upon rolling meadows and gentle fields. They rejoiced when the Protestants of Europe overthrew the domination of the Catholic pope. They survived the turmoil of the Reformation. They remained hopeful that the Calvinist creed would at last eliminate the scourge of Catholic ceremony from their plain style of worship. Desire for purity in obedience to You was shown by their dress and in every aspect of their lives. They strove toward You in a world of imperfection, as my father said.

Father spoke of a time when there was a hope that the Reformation would end the oppressive divisiveness of religious disagreements. Instead of freedom came new laws. It came to be that one king succumbed to the temptation to exalt himself by royal theological presumption. King James had a new version of the Bible made, and then by his decree, outlawed all other English versions of the Bible except his own authorized translation. Possession of our Holy Geneva Bible became a felony offense. With our Bibles open before us, our plain observance of Sunday as the holy Sabbath became a criminal act to the Crown.

Father said that many of our countrymen bowed down before the power of such earthly rulers. Our brethren stood firm, bowing our heads only in prayer. These stories Father told me as a child make me understand that we who are known as Puritans are different and are special in our relationship to You, God. I am proud to be among those called Puritan.

Father's best stories were about our own family. Father told me about a bad thing that happened to our very own relative, John Bliss. Father lamented that under the reign of King James it had become quite popular to celebrate Sunday as a holiday for games and sports and other follies rather than as a holy day for undistracted worship. That is how it came to be that one Sabbath, when Goodman Bliss was on his way to church, he happened upon a bear-baiting spectacle on the village green. He and the fellow who was with him looked away so as not to witness debauchery. They did not see that the enraged bear, tortured by dogs, had escaped. They stood in the bear's path. The panicked animal fell upon Goodman Bliss in its madness. He died of mauling there on the road, surrounded by gawking revelers.

Father said that even though our relative was probably a good man, he fatally ignored Your lessons meant to temper us to vigilance. Closing one's eyes to vulgarity does not hold its threat at bay. Father asked that I vow to him that I keep my eyes ever alert to the quiet workings of the hand of Satan.

To teach me that earthly kings were not our heavenly Father, my father told a story about himself. King Charles, who was King James successor, reacted to the steadfast resistance of our brethren by ordering his soldiers out into the country to enforce his laws. My father was among the brave English patriots who cut their hair to just below their ears as a sign that they were not King's men. The men's fashion at the King's court was for long and curling locks.

My Father said that, as a young man, he lived in a countryside growing increasingly violent with the King's excesses. Their only protection from the King lay in the Puritan domination of Parliament. As Father described it to me, one day all the men of his church rose up in full strength against the Crown. The thirty men of his congregation set out for London as an escort for their Parliament member. They intended to speak out their righteous concerns before the King and the Archbishop.

My grandfather, Father, and two uncles holstered their pistols into their saddles and rode with their brethren, mounted upon handsome matching iron-grey horses. Together in their battle against the evils that had beset England, the band of determined believers thundered into London astride their best horses. Their dark cloaks streamed behind them. Their black hats were set firmly against the wind.

They went to the floor of Parliament as planned. Father said they carried themselves with dignity as they stood as a group before the assembly. The most able speakers among them spoke pointedly and eloquently. They did not know that among the audience at Parliament were spies for the King, waiting to identify those who spoke out against the monarchy.

On the way home, before they even could reach the outskirts of London, an army of King's men overwhelmed the entire party. They were wrestled down and arrested. The last Father saw of the beautiful grey horses, they were screaming in wild-eyed fear and fury, rearing and lashing their heavy hooves against the soldiers attempting to subdue them. He never saw his horses again.

Upon hearing the news of what had happened to his son and grandsons, old Great- Grandsire rode immediately to London to pay the exorbitant fines demanded for their release. The King's men stripped him of his money, then they beat him. He was dragged through the streets as an example of what would happen to those known to be oppositional to the Crown.

Fortunately, all the men of my family were freed. Father said that after they had been in jail for many days, suddenly a key turned in the lock and they were told, without nicety or explanation, to go. They walked back to the farm all the way from London, carrying old Great-Grandsire in their linked arms. Father said that they were unaware that their punishments had just begun.

Soon thereafter, the King's men raided the family farm. Soldiers confiscated our family's whole herd of horses and all the flocks of sheep. Only one ewe was saved because, in her fright, she ran into the house. My oldest brother, Thomas, remembers how he helped to hide the ewe under a bed. My older sister, Ann, told me that she remembers following our flock down the road crying. She tried to stop the soldiers from driving away her lambs, but they would not listen, and they mocked her.

The King's men were not satisfied by their works of wrath, Father remembered bitterly. Soldiers returned to the farm to gather up all our family who lived there. They lined up my family for counting and recorded their names. My sister remembers that, as she stood there frightened, the soldiers yelled out taunts and insults. They called our men Round Heads because of their shorn hair. She said Father shouted back at them that they were Strange Children for putting their faith in earthly kings. The soldiers grew infuriated. My sister says it was terrible. Some soldiers suddenly attacked our men. Father and my uncles struggled against them. The women and children were screaming. The soldiers were armed. They overwhelmed my family. The soldiers took our men away. Our men were not arrested, but they were made to march through the marketplace at Okehampton, roped together at the neck like cattle with twelve other men from the village. All of them were bludgeoned by the crowd as they went. Even though they became weakened from their beatings, Father said they were not subdued, just as I must never be. Father made certain that I understood what had occurred, as if it had happened to me.

Father left the farm to find work in the city of Rodborough. In his heart, the farm was never left behind. Father always intended to take us back. He liked to tell us stories of the farm that was always a beautiful place, where there were no scars to mark all that had happened there. The endless fields were green and divided by orderly stonewalls or hedgerows. He assured us that Grandfather was slowly rebuilding his flock of sheep and cows. Although there were no longer fine horses for riding, there were a few hefty workhorses. Father said the stone barn probably still had the sour-sweet smell of hay and milk. Father imagined that the thatched roof stonehouse was full of the fresh aroma of Grandmother's baking. These faint recollections, these precious family stories, these are all that remain to me of my father's English legacy.

The blessings of endurance You have given my family in the past bind me to Your ways and preserve my life from the fear of those who seek to destroy my soul. Amen.

Chapter 3

No Promise of Deliverance

England, 1635

*Every day I meditate upon You, raising my story to You like the
bird that rises to dawn. I lift my eyes in the darkness, knowing that
from You comes my only light.*

I am caused to remember one early spring morning in England
when I was ten years old. The birds were singing. I was playing with
my brothers and sister, Hannah, outside of our small house in the city.
It was a lovely day. The air was light and warm. The ground was
fragrant and moist. Mother was nearby in the small garden she had
made. She was gently pushing dead leaves away from little herb
sprouts that had just begun to poke up from the ground. That morning I
especially wanted to help her because she had just told me that she was
with child. She had refused my offer, saying that she wanted to be sure
that not a single wee plant be crushed underfoot. I thought I could be
careful enough and was offended. Distracted by my feelings, I did not
at first hear the voice of Father shouting my mother's name.

Father's voice came sharply in a way so unlike him, yelling,
"Margaret! Margaret!"

We all looked up from the garden and turned toward the sound. I
looked down the narrow lane that led through the row of closely set
sooty houses and recognized my father hurrying toward us. I saw that
someone was with him.

Mother called out to him in response, "Thomas, I am here."

It sounded as if Father was hurt. As he neared, I was relieved to
see nothing wrong with him. I was surprised to see Uncle George
alongside Father. We had not seen Uncle George for a long while. He,
too, had left the farm to live in another city where there was work. I
had little time to think about any of this. Father began to speak in a
rush of words as soon as he came close.

"We just received word that the King's men have come again to the farm. They have taken Father and Brother Jonathan away. They are in prison now. We must go to get them at once, Margaret. Get yourself and the children ready, but first, give me anything that we can sell. There are fines to pay."

Mother responded, "Oh, Thomas! This is terrible. Of course, I will see what we have that might sell. I will make ready to leave. But, Thomas, where will we stay? Surely not at the farm?"

My father was adamant. "No, it is not safe at the farm. My mother has been taken to my sister's house. We will go there."

It did not take Mother long to take from our belongings whatever she thought we had of value. Most of the household goods Father owned had been Mother's dowry from her family, the Hulans. She offered the best of it to Father without apparent regret. Father went off to the marketplace to sell everything. Mother set us to packing for a long trip. Uncle George left to do the same at his house.

Despite all the sacrifices, when Father and Uncle George came back together to count the combined money from the sales of all our two family's best things, they worried aloud that the sum might not be enough. I cannot remember when exactly we left, but it was soon. We left in the grey light of morning. It was a long journey. We made haste, driven by the urgency to free Grandsire and Uncle Jonathan from the harsh hands of those who held them.

At last, we reached the farm. Father was relieved to see that it had not been ransacked. Members of Grandsire's congregation had sealed the door and were standing watch over the house and barns until our family came. We were greeted with a warmth that can only be offered by brethren. Wasting no time, Uncle George and Father went through the house and outbuildings with great urgency. They selected whatever they thought might bring the highest prices. Mother seemed sad at seeing what precious keepsakes they piled into the wagon but told me that we could not be sentimental in choosing what needed to be sold.

The next thing I remember is sitting in front of a church with all manner of chairs, tables, chests, tools, and dishes around me. I was instructed to keep watch that nothing was taken until it was purchased. I was to cry out if anyone tried to steal from us. Father and Uncle

George haggled fiercely to get fair prices. They sold nearly everything. The very next morning my father and uncle set off down the dusty road to pay the ransom for Grandsire and Uncle Jonathan. We could not go with them. Mother, Grandmother, and all the rest of us remained behind at the small farm of Father's youngest sister's husband. I did not have a good feeling about their leaving. Mother reassured me that they would be all right.

All of us prayed for the safe delivery of our menfolk. As we waited for their return, our Auntie cheered us with her sunny disposition and her ever-hopeful outlook. She did not seem bothered that our presence cramped and overfilled her house. Auntie, Mother, and Grandmother spent the days keeping us children busy helping with cooking and with house and farm chores. Working alongside my cousins was fun, even when we were under Grandmother's very somber eye. Several times we made her laugh.

Father and Uncle George returned in about five day's time. We were shocked when we saw that they did not have Grandsire or Uncle Jonathan with them. Neither of them said a word as they went into the house. They called for Grandmother. I listened as they told Grandmother that the money our family had raised had not been enough to pay the fines for her husband and youngest son.

Later, I heard Father in his sorrows as he confided in my mother. "Margaret, you cannot know how it grieved me to stand outside the jail so close to the dungeon where my father and brother are and not be able to see them. I could find no guard willing to carry a message or even a word of hope inside. We had no way to let them know that we were outside keeping vigil for them. We had to leave without being able to tell them that we will come for them as soon as we can. I feel like a failure, a helpless failure."

Father decided to bring us all back home to the city where there was work for him. We said painful goodbyes to our Aunt and cousins and parted. Father worried each step of the way home about the difficulties his father and brother must be enduring. It was a sorrowful, heartbroken trip. I was young but I remember it well. The painful long trip home has shaped much of who I am. It created a loneliness that has never gone away and an outrage that must not be vented.

Weeks passed into a month as Uncle George and Father appealed to every friend and every congregant for donations. It was not easy because other families were in the same situation, scrambling just as we were to free their loved ones from arrest. My brothers worked at every job they could find. They went from one job to the other, sometimes without time for food or sleep. Mother kept me busy carrying packets of food and containers of tea to them. Often they were difficult to find. The tea I brought to them grew cold.

On the very day that Father thought they had the amount of money needed to pay the fines, Uncle George and Father immediately struck out for the jail. We stayed at home with Mother. Father desired speed. He and Uncle George decided that they would not stop long enough to gather up Grandmother even though they knew she wanted to see Grandsire desperately.

I know because of what I have been told that when they reached the jail they had to wait a long time outside the prison until soldiers took them inside. They were brought before a well-dressed official. Father described the man as "a pompous person of some minor authority." He said that the man scolded them in a haughty voice.

According to Father, the arrogant man told them, "You have dallied too long. It costs money to keep law-breakers locked up so that they can do no further harm. You must know that you have to compensate the Crown for its duties to the public. What did you think? Of course, the fines have increased. Time has passed and if you delay, the fines will continue to grow. You Puritans do not seem to understand your proper responsibilities!"

They gave over all the money they had to the official. The man said it was only enough to free one prisoner. They had to make a dreadful choice, whether to release Grandsire or Uncle Jonathan. They chose Grandsire. The tragedy of the moment was compounded when the soldiers carried Grandsire to them.

As Father described it, "The man they brought to us was thin and crumpled, almost unrecognizable as my father. We helped Father to lie down in the wagon. He seemed sick and near to death. We realized that we had little time to save him. We had to ride away leaving our brother behind. We had not gone very far before we decided Father's life was in such peril that he could not make it to the farm. We had to decide where to go with him. We swallowed our pride and brought him straight away to the only safe haven we knew, the home of our disowned sister."

I had not heard my father speak of my other Aunt. Aunt Elizabeth was supposed to be dead to us. She had turned her back on our faith to take up the Anglican ways of her knighted gentleman husband. She must have been surprised to see her brothers when they suddenly appeared at her residence in Belstone. Father said she immediately opened her doors to them when they knocked. She had Grandsire brought in. She urged Father and Uncle George to fetch Grandmother to her immediately.

Father told Mother "All my former misgivings about my estranged sister seemed prideful and regrettably stiff-necked in the face of her fidelity. She cared for our parents in their need. I am humbled to say that my sister's husband discretely slipped a bag of coins into George's hands. Inside was the full amount needed to pay the fine for Jonathan. Ordinarily we would have never lowered ourselves to ask the husband of my sister for this kind of help. We offered our thanks, but our brother-in-law seemed not to want to hear of it. George and I wasted no time in going back for Jonathan. We were too late. In just the few days that we were gone, Jonathan had already been taken for public punishment at Exeter. We heard it had been ordered that he be given thirty-five lashes by a three-corded whip upon the bare back. We knew it to be a horrible punishment. Skin does not stand up to such a flaying. We were desperate to get to him. This time we knew where to go and what to do. We went before the same official we had spoken to before. He took our money from us. Once he had it, he proceeded to vilify us and to scorn our beliefs. We dared do nothing but to stand silently until he was finished spewing his gall, lest he take offence. He had all our money and our brother. The official raged and blustered with a terrible fervor. His spit flew upon our faces. We were certain that all was lost when he screeched an order that we be removed from his sight. We were roughly taken and led away. We thought ourselves arrested; instead, we were taken outside to our wagon and told to go. We were in a great trepidation until we saw that they had dumped Jonathan into the back of our wagon. We found Jonathan unconscious. He was not even aware that he was being saved. As we had feared, his flesh was deeply ripped right through into the muscle. Jonathan's wounds were a frightfully oozing and festering mess to behold. I nearly fainted to think that the man under all that smelly gore was my own brother. We wasted no time in bringing him to Elizabeth's to be ministered to by her physician."

Father told Mother all of this when he came home. My brother, Thomas, overheard what he said. Thomas secretly relayed the news to the rest of us. Soon, Father gathered us all together. He said it had been decided that our Grandparents would remain under the care of Aunt Elizabeth for the remainder of their days, and Uncle Jonathan for as long as necessary.

Father said, "Your Grandsire has called a meeting of the entire family at the home of your Aunt Elizabeth and… her husband." Father would call no one Lord except You. He found it difficult to say the proper form of address for his brother-in-law except out of polite necessity. "We will all go, even though your Mother soon will be into the time of her confinement for the baby that is coming."

One side of me was excited and curious about meeting Aunt Elizabeth. She had previously been an unspeakable mystery. During the long travel to her house, I was careful not to ask questions about her. I remained painfully obedient to the code of silence that befitted me as a child. As it turned out, her home was more wonderful than I could have imagined. The people around my aunt called her Lady Calcliffe. She lived in a real manor. It looked like a castle. The grounds far exceeded anything I had ever seen. The inside of the manor was breathtaking. I wanted to explore. That would have been too forward. I behaved. I watched quietly. Aunt Elizabeth was kind to us. She saw to it that we were well fed, and several times she even paid special attention to me. I remember that she reached her fingers out and smoothed my hair. She said that I looked like she had when she was a girl. I felt sad that she could not be in our family, but I did not say it.

We were not allowed to see Uncle Jonathan, but all of us were taken to the room where Grandsire lay. Grandmother was at his side tending to him with the help of servants. The big bed made Grandsire appear small. I hardly recognized him. His voice was faint. He coughed each time he tried to talk. We all knew without him telling us that the old family farm had been sold to pay the taxes and claims laid against it by the Crown. It was Grandsire's wish that what little remained to him from the proceeds of the sale be divided among my father and uncles. I listened as he went on to divide the few family goods he still owned between my two aunts. Feeble as he was, with proud dignity he bequeathed all that he had to his children, with provisions for his wife to be cared for to the end of her days. Grandsire's breath came hard. Before his head sagged upon the pillows, I heard him beg Father and Uncle George to leave for the Massachusetts Bay Company colony. He asked that they leave just as soon as Uncle Jonathan was fit to travel. Grandsire's eyes closed. We were led from the room. Outside the closed door, the adults were very quiet; then they began to weep.

I was scared. No one seemed to see us children until a long time later when we were on the long trip home. As we rode back to Rodborough in our wagon, which was on loan to us because Father had sold his as well as the oxen that had pulled it, Father told us that he had something to say.

Father's words were few but they resonated and echoed in my ears. "Uncle George and I talked after the family meeting. We have decided that it is not safe to delay our departure until Uncle Jonathan is fit to travel. We must make ready to leave England immediately. We will await the birth of our baby."

I do not remember if anyone spoke further until we reached home. A swath of miles tore away in silence. I struggled to imagine that I was seeing the sights of England passing before me for the last time. I was only young. I could not change anything that was happening. When my parents raised a prayer to You for comfort and courage, all I could do to help them feel better was to say "Amen."

Father and Uncle George arranged for our sailing. Aunt Elizabeth generously offered to provide us with the money to buy the tickets for our passage. She also gave Father and Uncle George each an ox and a young bred cow so that we would have a start in the new world.

We began to pack what we would need for our long trip and our new life. I knew Mother was worried about her own father, Grandfather Hulins. He was old. She feared she would not see him again. As painful as it was to leave him, she did not lament her grief. Even though Mother was uncomfortable with the weight of the baby inside her, she kept us directed to our tasks and to our obligations. She gave us little time for regrets or for worry about what lay ahead.

My older brothers, Thomas Jr., Nathaniel, and Samuel were eager to leave for the Bay Company. My poor sister Ann was in love and could not make up her mind whether to go or stay. When she talked to me about leaving, she cried. Our family was splintering into pieces. Had You not put Your wing over us, our strength might have failed.

We came to know the breadth of our love for those who would be left behind by the measure of the aching hollowness inside us that grew as we anticipated our parting. My dear friend Emily made a rag doll for me out of clothes she had outgrown. She asked me to remember her by it. As I held the soft poppet, I could smell the familiar scent of her. The poppet's face was embroidered with a smile that crushed my heart, a grinning reminder of our friendship.

Father promised me that we were going to a beautiful place where we would live as a community according to Your true will. If we responded to Your call to restore the covenants, You would reward us with a life of faith and opportunity. Father believed completely in the rightness of this venture. With a child's earnest commitment to family dreams, I gave my promise to help Mother make our new home. I meant my promises to my family and to You, but as Mother grew closer to her time, I began to wish that the baby would never come. Its birth would mark the time when we would sail.

I admitted my worries to Mother. We had stayed late at a prayer meeting one evening because Father could not stop talking with other men who were going to the Bay Company. It was dark when we started for home. Mother was very tired. She walked slowly, holding her belly with her hands, sighing. Father had not wanted her to come along. She had insisted. Time here was short. She wanted to be among her friends at every opportunity whether it was seen as immodest or not. She could not carry Hannah, so my baby sister toddled along beside me holding my hand. Father walked ahead with my brothers, Thomas, Lawrence, Nathaniel, and Samuel. We were not far from home but it seemed to take so many more steps than usual to get there. Before us the moon rose, huge, red, and round. It alarmed me that all the familiar places I knew were half-invisible, dark against the light. I realized that soon I would not see these places at all anymore.

"Mother?"

"Yes, Mary."

"Mother, how long before the baby comes?"

"Soon, Mary, very soon I think."

"Can you wait, Mother? I don't want the baby to come yet."

"Oh, my little dear, when you were a baby you came when you were ready as will this one."

"Yes, Mother, but when this baby comes we will leave here. I wish the baby would wait. I am afraid. When we leave everything I know will be gone."

"Mary... look at the moon. Are you looking at the moon? See how it shines on you and lights you up?"

"Yes."

"The moon is shining on you here, and the same moon is shining over the place where our new home will be. Even now, the moon shines upon where we will live one day. When we build our new home, you will only need to look up to see the sun, the moon, and the stars. They will still be there as evidence of God's promise to us. You must always have that promise in your mind. Did you hear the psalm we sang tonight? Let me sing it to you. It helps me to understand what we must do. Listen.

When I behold Thine heavens, even the work of Your fingers,
The moon and the stars, which You hast established,
What is man, say I, that You art mindful of him
And the son of man, that You visiteth him?
For You made him a little lower than God,
And hast crowned him with glory and worship.
You hast made him to have dominion in the works of Your hands;
You hast put all things under his feet:
All sheep and oxen: yea, and the beasts of the field:

The fowls of the air, and the fish of the sea;
And that which passeth through the paths of the seas.
Psalm 7: 3-8.

As Mother chanted the last, Father said out of the darkness, "Who ever passeth through the paths of the sea… by the work of their hands…will have all things put under their feet. We are the chosen ones. We will live a life set apart. The eyes of all peoples are upon us. We will create a Biblical Commonwealth that will benefit all of mankind. Do you understand, Mary? This is what we will do."

We walked on amidst the sounds of Your creation, the soft drone of insects and the pleasant songs of night warblers. I felt myself grow solid with a determination that has never left me. I would be an unbending defender of Your commonwealth. Even children were being called. I would be among the steadfast. The moon had risen and grown smaller, hard, and silver before we got home that night. The sight of it gave me a nervous sense of being slowly pulled away.

Now so many years later, here in this cell there are no heavens to behold. Into this void my husband visits daily. He speaks to me through the bars. He brings me food, cider, and clean clothes. What can I say? What makes me different in his eyes from the others around me; the wretched thieves, harlots, murderesses and accursed witches with whom I huddle in the night for warmth? The vermin feed upon our bodies as if we were one living mass. Our wastes mingle to overflowing in the slop pail so that our skirts are encrusted, one just as much as the other. The straw upon which we lie is saturated with snot and vomit, woman's monthly blood, and tears. How can I spare him this knowledge? He comes here to protect me, but he cannot save me from what his nostrils surely must tell him.

I know there is nothing Joseph can do to control or change my circumstances. I fear that soon he will begin to resist the pain of his powerlessness by becoming hard and distant. Our love must not become his prison.

Oh, my Divine Father, without You, there would be no promises here or any reminders of our noble vision. There would be no honor except for that which I have in my mind. You are in the remembrance of that high cold moon of long ago, and in the thin melody of the psalm that trailed its retreat. Until the day that I am free to walk out under Your sky, have my mind to Your breast that it not fly away into the abyss of swirling doom that curls at the edges of my thoughts. Remind me that the lights of Your stars and Your moon still pierce the darkness that silently beckons me to all the ways of death. Amen.

Chapter 4

The Paths of the Sea

August 1635

Lord, You know that with You before our eyes we left the place of my birth to travel to the port city of Plymouth, England to meet the ship that would take us to the Massachusetts Bay Company.

I was ten years old and remember the journey well. With the new baby, John, in Mother's arms and Emily's poppet in mine, my family stood on the dock waiting to board the ship that lay anchored before us. Staring nervously at the ship, one of my brothers asked again how long we would be at sea. I already knew the answer, as did we all. Father said again in his most reassuring voice that usually the crossing to the Massachusetts Bay Company took six to ten weeks depending upon the winds and weather. I had counted on my fingers how many days that would be. I tried to push away thoughts of any storms.

The likelihood of bad weather did not seem at all remote on the day that we left. A stiff breeze chattered my skirts around my legs. I had to clutch my hat to keep it from swirling away. I had never been to the coast, never seen the ocean or a ship. The ocean looked terribly unquiet.

The ship to which we entrusted our fate was large but when I saw how many people, animals, and things were to be put aboard, I wondered how we would all fit. Nevertheless, the thick masts were impressively tall, and the heavy, furled sails reassured me that we would move across the sea with great power and speed.

I watched the sailors laboring busily about the ship. Other men on the docks had taken our animals and our most bulky belongings from us to be led, lugged, or hoisted aboard. The sailors' shouting was rudely jolly. The way they moved and dressed was very different from those of us who waited somberly and darkly clad upon the dock.

A man high atop the plank that leaned across the water from the dock up to the side of the ship waved toward us and yelled something that only the people in the front of our group heard. All at once, our people began to press toward the ship. One by one, we went up. Our strange journey had begun.

Once onto the ship, we were motioned to cross the deck to a small door. A narrow ladder led down to the inside. There was no chance to look around the ship before we were swallowed into it.

At the bottom of the ladder, we found ourselves in a great open cabin. After some confusion about what to do, we moved forward with Uncle George and his family until we found a place to set ourselves down upon the planked floor among a hundred or so other travelers; Puritans and strangers all mixed. We piled the things that we had carried on around us, a small wall against the surrounding people. We were told that our animals were below us in a large hold with all the other animals. I knew that was so because, as we waited for everyone to come aboard, I began to notice the rising stink of manure.

We helped Mother shuffle our things. She worked to make our small area organized and comfortable as best as she could. Mother turned a deaf ear to any of our questions. After a long while, I heard and felt a heavy clanking rumble. Mother rose from her stacking and smoothing of blankets to turn and look at Father. Father said the anchor was being pulled up. The ship began to move. Everyone cheered that we were at last underway.

Time passed quickly in the first days when everything was unfamiliar and exciting. We had to eat and sleep and tend to our bodily needs in ways that were new. The motion of the ship was gentle and pleasant as it traveled out of the long bay. At first, we children had a fine time staggering upon the moving floor as we learned to stand and roll upon it. As the days went by there was less that was interesting and more that was the same. The ship was too cramped for running and too crowded for playing. I became restless. Most days we were not permitted to come up on to the deck to see the sun or to take air. I began to think that perhaps this might be like being in jail. I dared not remind Father of his days in prison by asking if this were true.

The only change in each day was our increasing discomfort. When the ship came out into the open ocean, it began to sway and pitch violently. We children no longer thought walking against the waving deck was funny. People were hurt when they fell down. Everyone was either sick or very cross. As the ship rose and fell it also tipped side to side. The hull creaked dreadfully as if it were being pulled apart under the strain of the wind filled sail. Waves crashed against the boards beside us. Sometimes seawater sprayed or poured over us through open hatches. To close the hatches against cold and wind meant suffering to breathe the overwhelmingly smothering dank. Our herb bouquets, picked from gardens left behind could not mask the fetid smell that rose from us.

The old crippled sailor who emptied our chamber pots overboard also brought us buckets of water. Women used it for rinsing out baby diapers and personal items. There was no bathing or washing up at sea.

The water from the ship's barrels began to grow green and scummy. Our food became infested. Before long, we picked wriggling weevils from our hard bread as we did lice from our bodies.

There were rats. Even though there was a terrier dog on board to kill them, the rats multiplied like a plague. I could see rats sneaking out to sniff my things. A little boy was bitten badly one night. He woke us all with his shrieking.

In the close quarters, a feverish sickness spread among us. There was one very old woman who curled up shivering and coughing, not able to keep down food. Her daughters could not warm her. After a few days she died. They wrapped her into a bundle in her blankets. We held a prayer service after which the men carried the woman to the deck above us. They say she was thrown into the storming sea. I thought that was very shocking, to be dropped into the sea and left behind.

We also heard that some of the animals down below were dying, precious cattle and other farm animals. I felt badly that some families would not have a cow or ox when they got to the other side. I worried how the ox and the cow that Aunt Elizabeth had given us were faring.

One morning a little baby who had been whimpering died in his mother's arms. There was much weeping. It was so sad. I knew the baby also went into the sea.

We sailed on and people grew listless. I wondered if every ship left a trail of people and animals behind it. I do not think Father or Mother had thought of these things when we were getting ready to take ship.

The death of the baby made me remember how I had asked Mother to wait to have our baby John. That seemed very selfish now. I tried to make up for it by being especially helpful with little John and Hannah. I could not imagine what it would be like to lose our babies, a frightening thought. Little John seemed healthy and loved the attention of the people around him. He never got sick except for a runny nose. He suckled from my mother's breast so maybe his food was better than our terrible stuff.

Father made sure that Mother got her portions. We received rations every day from the ship's provisions, which we cooked for ourselves in little groups. Meals were cooked in what was called the ship's firebox. The firebox was an iron tray filled with sand over which a fire was built. Firewood was guarded jealously so that it would last as close to the end of the voyage as possible. There was always the danger of fire when the seas were rough. We lived on such foods as hard tack, boiled salt pork, dried meats, pickled foods, and peas porridge, or oatmeal; whatever could be cooked in one pot. We were also given beer several times a day. Mother said beer would keep us healthy, and warned us never to drink water. Water would make us sick. Children were given beer to drink as soon as they were weaned. When Mother was not looking, I began to give her a little extra of my food, or would pour a little of my beer into her cup. Father caught me doing this. He did not object. We shared that secret.

Father would call my mother to stand and pray among the others. The constant nearness of people upon us upset me but Mother could calm me with her hands and eyes. I felt secure in the nearness of my pretty fair-haired mother, and was comforted by the sound of my Father's prayers. As he stood among the men chanting psalms, the low tones of his Preston Capes brogue resounded strongly beneath the voices of all the others. His hands upon the soft pale leather covers of the Geneva Bible and his melodic voice were the center of my world on that endless voyage.

Like my parents, I was serious and respectful when offering You my prayer. Trying to stand still, swaying with my hands clasped, I was distracted by the waves that rolled the ship beneath me. I sensed the presence of a powerful surge welling up from the depths of the ocean's bottom. By raising my elbows just a little bit to center my weight, I found a fragile balance upon the waters. I wondered that You came to me through my feet. I soared upon the heaving sea and holy song. While Father read, I flew. The warm flood of safe words and the dangerous ocean swells lifted me up in moments of breath-taking gliding rapture.

The earth is the Lord's, and all that therein is; the world,
and they that dwell therein.
For He hath founded it upon the seas,
and established it upon the floods.... Psalm 24: 1-2.

In all other ways, living on a ship was unbearable. I kept a count of the days but the meaning of time changed because each day seemed so endless. I wondered over the fact that there were some wealthy people on board who were returning to Boston after voluntarily making a trip back to England. I thought that it must be easier for people who could afford a private cabin.

As for me, I decided that I would never sail again. This being so, everything in England was lost to me forever and forever. I tried to picture the faces of family and friends we had left behind. I could still imagine Aunt Elizabeth's tidy hair and the combs that had held it up and away from her frilly stiff collar, but I could not remember her features. I hoped that forgetting her face would not somehow diminish my prayer that she take good care of my grandparents and uncle.

Even the grinning poppet my friend Emily had given me began to lose Emily's fragrance. Its expression went empty of any resemblance to hers. Rocking back and forth endlessly within the ship, the sea in control of us all, we drew further and further away from everything we knew.

During the long days, I watched the behavior of others, touched and affected by the nearness of them. A feeling of tense criticism grew within me. Sometimes I complained about other people to Mother. She always shushed me and reminded me quietly that we must sacrifice our personal desires for what was best for everyone. When she chastised me, I could not argue, but I did not believe that I was the one making problems. I was trying to be good. It was other people who were not measuring up to the standards that Mother expected of us. Some other people selfishly crowded the people around them. Others were argumentative. It was not right!

I had one friend on the ship. Her name was Anna. Without anyone else I wanted to talk to more, I talked to her. Her family had taken up a space next to the opposite wall of the ship. Their spot was better than ours was because they were not completely surrounded by other people. Her father was a grumpy man but her mother was nice. I spent a lot of time over on the other side of the ship with her. Her brothers paid no attention to us at all and that was good. We could make everyone around us disappear by putting blankets over our heads. Underneath, we created imaginary worlds and made up little stories in which my poppet and the two of us were the main characters. We talked to each other in funny voices, which made us laugh.

Next to the place on the floor that my family had taken, there was a woman who caused me vexation. It seemed to me that she took advantage of my being smaller to take more room for herself. Night after night, I felt her sharp knees or windy backside pushing me off my blankets into my brother. She spread herself out largely, snoring and gurgling, much to my indignation. I lay in the dark glaring at her. She was filling up her place and mine. Was my discomfort not plain? Surely being covetous of a neighbor's only bed broke a commandment.

One morning I could stand it no longer. I waited until she lumbered to the night soil bucket and back. I waited until she lowered herself onto her blankets to sit, smacking her lips in her maddening way. I fixed her with a look I imagined full of Christian authority, took a deep breath, and spoke, using Mother's tone of voice.

"Goodwife, you have taken over my sleeping space and I have no place to rest because of your kicking. We all must see to each other's comfort. You have forgotten your duty. I am only a child, but this is my bed and you are in it. Please, give it back to me."

She snapped back at me, "You naughty rude girl! It is not your place to scold your elders. Has your mother not raised you with any respect at all? It is you who disturb my sleep. I will see that you cause me no further trouble. Now be quiet and say no more, you shocking little brat!"

The horrible woman got up and went off to make loud accusations about me to her friends. I saw them all looking over their shoulders in my direction. Knowing I was right, I sat rigidly and made certain that they saw I ignored their stupid gossip. Mother had heard and seen it all. To my amazement, she did not support me, as I would have thought. She reprimanded me instead.

"Mary! Mind your tongue. Do not speak to others like that. You must learn not to be so critical of people! Your mouth will get you in great trouble one day. You must go and apologize at once."

It was humiliating. I had to walk through all the people with everyone watching. I stood stiffly as I presented my apology to her.

"Goodwife, I am sorry that I spoke to you…so. I will not do it again."

Time seemed to crackle and swirl. My head felt as if it slid sideways off my shoulders. My breath was smothered. Only my righteous resolve kept me from falling into the black centers of her eyes and disappearing.

When I could think again, I had somehow returned to my blanket and was sitting in my own rightful spot. I would not relinquish it again to anyone or look at those who offended me.

That day I knew that, as a person, I was alone. It made me sad and nervous. Knowing the women had cackled and huffed about me caused me to realize that I must either hold on to what I personally knew to be right or else disappear piece by piece into the chewing of their bitter mouths.

It appeared that others, even my beloved mother, could not be trusted always to defend the commandments. I would not ever be like that, I promised myself. I told my friend Anna about it. Anna agreed with me, but I knew she was not as smart as I was so I was not sure if her opinion counted.

Later that night, tired but vigilant, and not able to sleep for all the rolling and the snoring, the coughing, and the creeping about of things in the darkness, I wondered about grown people's imperfections and their seeming hypocrisy. My own mother had called me "too critical." If people complained about my small opinions, would they also scold You when they had to face You on Judgment Day?

While I was thinking about my own nature and having to justify it before You, the realization of the certainty of my death came to me for the first time. I had always thought about salvation and my hope for eternal life but never about becoming dead. The thought froze me. One day I would be on this earth no more. My body would be as lifeless as those limp corpses I had seen carried past me to be dumped into the sea. Would the places that I had been be empty of me completely? Was it true that one day I would not be able to see all that I loved on this earth again?

Painfully awake, it finally came to me that perhaps I could forestall such things. I began wondering if I might please You by building such a beautiful life that it would give You no pleasure to take me away from it any time soon. My idea seemed a good one except for the hopeless obstacle of trying to improve this time aboard ship.

I decided to wait until the day when we came to the new home to begin my promise to live a beautiful life of grace. My parents said that there would be green grass where we were going and that one day I would lie in the softness of it. When this day came, I would be so thankful that I would know at once how to start becoming a much better person than ever before. With that thought, I offered myself to Your mercy.

"Where," I asked my parents, "will we live?

Father reminded me repeatedly that he had a plan, that we were all part of a bigger plan. He promised me that we would be surrounded by people whose beliefs were like ours, people like us. I did not ask if the people there would be more like us than many of those traveling aboard our ship. I accepted his answers. I knew I would have to wait to see for myself.

Every day aboard ship, we prepared for our mission with prayer and sermon and chanting of psalms. In my mind, we were nearing the land of Your reward for the sacrifices of Your true believers. I awaited what I would become.

During those dreadful weeks, I became the focus of my neighbor's irritations. She noticed everything I did and found fault with me to her friends. Mother and I both overheard her gossiping. She flapped her tongue about my poppet. She said that it was a sinful attachment to trifles. Her friends decided that I was an unnatural child, likely to become prone to the enticements of evil.

Mother's advice was to stop my ears and allow the just punishment for caterwauling to come Providentially. "A harsh tongue," Mother reminded me, "is an abomination to God. Remember Proverbs. The forward tongue shall be cut out."

My personal lesson in this, and something important I must learn, she admonished, was the value of silence. I tried to possess Your silver silence. Whenever the woman came near to me, my heart pounded so painfully in my chest that I was afraid she would hear it.

I began to have wrenching hiccups, which would not still no matter how I tried. I was exhausted. The hiccups angered the woman and aggravated her gossip. It came as a huge relief when Mother and Father changed places with me so that I no longer had to sleep next to the viperous woman. My hiccups stopped. If the woman complained about me further, I did not hear of it. I hid my poppet under my blankets for the remainder of the trip and did my best to become invisible from critical eyes.

I was taught that You raise from darkness those who have made themselves ready. I behaved as best I could. I prayed that You would notice and see no need to delay our deliverance to the new world because of any need for me to become ready.

One morning the old sailor spread the word among us that the ship was "drawing near." He said the birds that marked the nearness of land had been seen. Upon hearing this report, the adults seemed to wake up and began smiling at us children, touching us with pats on our heads.

Above the crowded stink, psalm melodies swelled up in a joyous full-throated harmony of men and women and children raising our voices to our fullest as we waited. When it came time for the regular prayers that marked our days, the words were vigorous and overflowing. Later in the afternoon cries rang out that land could be seen.

Our elders who had made friends among the crew took turns going up on deck to report our progress to all of us below. They said that the land looked like a thick dark line on the horizon between sea and sky. It was growing steadily larger as we drew closer. The last man allowed on deck before being made to go below by the sailors working the ropes and sails said that he had seen arms of land reaching out to our ship.

Would such memories ever cause You to enfold me in Your hand. Amen.

Chapter 5

The Massachusetts Bay Company

Fall, 1635

My Lord, just as You delivered Jonah from the belly of the beast, so You rescued us from the sea.

Within a day of sighting land, we landed at Boston Harbor amidst the sounds of seagulls screaming and people yelling. The ship seemed to be moving very slowly as it came into the harbor. Suddenly there was a heavy bumping. Everyone cheered. The ship had touched against the dock.

I waited expectantly for our release. I wanted to see the new land! The old sailor told us that the Captain of the ship would give the order when he was ready to allow us to come up onto the deck. I waited restlessly among all the others below decks for a long time.

"Mother..." I fidgeted, anxiously.

She whispered to me, "Be patient my child and be grateful that we are yet together and safe. There are official things that the Captain must do before we can be let off. It takes time for the news of our ship's arrival to reach the ministers and friends of our congregation who may gather here to help us. God preserve us, once we step off this ship, we have no other home or sanctuary. We must not be too eager to go until the time be right."

At last, we were allowed to file up into the blinding brilliance of a sunlit afternoon. Everywhere about us was the movement of people, animals, trunks, and bundles. After weeks of sameness, I was beset by the overall confusion and overcome when at last I looked upon the citadel of Your chosen people. All the ships of England seemed to have been summoned to dock at Your shores. There was a forest of masts, and beyond, a wall of warehouses. I could make out many buildings upon a landscape of slight hills. It was glorious. We climbed down on to the dock to make our way to where we could touch the land. Mother warned us to stay together.

I was numb with an over-abundance of emotion. Around us, some people were already reuniting with parts of their family who had come over earlier.

"Father, where are all the people going?"

Looking over my head at everything around him, he answered. "Most of the families with set plans are going to a town south of Boston called Dorchester. Our congregation has known from the outset that we will not all be settling together as a group. No one place could absorb us." He looked down at me. "Daughter, hold your tongue for a while. You ask too many questions. Leave a man in peace! Look at your brothers and sisters. They are waiting quietly and obediently. Be like them."

Mother took me aside. She said, "Mary, before we left, Father and Uncle George posted a letter to a friend already settled here asking him to meet our ship when it docked. Our letter went into a mailbag with everyone else's letters. You see that many people did receive those letters and came here. Your father's letter was sent so long ago that anything could have happened to his friend since then. If no one awaits our arrival, we will have no idea where to go. We are prepared for uncertainty. Do not disturb your Father any more. He is watching for his friend to come. What will happen to us depends upon it, so shush, my child."

That first day of our landing was very exciting but for us nothing happened that would open our way to Your refuge of truth. I watched what other people around us were doing. Many were praying, asking that all our travails be acceptable to You. I prayed that Father's friend would come.

I had imagined that when we landed a presentment of the angels in heaven would greet us at the gates of the new land and lead us to the ground where we were to work and build Your blessed new sanctuary. The enormity of what I saw scared me. There was no sign from the expansive land that lay before us that You knew or cared that we had come. It was a struggle to set aside my worldly fears and let Your hand steer the way.

We were told that there were little provisions for the steady stream of newcomers, especially now because the first killing frost had already come. Boston, it was said, was over-settled. I began to feel small, like a fallen leaf that could be crushed and never missed. I thought it would be easier to be a leaf because at least Your winds would blow it to where it belonged. I wondered how long we could stay on the ship before it left to go back to England. It was only somewhat reassuring that we were not alone. When night fell that first night in the Massachusetts Bay Colony there were many others like us who had to go back inside and sleep in our old places below deck.

The next day more people came to the dock inquiring after passengers. Mother and Father scanned the small crowd that was continuously coming and going, looking for anyone we might know, hoping to see someone who might be able to help us. I could see that my parents were nervous. Father reassured Mother that his friend would come if he could and that if he were unable to help us, of course our elders would prevail upon those of our congregation who had come earlier to do their Christian duty toward their fellow brethren to provide such aide as was necessary.

Oh, my Lord, it was a great relief when You helped us in our plight. On the third day after we landed, Father was told that a man was looking for him. We all went to see. Father recognized his friend. I did not remember the man. Father and Uncle George did, and they were very emotional in greeting him. They thumped him on the back and they all were laughing. My eyes were on a large basket full of food. The man told Mother that his wife had prepared it for us. We children gathered around the man's wagon, eating and listening as he advised Father and Uncle George about what he thought we should do.

"The news is not good," I heard father's friend say. "People have been fleeing to these shores for many years. The coastal towns are crowding in on each other. The tillable land close to Boston is already claimed and overused. Pastureland is overgrazed and available harvestable wood is further and further out from the towns."

In his opinion, the whole colony was finding it difficult to support their existing ministries, much less to accommodate the press of new immigrants. They talked for a long time about which of the names given to us by our elders should be contacted first and which places would be the most likely to start the search for land.

I realized that Uncle George and Father were planning to go off with the man in his wagon. We could not all go. There was not enough room. The thought of separating was terrifying. Father refused to make much of a goodbye. He and Uncle George went back to the ship to get a few things and then climbed into the wagon. Quickly the wagon turned a corner and disappeared. We were left to Your mercy.

We were far from home in a strange place and now Father had left us. The only thing we could do was to follow Mother back onto the sour ship, carrying our basket of food. We lived over a week onboard waiting expectantly for Father to return. We watched as others departed in small groups, including Anna and her family. Once we said our goodbyes, I was bereft of any friend.

I remember that as an anxious time. Other people were leaving and we were not. The fetid ship was emptying, but we were still there. I worried about what would happen to us. What if there would be no place for us? I wanted my father to come back. One day I looked up and there he was. He was alone, no Uncle George.

"I have found a place where we can stay. There is no unclaimed land to be had around here but I found a place where we can go. The lot I found has a small house and barn. It will have to do. We cannot all stay together. There is no place large enough, and there is no time for us to search any longer. George has gone north to see about renting a house lot he was offered in a place called Salem. We are going south of the bay to Boston Mount."

Finally, it was we who were gathering our bundles to go. It was hard to say goodbye to those travelers left on the ship. I felt sad for them because they had no place to go yet. I could not show how happy I was that we did.

The crew hoisted our few heavy trunks down to us. We had no wagon here to carry our household goods. Father said that we would go by boat to our new home.

I was glad to hear this because our poor ox and cow looked so very weak and wobbly from being tied in the hold of the ship with the other animals for all those weeks. I doubted they could walk very far, even for food. I had noticed that there was no grass anywhere in sight of the docks, not even enough blades of grass for one cow to snatch a mouthful. The earth around the docks was bare from the movement of so many travelers. I hoped the boat we were waiting for would take us to a place where we could find food for our animals and ourselves.

It was not long before a man rowing an open boat came toward us. I wondered how everything we had could get into a small boat, especially the animals. I did not catch the man's name, but he knew just how to put the cow and ox aboard without much fuss, with the help of Father and my brothers. The man was very particular about how the load was balanced, and where we should all sit. Little Hannah sat in my lap, and my entire family settled down among our things, the trunks making a solid fence to keep the animals from possibly moving into us. We drew away from the docks, staying close to the shore. The water was calm. We began to observe the land around us. The trees here were fantastic colors: brilliant red, yellow, gold, and russet.

Father said we were going to the other side of a neck of land in another bay beyond a large tidal river. The boatman strained and spoke little. Slowly, we passed marshes full of grasses along the shore. There were many birds wherever there were rocky places for them to sit. I could see small islands out toward the sea. The man who rowed the boat said that his brother would be meeting us when we landed at the beach. He said his brother would take our trunks in his wagon to where we were going. We rounded a long point of land. Father pointed across the bay to a hill.

He said, "We are going there. That is where we will live."

I could see across the bay that there was a little village beyond a rim of sandy beach. I strained my eyes as we grew nearer, trying to make out the features of our new home. Our boatman rowed in a straight line toward a small dock. He hooted as we drew closer. I was surprised to hear an answering hoot come across the water. I could just see the outline of an ox and wagon. A man stepped from the dark shape of the ox and began to wave his arms. At last, someone was waiting for us and greeting us. We were expected. The rest happened very fast. The tide being high and the wind slight, our landing was gentle. The boatman poled us the last yards to the dock and handed a rope to my father to toss to his brother. With a quick flip of the brother's wrist, we were tied tight to the wooden dock. Our trip upon the sea was over.

The brothers were very jovial. They made quick work of unloading our beasts and baggage. They joked about how much they wanted a drink of beer. I realized that I was thirsty too. The brother told us his name was Elijah. He laughed as he pulled out a round jug of beer, popped out the wooden plug, and passed it among us. To this day, I remember that drink, Lord. The entire world shrank. All there was became the thin stream of warm liquid falling into my mouth. I was grateful.

The next thing I remember is walking behind the wagon up the slope of a seaward facing hillside. My legs were not used to the effort and began shaking. Finally, Father bid Goodman Elijah to stop. We had pulled up in front of a small house surrounded by a rough wooden fence. The house looked barely big enough for all nine of us. Behind it was a little barn, just as Father had said.

Father seemed a bit dismayed at having to show us that we had come so far for so little. I knew Father had hoped to re-build a family estate with his brothers. Before us was the truth that what Father had found was only a patch of land to perch on, rented from someone who lived in Boston. After all that had happened to us, this was where we were to live.

Elijah helped us to unload. When the job was done, he received his pay. Elijah wished us well and left us. I hoped we would see him again.

My mother looked at Father's expression. "Thomas, be not so humbled. The Lord has shown His generosity in causing you to bring us safely to good ground. It will be enough. Look, someone has kindly cut and stacked some wood for us. I am grateful for a roof and for the people who have welcomed us. Let us go inside and see to the hearth."

Mother declared the fireplace well built and began to build a fire in it. I was sent with one of my brothers to fetch water from a nearby stream while Father and the rest of my brothers saw to the animals. They were carrying the trunks to the house and barn when they discovered several loaves of course brown bread and a grass basket filled with eggs. Goodman Elijah must have left them for us without saying a word. Mother was very glad and began to cook immediately. It was not long before there was food to eat. We gathered around and gave our prayers to You for seeing us through our difficulties and then we ate. We sopped up the sweet orange yolks with our bread. I can hardly remember anything else of that first night because of the heavy exhaustion that came upon me. I know I spread blankets on the floor and lay down upon the solid unmoving land, surrounded by four walls and the quiet privacy of only my family around me. You had found a place for us upon Your earth. I hope I offered my thanks to You before I slept.

When I opened my eyes, it was morning. A thrill ran through me. I knew that as soon as I pulled the blankets from over my head all things around me would be new. The growling in my belly made me wonder how we would find food in this unfamiliar place. We had stores of dried beans and such, but no meat.

My brothers had already slipped out and were gone. It was not long before I heard them returning. They were excited. They told how some other boys had shown them how to catch fish that were spawning in the river. My brothers lay before Mother a row of fantastically colored sleek fish. Some were quite orange on their bellies and black on their backs with wavy markings. Their fins were red with a thin black line and a broad white front edge. The most amusing thing to behold was their sides, which were spotted in hues of brilliant yellow and blue. Each blue spot had a bright red dot right in the middle of it. Their eyes were big and they looked very cheerful for fish. My brothers said the other boys had assured them that these fish would taste very good.

Mother boiled the fish for breakfast. There was enough for all of us to feast. I still remember the sweetness of that delicate pink meat which we sucked from the bones in celebration.

My brothers went right back to catch more of the colorful fish that had been our first meal. I kept my eye out for their return. When I saw that their baskets were heavy, I ran to greet them. I looked into the basket and screamed. Inside was a foaming mass of wet and writhing black snakes.

My brothers laughed at me. They said it was not a trick. These were eels. Everyone told them that eels were good to eat. My brothers went to get Father to show him. I was glad that they did not show Mother. My father and brothers nailed the triangular shaped heads of the thrashing monsters to the side of the barn to skin them, but the eels would not die. Even when hacked into chunks with the axe, the flesh was quivering as it was tossed it into the boiling water of our kitchen kettle. Mother had insisted that they make the cook fire outside.

That evening those eels were our meal. I watched my mother and father as their spoons were lifted to their lips. Steam rose up from my bowl of stew. The vapors touched my face with clammy heat. I was afraid. I gagged at the thought of ingesting loathsomeness. In a wretched battle with myself, I opened my mouth to a small bit of the flaking meat and swallowed it with a large gulp of broth. Instead of being a nightmare of evil, the stew was actually pleasant, delicious even. I got through it. We ate a lot more eels in the days to come. Nothing bad seemed to happen to us because of it. I wondered why You desired us to eat such ugly food in this place.

Some families hunted ducks and geese in the cold treacherous marshes. Fowling had been illegal for us in England. Father did not have enough powder or balls for his musket to waste shooting into the sky. On days when we had little for our pot, we began to do what we saw others doing. We went to the seashore at low tide to scratch for clams in the cold sand. We picked mussels from the slippery rocks. These were other odd foods for an English farmer's family. I did not like the feel of small lumpy sea creatures in my mouth or the funny smell of them cooking. It was a diet for poor people. All I can say is that You provided it amply.

I wanted beans and brown bread but we had to stretch that as far as we could. Fortunately, there were families around us who needed extra hands and were willing to trade food or necessities for a day's work. Sometimes I was sent away to another family and was fed at their table in exchange for the help I could offer. All children were expected to go to live and work with other families. The experience was intended to humble a child's selfish nature. I grew to look forward to living with neighbors who had been here for a season or more because they usually had better and more familiar food, like meat dripping with pot liquor and peas porridge.

Father made a yoke for our ox so that we could pull wood out of the forest more easily. The small stacks of wood piled by the house needed to grow higher and longer so that when the deep snows and cold came there would be a fire in the hearth to keep us from freezing in our beds.

The weather was already turning inclement. Father and my brothers were in the woods every day that they were not working for someone else, cutting both hardwood for firewood and pine for knots to make candlewood for our lamps. Every one of us able to drag a bundle or carry a basket went to help. Mother and I also gathered tree nuts. We filled our baskets with beechnuts, chestnuts, and acorns. Later we would shuck the nuts and pound them into a moist nut meal.

On our way home, my brothers poked around in thickets looking for the remnants of a climbing vine called groundnut. It was easy to pull up the roots, which were loaded with clusters of starchy bumps. We pulled up armloads and broke off the clusters to bring home to store for slicing into stews. Any starch to fill our bellies was good.

The excruciating effort of dragging home our gatherings was greatly eased when Father acquired an ox cart of our own. It was then that I really began to enjoy going out to the woods with my brothers. I had nothing that gave me more comfort than my legs, and I made use of them, enjoying the warmth of running. On our way out to the woods, dodging wagons and people, we conquered the cold and the strangeness of a new land by overpowering it with reckless speed.

We made one last foraging trip before the snows came. That time Father went off by himself into the woods to hunt with his matchlock musket. He said he had noticed the signs of deer feeding on mushrooms and fallen acorns. He had seen some well-beaten trails leading to a sunny wooded terrace where it looked like deer often bedded down in the afternoon.

We had not had red meat in our diet for a long time. We were hopeful for his success. Back in England, it had been illegal to hunt, but we knew Father had secretly poached the King's deer. Father relied upon his stealth and his steady aim.

Late in the morning, we heard the sharp boom of a gun up on the ridge. Shortly we heard another shot ring across the valley.

"He might have gotten one! Oh, he got one," said Nathaniel.

After what seemed a long time, we heard a distant whoop. In a little while we heard several more. Thomas gave response to Father's cries. We looked at each other and hoped. We watched for Father expectantly. How great was our disappointment when we spied Father coming through the woods toward us empty handed except for his musket.

He stepped into the clearing. He was out of breath. "Boys," he said, "I need your help. Unhitch the wagon. Bring the ox. There are two. Two deer...up on the ridge."

We yelled out with joy. My heart was pounding. The prospect of such bounty was unbelievable. I had to stay with my mother and sisters while my father and brothers went to the hillside above us. I wanted to go with them to see and be part of it all but instead I had to wait in a flush of excitement beside our baskets and wood gleanings. Finally, Father and my brothers came leading the ox. I could see for certain that the ox was dragging two limp deer behind it. Father led the ox to a halt before Mother. He looked at Mother and bowed politely, as if giving her an offering. "Margaret, I guess this will fill the pot for us."

Mother was radiant. "Yes, Thomas, this will fill the pot aplenty."

There on the ground before us lay a very large grayish buck with spreading antlers. Beside him was a small golden doe. We stood gazing at the deer, amazed at the sudden change in our fortune.

Father began to relate the story of the hunt. "I was crouched behind a big blowdown that overlooked a strong deer trail on a hillside terrace of oak trees. I could see that the leaves in the grove were tumbled, showing where deer had been grazing on fallen acorns. The wind was right, blowing at my face. I waited for a long time. I kept my eye on the sun's movement so that I would know which direction led back to where you waited."

"I began to be tormented by thoughts that I might see better from a slightly different vantage point, but I stayed and did not move anything but my eyes. I strained to watch and listen. I began to worry that the deer might only be feeding there at night. All of a sudden, I thought I heard a shuffling of leaves. It could have been only a squirrel but then a twig snapped. I knew something big was coming."

"The hair on the back of my neck tingled. A doe came through the trees right toward me. She stopped and then lowered her head to browse. I lit the match and fired. I was sure my aim was true. I saw her rear up as if struck but when the smoke cleared, she was gone."

"There was a crash, crash, and a big white tail flipped up and sailed off through the woods. Chasing her was hopeless. I held still. The deer ran into a patch of thick brush and knelt down. I reloaded as quickly as I could behind the blowdown. I waited, listening, afraid to move lest I chase the wounded animal away."

"After a while of hearing nothing, I started to creep toward the deer. I saw an ear flicker. I froze. The deer rose up but it was not a doe. There before me was a buck with large spread of horns! I did not dare even to breathe."

"I was not quite certain how one deer had turned into another. He saw me and disappeared like a ghost. Then I saw him again. He was sneaking away broadside to me. His head went behind a tree long enough for me to lift my musket. A second later and it would have been too long a shot. I lit the match, took aim where I thought his head would come out, and pulled the trigger as soon as I saw the neck."

"The deer lunged forward and took off, running low and strong. I went to the spot where I had shot. By the hair and the patch of pinkish blood on the leaves, I knew he was hit. It took everything in me not to give chase."

"After a solid good wait to let the deer settle down, I took my bearings by the sun and started to follow the blood trail up the hill. I must tell you, I was worried when the sign grew sparse. I hoped I would not have to track him far because I feared I would have a job to find my way back. I hated the thought of not being able to find an animal after I had hurt it."

"I kept on. At the top of the hill I could see where he had stood, probably looking back at me. He had begun to bleed. The blood trail became clear to follow. I thought he could not go far like that. Fortunately, in not too long a distance I found the buck lying in a thicket just below the crest of the hill. He was dead where he had fallen. I think he went so far on courage."

"I yelled out and was relieved to hear one of you yell back, right where I thought you should be. I was deep in the woods but I was not lost, and I had taken a fine buck! I did wonder how I had missed the doe. I marked the place where the buck lay, and then I backtracked to look where I had first shot to try to sort out what had happened."

"You would not believe how surprised I was. She was right where I had first shot. I had hit her high in the spine. It looked like she had fallen backwards and dropped right down. That is why I did not see her. When I shot, he must have been right behind her. So, look. I have two deer! She is a little small, but what a size he is! Between the two, we will have meat! Two deer! We have truly been blessed by a miracle!"

I circled around the deer admiring their wondrous beauty. The deer's pretty eyes, black moist noses, and long soft ears made me sad that because of us they had been killed. As I stroked the doe's stiff fur with my fingers, I also felt hunger and then gratitude for the meals they would make. Our bellies would be full for a long time.

Father and my brothers had gutted the deer up on the ridge and washed out the inside of their bodies at a stream at the bottom of the hill. They had saved the heart, liver and kidneys for Mother to cook for us that night. That thought and all the excitement helped make the trip home easier. Thine hand was upon us that day. We took the two deer to be a sign that You would hold us in safety through the winter.

Back in the village, the men gathered around Father and the deer. It was truly remarkable that a man could have gotten two deer. As the word spread, more men came to see. Deer were not very plentiful anymore, under pursuit by both Indians and settlers. The men helped Father to put a stick between each deer's hind legs to hold them apart. They tied a rope to the middle of the stick and then tossed the other end of the rope over a stout branch of the shade tree growing outside our house. They hoisted each deer so that it would hang up and out of the reach of any dogs or beasts overnight. It was almost dusk, too late to begin cutting the meat. That would begin in the morning.

The men stood around telling stories about other deer and discussing the antlers of Father's buck. The antlers were thick and rough at the base with forked brow tines, curving up and out in identical broad branches that ended in five long, slender, polished white tips. Their graceful beauty made me feel solemn and awestruck. A magnificent creature had been sacrificed so that we could live.

I went inside when the men began to argue about the quality of these antlers compared to those of another deer previously taken. I had seen that the men respected my father for his successful hunt, but I had grown tired of listening to all their boasting. When Father came inside, he told Mother that one man wanted the antlers so badly that he had offered to trade black powder and a sack of dried corn for them. In the end, Father agreed to trade the buck's hide, head and antlers for the black powder, the sack of corn, and another of peas. Mother told Father that he had traded well. The antlers would have made buttons and handles and she could have used the hide for clothing but we needed the black powder and dried food more. We gave thanks to You for the unexpected increase in our stores for the winter.

The next morning we all rose knowing what our day's task would be. Meat that is to be dried must be cut off the bone immediately, and every bit of fat scraped and cut away. We had to work together as fast as we all could to make certain the meat did not spoil. The meat had to be cut into thin strips and hung to dry on racks made of slender sticks, which we watched and tended carefully for three or four days until the meat dried all the way through without rotting or wrinkling. We hoped it would remain sunny. We were fortunate that the weather did not turn damp. We were relieved when the meat was finally put up into a cask, bedded in salt. Had the weather turned, we would have lost good meat.

The weather here was troubling. It could be severe. Already it was colder than we had known in England. In the woods thousands of ruined trees bore witness that a mighty tempest had hit these parts just before our arrival. Men were still busy cutting up tangles of trees that had been ripped up by the roots, broken off at the tops, or twisted into flayed shatters. During the violence of wind and storm, many homes had been blown down or lost their roofs in a misery of flooding rain. The sea had swelled up onto the land causing people to flee before it.

Upon the ocean, ships had been lost in the waves. I shuddered in terror at such stories, especially upon hearing that this fearsome mid-August tempest had been followed the next night at the close of the Sabbath by an eclipse of the moon. Not only this, people also told me that the ground had been known to shake.

Mother reminded me that when Israel went forth from Egypt, the sea had fled and the mountains had skipped like rams, the hills like lambs. She said that perhaps all of this was evidence of the Lord showing great notice to the peoples of the earth that the Lord's faithful were coming out of bondage to build a kingdom of the Gospel in the wilderness. I tried to imagine how this idea gave her comfort because I hoped not to experience any such announcements. The wind that lashed rain against our trembling door was ominous enough to me.

Our little house was usually draped inside with wet, clammy clothes. At night, when the fire was banked in the hearth to conserve wood, we shivered. We had to crowd all together under our blankets to keep warm. If it became necessary to make water in the night, it was hard to leave the huddle. I could never lie back down on the precious spot I had warmed. Everyone else would roll in to the warmer middle leaving only the cold edge. My family pressed so tightly together that it was hard to get back in under the covers at all. Anyone sleeping on the edge of the bed had to keep a tight clutch on the blankets lest they be pulled away.

Winter came early that year, cutting our preparations short. By the middle of November, the snow was already deep. We suffered storm after storm. It was so sharply cold that even the salt water in the bay froze. Our world became very small, ruled by the storms that roared across the bay. The heat from our fireplace warmed our one room, but when the wind blew, the drafts came through the walls. Our backs were very cold no matter how large the fire or how close we huddled to the hearth. Some days just getting to the barn to feed our cow and ox required great exertion. The worst days brought certain work for my brothers because several older farmers needed help with their winter chores when the snow was deep. My brothers were compensated in trade with hay for our own animals or by more firewood and foodstuffs. In the intense cold, the animals ate more hay.

Our firewood dwindled faster than we had expected. Our house was so crowded that when my brothers decided to board out with other families it was honestly somewhat of a relief.

We were ill prepared for this unfamiliar climate. We were most grateful when we received a packet from Aunt Elizabeth containing stout shoes and warm clothing for each of us as well as other necessities hard for us to obtain here. With the packet came a months-old letter bearing bad news from England. Grandsire Bliss had died of the sickness he had developed during his time in jail. Uncle Jonathan was sinking away. He was so gravely ill and feverish from his wounds that Aunt Elizabeth expected he would be gone by the time her letter reached us. She reported that opposition to the King continued and that economic hard times were having an adverse effect upon the general morale. All this sorrowful news affected us greatly. Although we could not be there with Grandsire in his final days, we hoped that he had taken some comfort in knowing he was the cause of our escape to safety. Father grieved the loss of his father and brother. The pain of separation from family, friends, and country heightened as the winter raged on with brutal disregard.

Father left the house whenever he could to go out and talk with the other townsmen. He reported his news to Mother.

"Everyone is shaking their heads about how fast and hard the winter has come on. There is a great general worry about the welfare of a group of sixty families from Dorchester who struck out this fall with a large herd of cattle, swine, and horses to make a new settlement along the Great River in Connecticut."

All fall Father had listened raptly for any word about the departed party. As a new arrival himself, he was struck that these people had been driven to leave by shortages of land, food, and pasturage for their animals. They had chosen to leave the crowded coast based solely on rumors from English trappers that lush meadowlands awaited. Father was a man who craved news almost with the same desire as for food. He asked every trader coming back to town about the settlers. The party had been encountered at various points along their overland journey. Apparently, they were making slow progress. Trappers warned that the way over the mountains, rivers, and swamps was

rough any time of the year. One day Father reported to N
had heard that the party had reached their destination. Tl
encampment on the west side of the Connecticut River near the
riverbank at a fording place at Windsor. The shelters they had built
were described to Father as being little more than earthen huts in the
ground, walled in the front with posts, and covered with reed thatching
on the roofs and sides to keep out the winter snows. It seemed there
had been trouble in their crossing of the Great River. Many supplies
and cattle reportedly had been lost or were not able to be brought over
at all. The settlers had sent their principal supplies by small ships to go
by sea with the expectation of a rendezvous with the planters up river.
Father hoped that the people would get what they needed in time.

The sudden storms that hit us that year nearly trapped us all inside
the house. Our discomfort was great. Father chided us for
complaining, reminding us that some of our brethren were living in
scooped out holes in a riverbank.

Father waited for news. When it came, it was bad. Some of the
settlers' supply ships had sunk in the storm; others had been washed
over by waves, sending household goods overboard. It became clear
that many families in Windsor were waiting for supplies that would
never come. Father fretted about how such a winter could be survived
by those so severely lacking in clothes, tools, food, and all essentials.
We were horrified when a few settlers from Windsor began to return to
Dorchester, sick and starving, with distressing stories of suffering.
Most of their cattle had died. The few people who made it back to
Dorchester had struck out overland into the snowy wilds in extreme
hunger, fearing that death was upon them. One of their party had fallen
through the ice as they fled and had died before their eyes, just out of
their reach. All would have perished had not some passing Indians
rescued them. The settlers told that some of the people they had left
behind planned to escape starvation by taking refuge in a supply ship
frozen at anchor in the river. Others had chosen to dig in at the
settlement. They had said they believed they could survive by hunting,
scratching for acorns, and begging from the Indians.

When Father heard these stories, he became quiet and tense. With
the bad news from England and the bad news from the western

settlements, Father had little information to share that was fit for the ears of children. He became broody. Amidst my own worry about just trying to stay warm, I knew I had better listen carefully whenever my parents spoke. I had seen great changes in my life come after only a few words were spoken.

Several times my parents quarreled that winter. That was unusual. It made me uncomfortable. Mother thought it incredible and irresponsible that Father, like many of the other men, had been speculating about those vast meadows along the Great River. Father maintained that most of the settlers' problems that Mother worried about were brought on simply because they had set out too late in the year. With quiet voices, my parents argued about it. They whispered harshly at each other after they thought we children had gone to sleep. Father resisted listening to Mother's recital of the events being told to her about the settlement at Windsor. He could hear about all of it from his men friends but not from her. Finally, Mother shouted. It was the only time I ever heard her do so.

"Mr. Bliss, you stubborn man. You can make all the plans you want but I did not come here to see my children starve!"

The next day my parents did not seem to be speaking to each other. I held my breath and felt upset. Sometimes, I decided, it was difficult to know when You tested us with Your trials and when You rewarded us with survival, the margins between being so thin.

Father's mind was set upon acquiring land where we could prosper. When spring came, he convinced Thomas Jr. to go with a small group of Puritans to help them build up the plantation at Windsor. Led by The Reverend John Wareham of Dorchester, Thomas Jr. set out.

After Father left, our cow produced a healthy she-calf. The jolly twitch of the calf's dear little tail as it suckled made me laugh and filled me with a huge love that overspread me with joy. The baby nuzzled me and sucked on my hand with its warm little raspy mouth.

That rapture of perfection was soon over because when the time came to wean the calf, Father traded it for supplies. I was devastated when the calf went. The mother and babe called to each other pitifully as the calf was led away. Mother comforted me and reminded me that they would see each other again on the community pasture. It was true that I did enjoy our cow's milk that became abundantly ours once we did not have to share it with the calf. It was my chore to churn the cream into butter for topping our biscuits.

The warming days of that spring brought welcome fresh wild greens to eat. Mother planted a garden. Father and my brothers went to work with other farmers to supplement the expected harvest of our small field.

Our ox and cow went to pasture on the common. I went morning and evening to tend to them and to milk the cow. They knew me and came to my call. The calf was there, grown much bigger. It still remembered me.

Late in the spring, one of my brothers worked a day in exchange for a basket of tiny cheeping chicks for Mother. I guarded them as best I could but it was difficult. Seagulls, hawks, raccoons, and foxes made tries at out precious flock. We lost a few chicks, always my favorites. By the fall, we hoped to have roosters big enough to eat and hens laying eggs. We would save the best rooster so that we could hatch out new chicks the next year. I already had picked one. I hoped it would be Mother's choice as well.

That summer was long and busy, but not long enough. The frost came suddenly, killing all but the hardiest plants in the garden.

The leaves of the trees were turning to the brilliant colors of fall when Thomas Jr. returned to us full of news from the valley of the Great River. The reports of plentiful fertile land, tillable and rich were true, he said. The forests abounded with game and there was wood aplenty. The huge fresh river and the smaller ones that fed it were full of fish. Fine land was available for those willing to risk a life in the wilds.

Mother turned her back upon such conversations. She was firm in her conviction that knowledge of riches was only a temptation if not offered by the Lord's calling.

We remained on our lot south of the great harbor of Boston. We worked to fulfill our obligations to the proprietors of the colony so that Father would remain eligible for his own land grant. Father became known as Thomas of the Mount, a planter. He poured every bit of himself into creating his own little heaven on earth, as if by the sweat of his brow and the prayers of his lips he could recover what had been taken from his family in England. We labored by his side.

It was a sad thing to see Father slowly begin to realize that the promises made to the settlers by the town developers about the availability of land at Boston Mount would not be fulfilled. Instead of acreage being granted to settlers, much of it was instead set aside for the use of Boston. Rich absentee owners took over control of most of the finest lands. Father chafed under the knowledge that the years we worked our lot at Boston Mount would prove of little betterment to our future circumstances. Father continued to keep his eye to the western horizon. I noticed that he included in his prayers the hope that Your will would be made apparent.

Father was as concerned about the weather as he was about the Indians. I had never heard of Indians in England. Here in the Bay Company there were many Indians. Some were friendly to us and some not. Every nation had a different, baffling language. Father explained that along the long fresh river called the Connecticut there were even more diverse tribes of Indians. Some of these tribes had earlier sent emissaries to both the Puritans and to the Dutch inviting them to move to their lands to help protect them from their enemies. The Dutch had built a fort along the river in the friendly Indian territory to defend the fortune in furs, timber, and crops. Our Englishmen from Plymouth and Dorchester also went to the distant land to lay vying claims north of the Dutch fort. Father thought it an interesting symbol that the fort the Dutch built along the river was named the House of Hope. To the local Indians it had brought not hope but death. Father described that a gruesome plague of small pox had spread outside its walls to rage among the tribes. He had heard that the abandoned villages and fields were scattered with Indian bones and skulls.

We wondered over the horror of a valley of dry bones. Father believed that there was a direct Biblical message to us in Ezekiel's similar visions. Mother watched Father pondering over the verses from the Bible. She told him that God's Word was scarce in the wilderness. There were too few English there to carry it to the ears of heathens.

Father said, "It might take years for our English ventures to prevail but they will. Our traders are establishing good business among the tribes. They will eventually over-reach the Dutch control of trade. We English purchase our lands from the River Indians, not so the Dutch. Moreover, we bring our Savior to them. We teach them to pray."

Mother said, "Yes, but there are nations of powerful Pequots to the east of the Great River, and Iroquois and Mohawks to the west who either do not hear or do not want to hear about the Holy Spirit and God's laws."

"Oh, they are feeling God's wrath well enough. Disease has killed many people from the local tribes and weakened even the fierce Pequot," Father reminded her.

Father listened to everything about what was happening along the river. He and Thomas held many a lively conversation around the fireplace in the evenings, smoking their pipes, discussing the complicated alliances and schemes that were in the making. Father believed that the river lands held promise for our own future, and that the Indians would come to rejoice with us in Jesus in the holy commonwealth that was our destiny.

Mother listened to all Father's talk silently as the troubles with the Pequots worsened. She cast a long warning eye at Father when we all heard that the Pequots had killed a trader along the Great River. The man had earned a bad reputation for trickery but his death was a dangerous justice. Mother's opinion was that the brazenness of the killing showed that there was no safety or peace along the river for our kind.

The Bay Colony was not a gentle place for the building of the covenanted society for which we had all hoped. Father's dreams and prayers could not feed us during the times when there was little to put into the pot.

I heard Mother ask Father one day, "Thomas, do you really think this life is better than what we left behind in England?"

I craned my ears to hear his answer. I had wondered that too. Father had no answer that day or ever.

Father believed it was our duty to be an example to all Your children. He did not approve of treating the Indians in any other way but as a Christian parent would to guide a child. Father's ideals conflicted with what we were doing to survive in this land.

The increasing numbers of men fighting over the rich meadowlands seemed only to bring more news to our ears about worsening ferocities. We heard more frightening tales about deadly encounters between the settlers and the Pequots. In April at Wethersfield, a party of Pequot warriors attacked townspeople as they went to work in their fields. Nine Englishmen were massacred and the savages took two maids captive. The raiding party slaughtered the town's cattle.

My brothers heard things from their friends at school that our parents would not have wanted us to know. We knew that death came to Indians and settlers along the Great River and that it was often grisly.

The discussions that filled our home grew more troubled. In addition to the fears about the war with the Pequots and the disappointment about divisions of land at Boston Mount, there was another problem. A controversy had begun that was dividing our community and all of the Bay Colony. The dispute was about the proselytizing of a local woman named Anne Hutchinson. The Hutchinsons had a large farm up on the highland above us. We knew Goodwife Hutchinson as a gentle midwife and a mother. She was the wife of a wealthy merchant who came to Boston Mount in the summer. She was also a student of the Bible. We heard that her home at Boston had become a gathering place for women to meet and discuss recent sermons, particularly those of The Reverends Cotton and Wilson. All the gossip about those interesting Bible study discussions was much easier to listen to than talk about the Indian terrors.

I remember that Mother told me "Goody Hutchinson's interpretations of Scripture are daring. She believes that the Holy Spirit speaks directly to her and she believes the Holy Spirit will speak to all individuals. Goody Hutchinson is gifted with mystical ability. She receives direct revelations of salvation through faith. She wants to show us the way to become 'Godded.' She believes that any person can open their mind to the intuitive covenant of grace. She teaches that women should not be kept silent, that Indians should not be enslaved, and that no minister need come between the mouth of God and the ears of the faithful saint; man or woman!"

It seemed to me that Goody Hutchinson was inspiring Mother. Mother was not alone in this. I also heard many other people talk about how thrilled they were by Goodwife Hutchinson's message. The mothers of almost everyone I knew had been to her. Even the men had begun to go with their wives to hear her speak. Such mingling of men with women was usually considered an immorality. A great change had come. I heard that the Governor of the Commonwealth, Henry Vane, was often seen by her side. Our own minister, Reverend Wheelwright, invited the discussions to move into our meetinghouse at Boston Mount when the groups of people who gathered around Goody Hutchinson's skirts became too large for the Hutchinson home. It was very exciting. I remember that whenever Mother congregated with other women, whether over the quilting frame or the flax combs, there were always new believers ready to share Goody Hutchinson's ideas. Most people who heard her agreed that her message was sweet to the soul, but not everyone felt this way.

Father said, "Many are upset by Goodwife Hutchinson's criticism of the Massachusetts Bay clergy and magistrates. She claims that they have unrighteously set themselves up as legal interpreters between God and His faithful. The clergy and magistrates fear that she and her followers could form a cult that might challenge their authority within the colony to uphold the laws of our holy mission. Many important Boston ministers are crying for her to stop. People are calling her a heretic and a Jezebel. I do not think it would end well for any of us to attend her lectures. Her detractors are very powerful, even though she seems to be under the protection of Governor Vane."

I suspected that long before Father asked Mother to promise that she would never go to hear Goody Hutchinson, she had already been to lectures. I believed this because all of a sudden one day Mother had taken to speaking with a new intimacy about the Holy Spirit. Whenever she experienced something that pleased her she would exclaim something that she had never said before, "The Holy Spirit illumines the heart." At such times, I noticed in my mother's voice a tone of tender peacefulness. A flood of smooth radiance would shine upon her face.

It was rumored that Goody Hutchinson had begun to preach that only two of all the ministers of the Bay Colony were elected by You for salvation. One of these whom she saw as "Godded" was her teacher, The Reverend John Cotton. The other was our minister, The Reverend John Wheelwright, her brother-in-law. People said that many of Goody Hutchinson's other clergymen friends were beginning to withdraw from her. In January, The Reverend Wheelwright preached such a brilliant sermon in defense of Goody Hutchinson that all her followers rejoiced in the hopes that a resolution to the controversy might be reached.

In May of 1637, something happened that would change our lives. One morning the call of the drum and horn was heard passing throughout our streets. This was the signal to gather at the meetinghouse. It not being a lecture day, I was nervous to know why we were being assembled. I could not remember that such a thing had ever happened before.

"This is not a day we have to go to meeting," I protested.

No one in my family knew why the call was being sounded. There was no question that it was the signal to assemble. With a single mind, everyone around me hurried to respond. Father and my brothers grabbed their muskets and hats. Mother made certain that each of us had our cloaks on and began to herd us all toward the door. From every house, people were pouring into the street with unusual urgency. At each crossroad along the way to the church common, the crowd grew in numbers and in noise. Because it was not meeting day or the Sabbath people began to raise their voices in excitement, calling out to each other with wild suggestions about the cause of the signal. Upon reaching the common, the crowd pressed in on each other. I was uncomfortably pushed up against my family and neighbors. People began to look toward the meetinghouse steps. The Captain of the town militia stepped forward with the minister and a strange man. I strained to see. The trumpet sounded a small burst for our attention. The milling crowd stilled to hear. The stranger began to shout out news.

"Two days ago at daybreak, a company of eighty of our militia and about three hundred of our Indian allies from the Narragansett and Mohegan tribes surprised a Pequot stronghold. Their fort was set afire. All inside perished. More than six hundred Pequot were killed." He proclaimed jubilantly, "The Pequot nation is wiped out! No more will they threaten the lives of our English settlers and our River Indian friends. The Indian threat is destroyed!"

A cheer rose up from the crowd. Men shook hands with each other, the women hugged and cried. The minister called for silence. Our entire community bowed our heads. Together we offered our prayers to You, Lord, for sustaining us. Afterwards people were slow to go home. The crowd broke up into little knots of people visiting and chatting. Children and dogs ran among them playing. I walked around listening to what different groups were saying. The group where my mother stood rejoiced that no more men would have to go to battle. They remembered the names of people they knew who had died.

Nathan was in a group of young men who were imagining the final battle. They chortled, "The savages are frying in hell where they belong."

Father stood apart from such talk. The group of older men he chose to associate with were talking more charitably about the general impact of new hope and opportunity within the colony.

Someone in his group said, "A Garden of Eden is now ours to open with our plows, our laws, and our holy purpose."

Although Your ways seemed unfathomable, we offered ourselves to Your purpose and gave our thanks, as do I now. May it be that by Your trials and lessons I may come to know what I am to do. Amen.

Chapter 6

Stained Soil

Boston Mount, 1637-1640

This is the generation of them that seek Him
Of them that seek Your face. Psalm 24:6

Lord, to do Your will, families of good reputation were needed to inhabit the new settlements of the Great River meadowlands. We were such. We heard the word through our minister that Reverend Thomas Hooker and his congregation would welcome our church members and their families at Hartford. They had established a plantation at the feet of the once powerful Dutch fortress and trading house. We were reassured that the sheer number of English settlers pouring up the river had long stilled the cannons of the Dutch fort. Our settlers by now vastly outnumbered the Indians who inhabited the valley.

With the warring over, at last Mother consented to prepare to join our brethren at Hartford. When Mother agreed that Your call had come for us to settle at Hartford, it seemed to me that even the chestnut trees celebrated our decision. We went into the country to view the hills bursting into flower, covered in clouds of stinking white blossoms. That spring and summer, Father and Thomas farmed the land at Boston Mount knowing that the next spring they would be breaking ground in Hartford.

The end of the hostilities of the Pequot Nation did nothing to mend the divisions that tore at our town. We lived in a state of uneasy balance within our congregation because of the divisiveness of religious controversy that rose around Goody Hutchinson's preaching. The opposition against both The Reverend Wheelwright and Goody Hutchinson was rallying to new strength. In a public speech at Boston, The Reverend John Wilson spoke out his concern that the dissent of

Wheelwright and Anne Hutchinson posed "inevitable dangers of separation." Father, of course, followed all of these struggles very closely.

In his opinion, "The hands that rise against Wilson and Hutchinson will also push Governor Vane out of office."

Father and his group of friends had smoked many bowls of tobacco while discussing evidence that the powers of the colony were aligning against the threats of Goody Hutchinson and her followers. When they heard that the scheduled election of that year was to be moved from its usual location to a town unsympathetic to Vane's thinking they all agreed it was over for Governor Vane. Father and his friends puffed and pontificated about the appearance of sly maneuvering on the part of Vane's powerful opponent in the election, John Winthrop.

Mr. Winthrop was a man known to have little toleration for dissenters. Just as my father predicted, when the election was done, it was John Winthrop who was elected to be the new governor of the Massachusetts Bay Company. Governor Winthrop stepped into office and almost immediately filed charges of heresy against both Anne Hutchinson and The Reverend Wheelwright, ordering them to stand before a jury that he himself had appointed.

In November of the same year that the Pequot threat had been lifted from us, we felt a new kind of dread when Goody Hutchinson was ordered to go before the General Court of Massachusetts. Everyone had no doubt that it would be a heated trial. Never in the colony's history had such learned and oratorically skilled religious and political leaders lined up against each other so publicly. It was so fascinating and yet so awful. Everyone around me seemed to talk of nothing else.

People in our community drew apart, associating only with those who agreed with them, and standing back from those who did not. There was no place for a girl in her teens to escape the uproar of these events. It seemed that every day there were new points for people to mull over with agitation. I watched all that happened around me. It was painfully confusing to witness such conflicting loyalties and doubt.

When the date of trial came, many went to Boston to listen. Those who were there gave mixed reports. Goody Hutchinson had apparently spoken brilliantly and courageously, answering boldly to the charges and challenging assumptions, but many hurtful insults had been exchanged, especially between Hutchinson and Winthrop.

The trial ended with a dreadful verdict. Goody Hutchinson was found guilty of traducing the ministers by encouraging people to question the fathers of our colony in violation of the fifth commandment to honor the father and mother. By the vote of the most important clergy and government officials in the colony, she was ordered banished from our midst forever. She was judged a woman not fit for our society. Even The Reverend John Cotton, her inspiration, stood against her. Because it was late in the season and Goody Hutchinson was in her forty-sixth year and great with child, she was shown the small mercy of being placed under house arrest to be held through the winter until her appearance for a religious trial in the coming spring.

As for The Reverend Wheelwright, he was also found guilty and sent into exile. He packed up his family and went far north, out of the reach of the colony. Our former governor, Henry Vane, sold his home and left the colonies to return to England. We lost our minister, our governor, and our prophetess. As a result of the severity of these judgments and consequences, emotional rifts between family and friends grew deeper and did not heal.

I wondered whether all of these goings on were right with You. As a thirteen-year-old, I had very much entered a time when I was no longer a child. I saw myself as a young woman whom adults should be acknowledging as a righteous daughter of Zion. In turn, I expected people to live up to their highest beliefs. In all this battle about who knew most truly the laws of Your will, it seemed to me that each side had become more drenched in anger than in the grace and expectations of good works they expected from others. People I respected were pitted against one and other.

I wanted someone to admire. I wanted that person to be Anne Hutchinson because of all the beautiful things she believed in, but I had begun to doubt her. I doubted her because people I respected doubted her. I was not sure of what was true myself. I was not a Bible scholar. I did wonder how I would behave if I were being treated unfairly. Would I rise in anger as she had? How could a woman speak her mind with honor when men refused to hear a woman speak at all? Should Goody Hutchinson have bowed her head and mutely nodded her agreement to an apology prepared for her by men of the court and church? As unjust as I sometimes thought people had been to her, it bothered me that a woman so much more learned than a girl like me could ever hope to be had sullied her modesty by stooping to threaten Governor Winthrop. It was said that Goody Hutchinson had shouted out "...for this that you go about to do unto me, God will ruin you and your posterity, and this whole State."

I would never dare to talk like that. People who opposed her used this comment to laugh at her arrogance at seeming to believe that You acted as her servant. Those were not the meanest words that were said about her. Her voice had been an annoyance to so many, yet, if she had not spoken out many would not have found their way to knowledge of salvation. I pictured Goody Hutchinson as a fallen angel who very sadly had disappointed my hopes that she was someone even better. I wrestled with my thoughts about the lesson I should take from Goody Hutchinson. I was sad for her, all her family, and for my mother too.

With the peace of our congregation broken, my mother was ready to prepare our family for a departure from the Massachusetts Bay Company. Father did not hesitate to share his thoughts with her about what he knew of The Reverend Hooker in Hartford, a man whose teachings he admired. Disgruntled by the religious controversies of Boston, The Reverend Hooker had left with many of his followers to help build new more principled communities. Father contained his idealism by being practical; he spent the winter gathering the tools he would need for cutting trees, sawing planking, and building a house. I watched as he sharpened his axes and adzes, and then the plow blade for breaking up thick virgin sods.

Knowing Father was making ready to leave us reminded me of how I felt when he had left us on the ship at the docks of Boston to go off to find land in a strange new place. I noticed that the anticipation of his upcoming departure did not fill me with fright. Although my father would be far away from us for a long time, this time I trusted that he would be in Your hand.

As winter began to ease, Father was almost ready to go ahead with Thomas Jr. to Hartford to make the necessary preparations for us to follow. Clearing land and cutting timber to dry for the building of a house and barn was more than one season's work, but Father and Thomas were strong, healthy, and confident. They had waited a long time for this. We were all full of hope when they left us on the first day the muddy roads were dry enough for traveling.

Goody Hutchinson's religious trial came in March of 1638, just after Father and Thomas left for Hartford. All the ears of the Massachusetts Bay Colony were turned toward Goody Hutchinson the day she stood before the clergy at the First Church in Boston. She stood accused of blasphemy and of lewd and lascivious conduct for encouraging the mingling of sexes. They say her words of defense rang out courageously but her very eloquence was used as proof that she was an instrument of the Devil. By verdict of the church fathers, she was excommunicated.

After the judgment was reached against her, the joyous talk of faith and salvation was replaced by gossip and revulsion for Anne Hutchinson and her husband. The faces of people I thought I knew gaped open in strange contagious laughter. Spittle and ugly words spewed out from a blackness of soul I had not known they possessed. I had seen some of these very people praying at meeting. I had thought of them as kind brethren. Before my eyes they transformed into people who gloated that William Hutchinson was a mere wisp of a man who had lost control over his wife. Shutting out the awful sounds, I watched their mouths, noticing how the motion of their lips was like the vent of a chicken. Even after Goody Hutchinson, her husband, and all their children left us to move to a settlement at Rhode Island, a place of Quakers and other strange thinkers, the foul rumors about her continued to grow like mold on bread. Plenty of people scratched about for those last scraps of gossip, seeking to fill their bellies with proof that God's justice had been served. It no longer mattered. Goody Hutchinson was cast out, and her followers were silenced. Mother warned me to be careful how I spoke with my friends because feelings were very sore.

From the pulpit, our new minister warned that the stain of ungoverned speech must not be permitted to spread to all women. It was a message that he repeated frequently in the weeks that followed. We were reminded that only ministers were ordained to translate Your words. The peace and order of our commonwealth depended upon our ministers' continuing guidance to lead us to our Lord. Our minister said that only through the direction of the ministry would the courts of the Bay Colony continue to govern us according to Your laws. There were many in the congregation who nodded, casting sharp glances around them.

One especially painful Sabbath our minister delivered a sermon about the slithering seductions of the unbridled female tongue. The message was so strong that my own tongue began to feel horrifyingly fat and slippery and big within my mouth. I pursed my lips tightly against it, lest any one should see its dangerous restlessness. After the meeting was over, I noticed that all the women in the congregation left very quietly. They were subdued in a way I found frightening. I wished I could become a free man instead of an invisible silent woman. My mother shook her head at such talk. I knew she had feelings that she would not tell me.

She said only, "The Lord bends his ear to all who speak with a truthful tongue."

I believe that Mother was changed in her thinking by her discomfort with the ways powerful men of the commonwealth kept people in their places. Although guarded of speech to the end of her days, few ever saw that behind the veil of my mother's eyes she freely used her mind and her determination to guide our family through a multitude of dangers. I began to admire my mother.

One day Mother told me that a new baby was coming.

I asked, "How do you know?"

Mother looked at me. "Mary, you are old enough to hear."

She took me for a walk, just the two of us. Mother told me many private things. We talked a lot that day. She told me about my brother Thomas Jr. and my sister Ann. Mother explained that Thomas Jr. and

Ann had not been her babies, although she had felt for a long time as if they were her own children. Father had once been married, she said, to another woman who died after Thomas Jr. and Ann were born. When she met Father at Rodborough, his parents at the family farm were raising Thomas Jr. and Ann. She talked a little bit about meeting Father in Rodborough and how happy she was when they decided to marry. At first, she said, she had cared about Thomas Jr. and Ann because they were Father's, but she had come to love Thomas Jr. and Ann for themselves. She said that people would call Thomas Jr. my half-brother and Ann my half-sister. I told her that I could only think of them as my brother and sister, as I always had. She agreed that she felt the same. I asked if I was her baby. She said yes. Nathan was her first boy. I was her first girl. That made me glad. I was happy that I was hers and that I looked like her. We turned back through the field to return home. I felt tall, grown, and full of special knowledge. The bond of closeness I felt with Mother was stronger than I had ever felt before.

That summer an old woman told me about a time in the past, long before the present troubles, when Boston Mount had been known for sin. In earlier days, the village had been called Merry Mount. It had become a place fallen to loose and immoral ways. People were frolicsome and there had been revelry in the company of Indian women. One spring the men had dared to erect a pagan maypole upon the hill. They had danced and celebrated ancient spring rites until the Puritans of Plymouth put it all to an end by sending Captain Miles Standish to arrest the leader, Thomas Morton. They took Morton's land and ejected him from the Bay Colony. He went back to England in disgrace. The husband of the old woman grumbled that the whole thing had actually been blown up bigger than it was only because the colony at Plymouth felt threatened that the men of Merry Mount were better hunters and trappers. I had no way of knowing if that were true since most of the men of that time were gone. Boston Mount was presently in the care of men who strove to enforce proper Christian obedience.

It had been an eventful summer. Father returned to us at harvest time just before the birth of baby Sarah. He was clearly pleased that all our animals were fat and that the fields had yielded well. Father looked as brown and muscular as the ox he brought back with him. He and Thomas proudly related the great effort they had given to break up the thick sods that grew upon the dark deep soils of our lot. They had felled trees and dragged them to the sawpit to feel the blade of the two-man saw. Boards and beams lay stacked and shimmed to dry for building the following year, he boasted contentedly. Father liked the community he had seen at Hartford. He was certain that life would be better there for us in all ways. The church there was thriving and strong.

Father chanted words spoken by The Reverend Hooker that were inspirational to him. "The foundation of authority is laid, firstly, in the free consent of the people."

Father wanted us to understand and remember this principle. It erased forever the possibility that oppression such as we had suffered in England would ever be visited upon us again. Even before we moved, we were proud of the men who served upon the General Court of the River towns of Hartford, Windsor, and Wethersfield. They had drafted a constitution that guaranteed in writing that all free men would be ruled by a government that openly protected the rights of the individual. Governor Winthrop himself had carried the Fundamental Orders of Connecticut to England and presented them to King Charles II, who approved them. Such intelligence and exhilarating bravery thrilled my father and filled him with courage. After watching the expulsion of our minister and Goody Hutchinson, we were in need of The Reverend Hooker's hopeful vision.

Father and Thomas went again to Hartford the next spring to work our claim. They returned late in the fall. Father reported that our new house was completed enough to accommodate our family. As winter's howling winds came again across the bay, we took solace that this would be our last at Boston Mount.

The anticipated great land division at Hartford took place in January of 1640. Father was granted his six-acre plot and Thomas Jr. his adjoining four-acre plot by courtesy of the Town, with rights to collect wood, to keep swine, and to pasture cattle on the common pasture. Each grant was to remain in their name as long as the land was improved and we abided by the laws set forth by the town and by the General Court.

That same spring Father's claim at Boston Mount was also granted to him. Father arranged to sell the house and lot to another planter. With the house sold, we were ready to move to Hartford. I remember that the leaves on the trees were no bigger than a mouse's ear when the time came for us to prepare for our journey to the colony along the Great River.

Father cried out, "For this God is our God for ever and ever: He will be our guide even unto death. Amen."

Chapter 7

Into the Wilderness

Hartford, Connecticut, 1640

Lord, may it please You to remember the earnest hopefulness with which we undertook our momentous relocation.

Trusting only in Your sustaining mercy, the menfolk of families ready to settle at Hartford agreed upon a date of departure. We packed and made ready. Our urgent prayers that You guard us from harm and lead us in Your ways were upon our lips and in our minds with fervor.

Father and my brothers loaded beds, the loom, pots, and kettles, the casks of dried peas and other foodstuffs, household goods and tools, and our wearing clothes into the ox cart. The beer added great weight to our load, but it was a necessity to protect us from having to drink water along the way. Water carries sickness. Beer would keep us healthy. Mother watched how they packed, making certain that anything that might be needed along the way was not buried.

On our last night at Boston Mount, we slept on the floor in the empty house with just our blankets. We arose early at first light to find the morning clear and pleasant. The eastern horizon was just turning a delicate pink when Father stuffed the last of the carefully rolled bedding into one of the two battered, waterproof trunks packed aboard the cart. It would not be well for us if our bedding got wet. Father lashed the load to hold it securely. Mother looked around the house one last time. I left the house that had sheltered us for so long with barely a look over my shoulder. Lingering gazes and saying goodbye had been done aplenty in the days before. I was eager to go. It was my feeling that at last we were embarked toward the destination You had intended for us.

We were among the first to arrive at the meeting place on the common. I could see that most of the other families of our party were well within sight, herding their cows and swine before them. Only one family caused a wait. I looked upon the familiar sights of Boston Mount. Emotion erupted through my chest and caught in my throat. I willed back unwanted tears. Mother's call to eat some biscuits saved me from falling into an unexpected sadness. I held the biscuit she offered cupped in my hands. Its familiar shape and fragrance seemed very important to my life. Mother had made these biscuits in every place we had lived. She would make more no matter where we went. I accepted the biscuit as a sign of Your good will.

The straggling family arrived. The party began to move at once, all in the same direction, gradually forming into a line of no particular order. That is how we set out to cross into a land unknown to us. Father exalted and coaxed us onward with his favorite verses 3-5 from Isaiah.

Prepare ye the way of the Lord:
make straight in the desert a path for our God.
Every valley shall be exalted, and every mountain and hill shall be made low:
and the crooked shall be straight and the rough places plain.
And the glory of the Lord shall be revealed,
and all flesh shall see it together:
for the mouth of the Lord hath spoken it.

Lord, You did not subdue the way nor make it straight or easy for us. Once we left the coast, the terrain became more hilly and wild. I would never have been able to imagine the misery we would endure. Our animals had plenty of forage and seemed not to mind the little nipping insects that began to trouble us immediately when we drew away from the coast. The animals lashed away the biting pests with their tails. We made do, swatting with our hands or tree branch switches until too exhausted to bother. We built smoky fires at night but unless a cold night drove the insects away, the humming and buzzing of wings and the touch of little stingers kept me awake. My skin burned from my scratching.

For fourteen days, our party followed the old Indian trail, keeping to the high ground as much as possible. We followed the Old Connecticut Path, a rutted cartway that meandered southwesterly.

Sometimes in the boggy lowlands, the way divided into multiple branches, causing me to worry that we might lose our way. My shoes and the hem of my skirt became stained by sticky, black muck. It was a relief when we traveled on firm ground under the shady canopy of tall trees. In the forests there was little deadfall or brush to hinder us because the Indians burned the woods in the spring and fall. What frightened me was when we came to treacherous rivers. Once I lost my footing in the middle of a small but fast river and fell on my knee. My knee swelled up and pained me for several days. We got wet each time we made a crossing. It was always a blessing to be dry.

One day it started to rain and did not stop. We walked on all day, dripping with water, bowed under its soaking weight, shielding our faces from its streaming. The rain continued through the night. Everyone crowded under the wagons for shelter. Boughs of pine were laid down in an attempt to hold us above the water that trickled down the wagon and splashed on us. The boughs barely softened the hard bones of the earth that pressed into our bodies. We had to sleep sitting up, leaning against the spoked wheels of the wagon or against each other. The men slept with their muskets across their laps, trying to keep the power dry. I woke damp and shivering.

We had to move to keep warm. We pressed onward without starting any morning fires. My clothes were stuck to me. My skirt clung to my legs so that they moved stiffly. Everyone was wet and smelled badly. At the end of that day, the sun came out and the sky turned blue.

We stopped to make camp. The men separated from the women so that outer clothes could be dried on sticks propped near the fire. In our group, the women and children gathered near the fire and steamed their inner garments dry by turning around and around. I charred my chemise but it did not burn through. I stood by the fire until I was dry. Had I spent another night wet I think I would have gotten very sick.

I began to expect that at the end of each day our guide would always find us a dry flat camping place near good drinking water. I noticed that the fire pits of those who had camped before us marked our way. We used the fire pits gratefully, as we were always weary when we stopped for the night. The food we ate in the evenings was very simple. There was no time for making the long-cooked stew I so craved. I was hungry very often during that trip, especially after we went those days in the rain without any cooked food.

Our guide thought we should camp near a native village. He left us to go speak to the tribe. He returned with a small group of Indian men who came up to us and made greetings. I had to turn my eyes from the men because they wore only small skin garments. Their arms and legs were bare, and most of their chests, except for decorations. I glimpsed what I thought might be beads, claws and feathers. I had never seen so much of the nature of man. I was afraid I might see too much of them, even though I was curious. Our trail guide said we were being welcomed to eat with them and that we should go. He suggested we bring a gift to show our respect.

Father thought about what to give. We had nothing extra. As he stood before the uncovered belongings packed in the wagon, he touched what things he had. Finally, he began to draw out a hoe.

Mother said, "We will need that."

"What else is there? We cannot spare a pot."

Behind the wooden handle of the hoe, I saw the cloth bundle that held my poppet. "Give this," I said.

"A poppet? That is no proper gift." Father was shaking his head.

Our guide happened to passing by, and he said, "No, that will do. Have your daughter give it. I will tell you when and who to give it to. It will be fine."

We were led into the village to a large fire, around which were a great number of people; men, women and children. I noticed that the women were more modestly covered than the men, but I remained careful where I placed my eyes. Our guide directed us toward the center of the group to an older Indian man whom I took to be very important. Our men laid their gifts on a blanket before him. I was curious to see what our families had to offer. I saw several knives, a pipe, some buttons and needles, a shovel, some ribbon, an empty beer barrel.

Our guide came to me and said, "Come with your poppet."

I laid my poppet on the blanket in front of the man with the other gifts. Our guide said a few words that seemed to make the Indian man laugh. The Indian man called out a word, which caused a small girl to come forward. He pointed to my bundle. The girl picked up the bundle and proceeded to unwrap it. When she saw my poppet, her eyes grew large. My heart pounded. She brought the poppet to her chest and hugged it. The important Indian man nodded and smiled at her. The little girl went away, holding my dear poppet, stroking its face and talking to it.

After that, our women and we children were separated from the men. We were taken to another fire where Indian women were cooking in front of bark huts. As strange and marvelous as the dwellings, the clothes, and faces of the Indians were to me, what most drew me was the strong aroma of cooked food. The village smelled deliciously fragrant. An old woman with kindly eyes wrapped in wrinkles pointed that we should sit down. She talked to other Indian women in speech I did not understand. I saw that food began to be given out, first to the oldest of us and finally to us children. I was handed a chunk of tender stewed venison. The meat was rich and juicy. I fell upon it eagerly without question. My mouth overran with sweetness. No sooner was I was licking its juices from my fingers than another piece was offered to me. We were also given pungent greens smelling of garlic, which were mixed with fiddlehead ferns. It was the first fresh green any of us had eaten since the fall. I ate a slightly sweet mash that seemed to be a starchy root of some kind. The food was unfamiliar but plentiful and very welcome in my belly. I do not remember as much as I would think I should have. The big meal and the warm fire made me feel sleepy.

After the meal was complete, our guide gathered us all together to return to the big fire with the men. The guide spoke at length with the important Indian man. His words seemed to please everyone who could understand. In my sleepy haze, it seemed none too soon when our guide told us to smile and bow to indicate our thanks, and to then depart the village.

During our walk toward our camp, I admitted to my mother that I had some regret that my poppet was gone. My friend would never understand my giving it away. My mother told me that what I had done was good. As I walked in the light of the moon, I began to feel happy and amazed at what I had seen, despite my loss.

The next day we resumed our journey to Hartford. As I walked onward, I wondered all day over the kindness these people had shown us. The people who had befriended us were not brethren, not people who held the Bible, but they had acted toward us with what I had been taught to think of as Christian charity. I did not know how such a thing could be. I was sure it had to be of Your doing, and I thanked You.

With a full belly of fresh food for the first time since we had left the coast, I felt alive. I listened to the noise of our caravan, which was so constant that I had stopped hearing it. All around me was the creaking of swaying ox carts, the snapping of whips, the crying of babies, the blatting of sheep, the shouts of our men urging their beasts onward. I compared the small crunching sounds of my feet moving one in front of the other to the hollow thud of heavy hooves. The indifferent land muffled the sharp sounds of our passing with moss and mud. The effort of each step was much greater than anything that could be heard by the ear. I realized that many things were happening to me that I could not really understand. I followed my family onward through the lands of Thine own savage children as we made our journey to Zion.

Again, at the end of the day's travel we made yet another fire against the unknowns hidden in the long dark night. I remember that the woodsman who had been hired to guide our group along the path through the wilderness engaged some of our men in a particularly hearty discussion. What our men said was ordinary. What the guide said was amazing and has stuck with me. Our guide was trying to tell of his experiences with the many tribes who inhabited the woods and fields along the rivers. Some men had a hard time listening. They interrupted him with their own chatter. At best, they were argumentative, even as they sat so comfortable from the meal the Indians had provided to us just the previous evening. I noticed that my father sat quietly, nodding, and encouraging the guide to go on. Our guide gave examples of how each tribe was very different in its ways. He asserted that usually their compassion toward us could be boundless, and that it arose from the well-being of the land and from God. Some of our men scoffed that Indians had no God. The guide rolled his eyes and shook his head. He said that we would do well to understand that if we treated each Indian with the same respect as we would extend to one of our pastors, and did not interfere with their lives, that the Indians could show us the holiness of the land and how it could be urged to sustain us through all its seasons, not just in the good times. The guide was very serious when he said this. A few of the men laughed.

One man began to brag that he could plow a field better than any one; Puritan, stranger, or savage. The guide closed his mouth and said not another word to him or anyone. I wanted to thank our guide for what he had said, but I was just a girl. I knew I must be quiet. Later, as the guide put the last wood on the fire for the night I heard him talking to my father.

"We English, and the Dutch too, have not had an easy time of it along the Great River. From the beginning, we have known hardship in the winter and many of us have died. More would have died had it not been for the Indians. It does not sit well with me when settlers laugh at my gratitude toward the Indians. I was there and saw when a flotilla of tribesmen came silently out of an early morning river mist paddling canoes full of food to feed a town of starving Englishmen. How did we reward them for their generosity? We turned our muzzles toward them, and we barred them from the very harvests they taught us how to raise, in the places where it was they who prepared the soil. I have decided that this is the last group of English I will lead to the valley of the Great River. It will not be long until the woods here are pushed back and game becomes as scarce as it is along the coast. Once we come to Hartford I will collect my pay and go north beyond the reach of the company proprietors and their ministers."

After many long days, our guide declared that we were nearing the end of our journey. We had come upon the silty bottomlands of the Great River. Huge stands of spicy smelling white pines rose up to great heights there with trunks as big around as our wagons were wide. Father estimated that some of the trees looked to be over 150 feet tall, some maybe even taller. We were amazed at these giants and at the works of Thine hand evident in this place. We had come a long way.

We stopped when we reached the Great River. To me the river looked as if it were running high and strong, even at the fording place where our guide said it was safe to cross. Our men cut stout staves from tree branches and saplings that grew along the river and gave them out until each person had one. I found a long pale stick with no bark that had been chewed to a point on each end by a beaver. It felt good in my hand and gave me confidence. Our guide pointed out the way across and helped the weaker ones. I did as he said. There were dark places where the water was deep, and places where the current poured in strong spouts between the rocks. I avoided those. For me the water mostly came up to my knees. We slowly picked our way across, wading upstream toward the opposite shore, two abreast to steady each other. The larger animals and teams were led over. The pigs and sheep found their own way, which I never thought they could. By Your hand, we were delivered to the other side wet but unhurt. Hartford was within easy travel now. We reached the crest of a small rise and saw smoke rising from the Hartford settlement in the distance. The road continued alongside the Great River, passing wetlands of grasses and reeds. Finally, we reached a road that led up the riverbank from a landing at the water's edge. Before us was a line of storehouses flanked by rows upon rows of houses. Beyond we could see large pastures upon which many livestock grazed. Acres of plowed fields stretched into a gently rolling countryside. A small river divided the town in half. Father pointed in the direction of the southern back edge of town.

"My land is there, on the other side of the little river." When he saw that our eyes followed where he indicated, he opened both his arms wide and made a sweeping gesture, giving it all to us.

We were beautific as we rolled into the town. A group of children caught sight of our little group and began to run along beside and ahead of us. They clamored and yelled to their friends to come and see. Our party came to a halt when we came to a meetinghouse. We were haggard and rag tag, but just the same, people appeared out of dooryards and gardens to gather around our party to offer welcome. I even recognized a few faces. Men came forward to shake Father's hand and to nod at Mother. My heart pounded with excitement as I watched the people of our new town making a fuss over us. There were still people coming toward our wagons when Mother nudged Father. She was eager to go on to Father's house.

"See to the animals, Thomas. They are nervous. Watch them. They will bolt. We must go. Let us go, Thomas, before we lose them."

Our cows were shuffling their feet and the pigs were milling under our wagon grunting in protest, coming dangerously near the restless hooves of the oxen. We turned our attention to the business of herding them through the townspeople. As the crowd parted for us my eyes fell upon an all too familiar sight, something I would have thought would not be needed here in this community created in Your name by our own sainted brethren. There in the meetinghouse yard was a stocks and pillory. Aghast, I pointed them out to my parents. Neither Father nor Mother seemed disappointed to find evidence that sin existed in the town we had struggled so hard to reach.

Whether it be sanctified or not, as we passed through the town I was struck by its orderliness and found the small river that ran through it appealing. The houses were well built. Everyone we saw waved at us in friendship. We crossed over the Little River at a busy mill and went straight through a crossroads.

"Here. We are coming to my land now on the left. First from the crossroads is Thomas Seldon's. Next is mine, and next to that is Thomas Jr.'s. See, here is the edge of my lot, and there is my house!"

The house was smaller than those nearer the Great River were but much larger than that in which we had been living. It was sturdy and appeared snug and well built. I adored it instantly. Father had not seen the house since he left the previous fall. He cautiously examined the thatching, looking for signs of any leaks in the roof caused by the weight of the winter snow and ice. He was satisfied that the house had fared fairly well with only slight damage from melt water. The barn was cluttered in places with bits of litter from squirrels and mice, but otherwise it was stout and smelled sharply of clean wood. Father began pointing here and there, showing Mother what was and what would be.

"On this side of the house I want to extend the roof line and enlarge the kitchen with more sleeping space above. Over here is where I thought you might plant your herbs."

There was a small fenced garden area ready to be hoed and seeded. We drove the animals into the enclosure around the barn and released the chickens. Around us, we saw the acres of good rich meadow tilled by Father and Thomas Jr. Mother was smiling as she followed Father around the house. He showed her hewn wooden beams and posts and clay-daubed walls. Although Father had told her what he had built, Mother gazed as if in amazement at all that stood before her, running her hands over doors and oil-papered windows. As she stood before the fireplace, she suddenly threw her arms out and spun around in a circle on the hearth. She stepped to Father, took his hand, and patted it with joy and pleasure.

That night, long past sunset, I sat on the large flat stone that served as our front step waiting for the moon to rise. I watched as the moon cast shadows on the sweet new grass of our dooryard. I lay myself down upon the soft grass and let acceptance of the finality of our arrival fill me with wonderment and peace. Just as Mother had once assured me it would, the moon shone with cool assurance upon the roof of the solid home Father had made for us so far from where we had started.

From the first day, we flourished at Hartford. The church community adopted us immediately. Neighbors brought gifts of food and local knowledge. The Deacon visited. After we began to attend church, The Reverend Thomas Hooker himself called upon us. My father was greatly honored.

It was spring, the season to seed the ground. Within two weeks of our arrival, the garden and field began to show the first tiny sprouts. The rains came gently and sufficiently, keeping the plantings robust. We gave thanks. The ample and rich pasturage of the grazing commons allowed Father to plan how he would raise more animals for food, wool, and milk. We toiled, each of us doing the work of a man, cutting wood, digging in the fields, and building secure fences. Before winter, we would need a store of meat cured and smoked, vegetables in the root cellar, and a harvest of peas and corn put to dry. The townspeople were kind, but no one could save us from hunger except ourselves, and we knew it.

All the talk was about the civil war that had broken out in England and the hard times this was causing the Bay Company. Rich venture men who backed development on these shores depended upon filling their ships with wood, furs, and grains to sell in England. With the disruption of the great markets, goods and property lost value on both sides of the ocean, affecting everyone. It was said that immigration to the colony had slowed and that some people were returning to England because of the poor conditions here. Some worried that Winthrop's dream of building a city on the hill might not subsist. Father said that since we had nothing extra to sell, no money to buy anything, and nowhere to return, that we would go on as always, relying upon ourselves. By our own hands, we had hay in the barn and wood split and stacked by the time fall came. Even after we gave our portion due to the town, we thought we still would have enough for the winter if we were frugal and spared from unforeseen adversity. Under Mother's watchful eye, we managed our activities, traded carefully, rationed our supplies, and made it through that first winter without illness.

The next spring, salmon and shad came up the river in such numbers that we grew tired of eating the many meals we made of them. We fertilized our garden with the surplus. It was true that the forest was already being pushed back by our growing village and that the men had to walk a little farther to hunt as our town grew, but the hunger the town had known in its beginnings and the scarcity we had known on the coast seemed surmounted, at least for the time being. As if to give proof of our bounty, Mother bore twin girls, christened Hester and Elizabeth. She suckled both at the same time. Mother looked beautiful and happy.

As the babies grew, I helped by handing her a hungry mewing baby and taking away the sleepy full one to rock until they were both ready to be put down in their cradle to sleep. Father finished a matching second cradle for the girls. The babies were lusty and so were we. Unfortunately, that summer the rains came and drowned our fields. Our crops either rotted under water or grew stunted from lack of sun. Later that year, both Father and Thomas Jr. were granted additional land along the river but they were slow to put it under the plow because the rains would not stop. That winter was long because our food stores were less and our family had grown.

We hoped for better weather in 1642, but the spring thaw flooded the river and the waters overflowed the land. In the dampness mold grew. Planters could not go out to till fields of mud. Once again, the summer was rainy and our crops suffered. Not all was bad. That year Thomas Jr. was granted the rights of a freeman by the vote at the town meeting. My sister Ann came over from England. Our family was reunited, as much as it could be. Ann soon married Robert Chapman of Saybrook. Such were our joys and sorrows in those days.

One thing that was different about Hartford was living near to so many Indians. The community had to take care to protect the fields from them. For the most part, we lived in peaceful proximity with the local tribes, but even so, our men trained actively in the militia and all men were mandated to carry firearms at all times. My older brothers and my father were members of the militia, the "train band." In order to maintain the safety of our town, no one in Hartford was permitted under penalty of law to sell an Indian any crops, liquor, arms, or ammunition. Those who looked to trading any of these things with the Indians were found out, pilloried, and fined.

My family lived so as not to offend or cause damage to our neighbors. Father's livestock stayed within the fences. When the General Court ordered that all the planters grow flax and hemp, Father grew it. In terms of our standing, my family was not among the wealthy, but we were not the poorest. The milestones that marked our days were simple.

I had long wondered about the fate of Anne Hutchinson. One morning in 1643, her name jumped to my ears. Some women at the mill were talking about her. I went up to listen. They said that Indians had killed Goody Hutchinson and most of her children at a remote village in New York where they had moved. The Indians had appeared to come in friendship but then had suddenly attacked. Only one child, a daughter, was spared because of her red hair. It was thought that the girl had been taken alive to live among the Indians who had killed her family. I was struck that these neighbors seemed so unsympathetic about the tragedy.

One of the women gloated, "She told the ministers that God would deliver her from their hands. It looks like the Devil came for her first."

She snorted at her own joke. I did not. When I left them, they were recalling the fascinating but gruesome story about the monster Goody Hutchinson had reportedly birthed after she had been exiled to Rhode Island. From the pulpit, we had been told that the misshapen stillborn creature, a mass of hair and teeth, was a sign of the corruption that issued from those crowned by Satan. I did not want to hear about that again, especially upon the day of learning that her struggle had ended so horrifically.

I took the news to Mother. She stopped her spinning and sat for a long time with her hands in her lap. What her thoughts were she did not say. Hours later Mother spoke to me.

"Mary," she said with her eyes full upon me. "Know this. Anne Hutchinson lived and died believing she served the Holy Spirit. Her death proves only that the Lord took her. He may have taken her from an earthly hell to her reward in paradise. Do not believe anyone who says they know what justice our Lord metes out. Their mouths speak a presumption that does not come from the Divine. Beware of them."

I listened to my mother and nodded. She watched me as if to make certain that we understood each other. I have never forgotten what she said that day. I have found many since who give punishment in Your name.

As time went on and my brothers grew, Mother began to realize that our prospects here were good, but limited by the conditions of our land grant, which had been given as a courtesy without an investment on our part. Father would not ever gain the proportional share of land that would be granted to proprietors who had invested in the town. When the time came that my younger brothers would need their own land, they would have to look elsewhere. This concerned Mother more than it did Father. Father believed that answers came through hard work and obedience to Your plan.

Father was not at all pleased when Thomas Jr. abruptly sold out and left Hartford in 1644, looking to better his life by moving in with Sister Ann and her husband at Saybrook. Mother advised him against a move back to the coast because land was available on the frontier's edge, not in the settlements, but he went against her reasoning. Her warning would prove to be correct. We would seldom see my brother again, and he did not prosper.

After Thomas Jr. left, I noticed how much work he had contributed to our family. I could see that Father was aging and that he had relied on his eldest son in many ways around the homestead. The year of 1645 was hard for us because the river flooded in the spring. The weather was bad all year, and winter came early. There was no relief in the spring of 1646 when the river rose out of its banks again.

The unsettled weather seemed to make Nathaniel grow restless. He was the next to leave. The Springfield town meeting of March 6, 1646 gave its vote of approval for Nathaniel, being of desirable character, to join their plantation. He came to Father to announce very proudly that he had purchased over fifty acres of various allotments of good ground including a house lot for the price of thirty pounds. Father accepted his decision grimly. It meant the loss of another hand.

One unseasonably warm afternoon, I took some precious time for myself. I liked to walk along the Little River, through the town to the Great River to a place farther down the riverbank where the wetlands gave way to firm sands and overhanging trees. The freshly laid-down clays and silts of the previously flooded riverbank were pleasantly cool and smooth under my feet, and emitted a distinctively mysterious odor. Massive maples and sycamores leaned far over the water, reaching for sunlight. Under their heavy boughs, I could make myself invisible from the sight of men making their way in boats up and down the river. At the river, there was utter quiet. There was no boat or canoe anywhere. The wind was too calm to fill a sail, and the sun would surely have fried anyone who put a hand to a pole or paddle.

The river flowed strongly in one flat, barely undulating surface, broad and hypnotizing. No one was there to see me when, on an impulse, I dropped away my sticky clothes. I entered the river, holding on to the leafy branches skimming the top of the current. After the first shock had passed, the water began to feel delicious. I lay down into it. I relaxed and began to float.

The leaf clusters overhead made lacey green patterns against the deep blue of the sky. My submerged ears heard the hollow sound of my breathing. I drifted, bobbing up and down with the rise and fall of my chest. My hair fanned around me like wispy corn silk. The water wrinkled when I laughed at the funny little islands my body made where it poked out of the water.

After a long time I rose, dripping and chilled. Rather than trying to pull my shift over a damp body, I let myself dry in the warmth of the sun, naked as if I had just been born. There upon the riverbank was I.

Being in the state of my natural self seemed to make the sensations of the day more brilliant and personal. The soft air touched me. In my brazen exposure, I felt very much alive and timeless in Your creation. When I was dry I dressed in clothes freshened by their sunbath. I turned toward home. I thought about my life as I walked. It came to me that I was no longer homesick for England. As surely as the sun sparkled on the waters, I wanted to live this way forever, and thought then that I could.

Save me, oh God, for Your waters are entered even to my soule. Psalm 69:1

Chapter 8

Fears and Waiting

Boston, April 1674

My Lord, I offer these remembrances to You from the darkness of this loathesome cell. I mark time by the progression of my life's story rather than by the crawling passage of days. My practice of embracing the hidden gifts in the days You have given me is at battle with the pitiful part of me that is weak and seeping with worry.

Joseph's daily visit brings brief relief from the efforts of my inner discipline. It also brings me face to face with my worst fear. If I would let it, hideous doubt would taunt me with thoughts about how he must think of a wife named as a witch, a wife jailed, a wife who has brought a stain upon his reputation. I am grateful each time he comes. I try to push away the fear that there will be a day when he will not.

Each time I hear Joseph's voice say my name through the bars, I press my way through the women to come to him, trying not to step on the legs and hands of those who have not the energy or will to move. I reach my fingers out to him through the narrow openings that are my only access to the outside world. He knows I crave news, and comes ready with many stories.

Really what I want the most, so badly that it gives me pain, is assurance of his continuing affection. I do not beg him or nag him with my need lest it appear to be so great as to seem unquenchable and ugly. I know that he never imagined when we came here for my appearance before the Court at Boston that I would be held so long before trial. I pay attention to the breaths he takes and the rise and fall in the timbre of his words. I chide myself, knowing that there is nothing yet in what he says that should give my fears fodder in which to take root.

Joseph tells me that he has moved out of a room at the nearby inn and has bought a house. Imagine! He owns a home in Boston that I have never seen. It is good to hear that Joseph has sent for my brother Nathaniel to bring the children and Mother to live with him. I made it clear to Joseph that the children must never see me here. Just knowing that they are near will bring some relief. I await hearing the kinds of details about my children that only my mother can be relied upon to notice.

It is no surprise that Joseph has turned his hand to business. He is finding ways to profit from his time here. Joseph told me that he has been exploring the seaport. He has an opportunity to buy some large warehouses along the wharves.

Regardless of what happens to me, I know that at least Joseph will provide amply for our children. I must not think dark thoughts about the other women who would rush to him eagerly to fill my place should I be hung. I have no need to worry about the welfare of my Joseph. Even with his wife in prison, he is making money. No stain ever seems to remain upon him. I imagine him striding along the docks, the spicy smell of the sea washing away the clinging odor of prison, the distant gossip drowned out by the raucous laughter of seagulls. I am glad for his success, but the freedom and exploits of the world he tries to share with me seem so remote from this ugly cell where I now abide.

One day I dared to ask him, "Joseph, how do you do without our loving? You have not had to go without it."

"Are you asking if I fill my arms with other women? Could I do that knowing you are locked in here? I have been tempted; Mary, but I will not bring the glance of evil upon us. I hold fast only to you, trust me."

"I suppose I was wondering about such things. I apologize that I cannot be a wife to you."

"Do not say that, Mary. The days seem long now, but when we are past this, I will hold you again."

I heard the sniggering of women around me. A few jeered. I acted as if I could not hear. I summoned my dignity and did not speak of my doubts to my husband or anyone.

Make me to hear joy and gladness; that the bones which You hast broke may rejoice. Psalm 51:10

Chapter 9

Joseph Parsons

Hartford Plantation, Connecticut, 1646

Lord, I remember when You opened my heart to Joseph. I remember the days of falling in love with him in Hartford. To You I offer the memories of that love that my way may be lit by the light I have known.

I was twenty-one when my ordinary world was abruptly taken over by a consuming fascination with a man I met one late spring morning. His name was Joseph Parsons, settled at Springfield. I remember how his name spilled over my mind with complete lushness. Twenty-eight years old, he was seven years older than I was. He was handsome, energetic, and able. His confidence and his easy charm were engaging to everyone. He stood out from the other men. Not so much tall as well built, he held himself erect in a way that gave a sense that he possessed a quick supple balance. His dense brown hair curled loosely at his shoulders in the way of a trapper. His eyes were light blue and large, fringed darkly with heavy lashes. He was smoothly shaven with a ready smile. Other men seemed uninteresting by comparison. Everyone up and down the river seemed to know Joseph. He was a man of the forests and rivers. He was a man of ideas, vision, and intense spirit.

The day I first spoke to Joseph was in the spring at the Hartford river landing. He was examining stacks of winter furs with a trapper. His satisfaction with the furs and his enjoyment of them made me curious. I watched him with the trapper; saw the rhythm of their negotiations. I had not realized that he saw me. When the trapper loaded up and left, he turned to me and spoke, catching me by surprise.

95

"Hello. I see that you have a keen interest in trading. Let me introduce myself. I am Joseph Parsons. I would be pleased if I could be of assistance to you, Goodwife. "

"Oh, no. I am no one's wife. I am Mary Bliss. Surely, you know my brother, Nathaniel Bliss. He has land at Springfield. Those furs you have there are very beautiful. Would you mind if I look at them?"

"Not at all. Yes, Miss Bliss, I know your brother Nathaniel very well. He and I bought land at the same time and our home plots are near to each other. In fact, he has spoken of you and suggested that I make your acquaintance."

"Oh. I would have hoped that he would not have made such a suggestion without asking me first." I realized that I felt uncomfortable with the thought that my brother would talk to other men about me. It was likely that the tone of my voice showed it.

Joseph hesitated. With a wry smile, he selected one small dark shiny fur from the pile of beaver, muskrat, and otter pelts and held it out to me.

"The man who brought these furs is a very good and careful trapper. Each of these furs is top quality and well prepared. Here is a very special fur from a fisher cat. I do not see many of these. Fisher cats are a fierce animal, wary and not easy to catch. See how the guard hairs catch the light. This is a very good fur. It will bring a high price. Feel how sleek it is."

Sorry to have been so brusque, I stepped closer and reached out to touch the fur. Stroking the pelt, I was amazed at its softness and at the fluid way the hairs smoothed under my fingers. I felt the hollow of his palm through the fur. I saw him watching my hand. I knew he had noticed my touch.

I brought my hand back to my side. I said, "Thank you, it is very beautiful."

"Yes. Yes, beautiful." He was looking at me, smiling.

I felt wonderful under his gaze. I looked back at him with no embarrassment.

"Miss Bliss, I must secure these furs in the storehouse, but I would very much like to speak with you again. Would that be agreeable to you? I am going to the lecture later at the meetinghouse. I assume you will be there. Afterwards, may I walk you home?"

"I will be with my family. I would look forward to walking with you."

"Miss Bliss, I will see you this evening."

I was the first to turn. As I walked from the landing, I knew he was watching me. I had forgotten that I had intended to go to the market that was held each Wednesday on the grounds outside the meetinghouse. Halfway home I remembered what my errand had been. I could not go back and it did not matter now. I went home, breathing hard and saying "oh, oh" to myself. My fingers tingled where I had touched him. That moment went through my mind over and over. Mother was at the hearth preparing dinner. I was afraid she might talk to me and interrupt the pleasant memory.

As the hours went by, I was able to remain remote from the ordinary world. I hummed as I thought about the little nuances of our encounter. This evening he would walk beside me. It was strange that he had such an immediate effect on me, yet I felt no warning or alarm. After thinking for a long time about his appearance to the last detail, I began to wonder how he saw me. Looking into our small looking glass, I studied my face carefully, assessing it as if for the first time, trying to see myself as he might. I looked like my mother with her pleasant even features, wide brow, long pale yellow hair, and deep blue eyes. I was not as tall as my brothers were, but just as lean and hard, with a narrow waist and a woman's broad hips and bosom. I tucked my hair under my cap in case any escaping strands gave me the look of impropriety. I smoothed the collar of my blouse and checked the hem of my long skirt for any loose threads or tears in need of mending. Dressed in dark "sadd" colored clothes no differently than any other Puritan maid, it was only the bright flushing of my cheeks that made me unfit to be seen by anyone.

My family did not seem to notice. As usual, there was a rush to finish our chores before we could be ready to go to meeting. Our meal routine protected me from scrutiny. First, my mother served my father and ate with him. After they finished, she served the rest of us while she began to clean up. I helped with the meal, making sure to keep especially busy.

Our family walked to meeting, which gave me time to calm the feeling of growing anticipation. The activity of greeting friends and neighbors and the rush to get to our seats before the minister arrived swept me up and carried me along until I was delivered through the doors of the meetinghouse.

I caught sight of Joseph seated on a vacant bench. He turned his head and nodded, acknowledging me. I sat with the females of my family in our usual places and forced myself to enter into the order of prayers and line-chanted psalms that preceded the lecture. That night all our words of devotion strung together into patterns of sound behind my overwhelming awareness of his presence. I did not want to be seen staring at his profile. At the end of the service, he passed politely through those who greeted him and the girls who eyed him. He came to me as he had said he would. He introduced himself to Father and Mother. He asked them with easy comfort if they would give permission for him to walk home with me. My parents gave their consent. They looked at each other significantly, then graciously turned and began to walk home, the two of us following them many paces behind.

We walked quietly a short way, side by side. He carried a musket and his Bible, as did all men. I clutched my shawl around me.

He spoke. "Mary Bliss, I find I enjoy being in your company, although I do not even know you. I thought about you all day. I thought I should tell you this. If you are uncomfortable with my attentions, please tell me now. It is not my intention to overwhelm you."

"I, too, thought about you today. I would like to know more about you, Goodman Parsons."

"Well, maid, I am a man with no family. I travel up and down the river. I am a trapper, a trader, and a fur agent for Mr. William Pynchon. Mr. Pynchon buys and sells goods and does business between England and the colonies. He has warehouses here and at Windsor. Today I am here because I have purchased the furs you saw for Mr. Pynchon. What of you?"

"Oh, I am a planter's daughter. I would like it if you would call me Mary."

We made the simplest statements about ourselves as we walked the roadway along the bank of the Little River, crossing it at the mill. We reached home too quickly. My parents turned toward us. We all exchanged wishes for a good evening. Our time together was over. I watched as Joseph walked away in the dim light of the darkening sky. Father held the door for me. We went in. They made no comment. I offered none. That night I knew something important had changed. The wonder of it was more than I could imagine. It was difficult to fall asleep.

The next morning Joseph Parsons visited my parents and asked Father's permission to call upon me. Father gave his approval. Joseph brought with him rare treats from Mr. Pynchon's warehouse in Windsor, which he offered as gifts to my parents. Joseph was formal and proper.

Joseph left before we could speak together, but we saw each other. He bowed and smiled at me. Although I could not know what he was thinking, I felt strangely happy.

Mother was delighted when she showed me the two oranges and a yellow grapefruit. He had wrapped the three round fruits in pretty cloths that Mother could use in her quilting. We had never seen such fruits as these, nor known of them. Mother was eager to try the unusual fruits, but she waited until Father was ready.

Father left the fruits on the table. He went out to the fields to think and work. Around noon, Father came in for his meal. Mother laid the fruits in front of him. The family gathered around expectantly. Father cut and opened one for us with his knife, handing the slices all around. The room instantly filled with a clean bright perfume. The aroma was wonderful. We put our teeth into the slices. Juices erupted into our mouths. The flesh was sweet and tart, the flavor lingering and tingling. Swallowing hard, a sprayed orange droplet staining his shirtfront, Father stared at me in astonishment, as if I were responsible for bringing into this house such over-succulence of flavor and startling change. My brothers clamored for more.

My parents and I stood, savoring the sweetness of the fruits on our lips. The fragrant citrus lay on the table between us, flooding the room with scent. Mother waited for Father to speak, but he had no words for acknowledging the gift or its meaning. He wiped at evidence of the sticky orange on his fingertips in silence. He was an Englishman who had survived tyrants and storms. Now he stood in hesitation at the edge of his fatherly responsibilities toward his daughter's suitor. I swirled in the unimaginably spicy cloud of my breath.

Joseph Parsons came for me later in the afternoon. We walked with Mother to the gristmill by the Little River. We waited for her outside, sitting on a rock beside the stream. I saw that those who hung around the gristmill chatting in the warm sun were observing us blatantly and making comments to each other, inaudible to us. One girl glared at me, watching Joseph jealously.

We turned our backs to all of them and faced the water. Joseph told me a little about Springfield and his travels. He was fascinating, but we knew we had not much time. We stopped talking and looked at each other. It was comfortable to study each other's faces. He reached out and put my two hands into his, stroked them for the briefest moment, and then placed them back into my lap, gently. We smiled at each other.

Mother soon came out of the mill, motioning to us. We went to her and Joseph carried her bundle home. On the way, Joseph and I talked about all kinds of things. Mother walked beside us. Joseph included her in the conversation. When we got home, Joseph put her bundle on the table by the hearth and Mother poured us each a draught of beer. Joseph told us that he had to return to Springfield early in the morning, but that he would come back as soon as he could to see me. He seemed very serious.

Our time together was so short. I found it hard to part, even though I barely knew him. After he left, I heard Mother quietly humming as we sat by the hearth carding wool from this season's shearing. She seemed happy, but she said nothing. The world had changed. Only my chores remained the same.

Within the week, Joseph was back. He had not come by river. He rode his horse up to my parents' door. He hitched his horse and turned to knock firmly. Father was in from the fields for his noon meal and he went to open the door. I heard Joseph ask him for a visit with me. When I entered the room where he and my parents stood, he bowed. Again, he had brought presents: for Mother a fan, for Father a long-stemmed clay pipe. For me, he brought a pair of soft kid gloves, finely made. They fit perfectly. That meant that he knew the size of my hands in his mind. Nothing like this had ever happened to me.

Speaking to me, he said, "Mary," and paused. "It is a wonderful day. Do you have time to sit with me for a while?"

I loved the sound of my name when he spoke it.

To my joy, Mother said, "Mary, you have not eaten, and I am sure Joseph has not. I have just baked some bread. Why don't you and Joseph take your meal outside under the tree? I can get by without you for a little while. If you decide to walk, you can take Hannah with you. She would love a walk."

I felt amazed. I knew there would be no chance that we would ever be unchaperoned, but we had a whole afternoon to be together if we wanted. I was not sure how to entertain him. I paused to look at him. He blinked his two eyes at me and laughed. I realized he was teasing me somehow.

"Mary, do I remind you of an owl?"

"Why would you look at me like an owl?"

"Why would you look at me like a chipmunk about to be pounced upon? Are you afraid of me?"

"To be honest, I am not afraid of you, but I do feel nervous."

"Mary, this is an unusual turn of events for me, too. I think of you as if I know you, and yet we have scarcely spoken. I want to be near you, and it disrupts my work. I have had you on my mind since I first saw you."

"Oh, Goodman Parsons, I am alarmed that I disrupt you. There is danger when a person becomes distracted by earthly temptations."

"Oh, ho! So it is Goodman Parsons, is it? And are you not distracted by earthly temptations? Are you telling me you do not think of me? Do you not want to be near me? Do you think of me when I am away as I do of you?"

"Oh, I do, Joseph. In fact, I find myself thinking of you all the time. I wish my thoughts of you would go slower so that I could understand more clearly what is happening... I think we should take our meal here in the kitchen. Yes, I think it would be best if we stayed here where things will begin to make sense."

"Is it important to you that everything always must make sense, Mary?"

"I am a sensible person, and I admire that in others, yes. Being sensible is a comfort when life is confusing."

"If I am confusing to you, I apologize. I admit that I am as much a danger to you as any man, for surely many men have found you charming. However, it is my Christian duty to protect you, even if it is from me. You are as safe with me as you want to be, Mary. I believe I have an interest in you that is longer than today."

"I have not let men close enough for them to find out if I am charming or not. I find most people to be foolish or hypocritical. In turn, most people think I am standoffish and odd, I believe. I speak my mind. I do not have friends who are foolish or hypocritical. I have not found many women who will talk to me about anything but gossip or babies, and men do not talk to me about the subjects that interest me." I had not intended to sound so sharp, but I did not like the image of a silly chipmunk simpering under his attentions.

"I am content to talk to you about whatever you like. If you wish to talk here in this kitchen, let us talk in the kitchen. You can tell me what interests you. I like people with interests and ideas. If you are a different kind of woman, that is fine. Mary, I am a man who lives and travels alone. I have had many times to think and few times to converse, except with Mr. Pynchon, who is a thinking man of great depth. We talk for hours. If talking about ideas is what you enjoy, talk to me."

"I am embarrassed to find I have nothing in mind to say at the moment. I am thinking that we should eat."

"Well, then, Mary, I am hungry. That sounds like a good invitation."

We unwrapped the food and ate in silence. With the door open, and Mother clearly visible in the yard feeding the chickens and looking for eggs, I relaxed, even though I suddenly had little appetite. Afterwards, we cleaned the table together. The handling of wooden plates and cups brought me back to myself.

"There. Everything looks clean to me, Mary. The women of your family make good food. Now, let us take that walk your mother promised Hannah. Take me to your favorite place. Let me see what you see here."

I knew exactly where I wanted to take him, but it was farther than Mother would have liked, with only my young sister to watch over a man and woman alone. I could see she was uneasy when I asked, but she trusted me. I promised we would not be long. Mother admonished Hannah to stay close. I wanted to take Joseph to the Great River, to the place where the stand of arching trees remained uncut, overhanging the water. We walked fast, without conversation, matching step for step, my skirt snapping against my legs. It felt good to walk. Our pace together was easy. I felt a closeness with him in the walking that did not come from words. Hannah stayed right with us, pleased with her grown-up duty and excited by the unexpected adventure away from home.

We went directly to my favorite tree, a beech that leaned over the water and made a good seat. As we sat by the river, we talked, learning much about each other. During a pause in the conversation, I remembered that he had held my hands at the mill. Feeling a little guilty, it also occurred to me that the last time I had been here I had been naked. I glanced around at my sister to check on her presence just as he began to speak.

"Mary, I will be honest with you. I have reached a time in my life when I am looking for a wife. I would like to pass on what I know. I would like to have a son. I suppose a daughter would be fine, but I would not know as well what to do with her. I want to create a legacy. I want to share everything that I have with someone."

"Oh. And why do you tell me this?" Immediately I worried that my question was too bold. His answer told me that he was speaking to me more seriously than I had ever been spoken to before.

"The woman I would like to be with will be someone with your qualities; bright and curious, healthy and busy. I do not know where to find her, but I am looking. You are a beautiful woman. I cannot help but be interested in you, but if my interest is unwelcome, as I told you before, I will go away and bother you no further. I am not a man who is frivolous now. I have asked your father for permission to court you. If you wish to see me again, it must be because you want to; because you think there might be possibilities of a life with me."

"This is very soon to tell me this." I tried to laugh as I spoke.

He did not laugh in response. "No, it's not too soon. I am twenty-eight. I know what I want to do next."

"I came to show you the river, not to marry you." My tone was indignant, for I was a bit angry with myself for being so moved by his attentions.

He smiled at me. "I am not proposing to you, but, maid, hearing what I have said, would you agree to see me again?"

I did not answer quickly, but then I had to admit, "Yes, I would like to see you again."

"Ah!" He looked into my eyes. "I am very happy to hear you say that. I hoped you might. I cannot remain here any longer to convince you. I must go back to Springfield to see to the planting. I will be hard at it for the next two weeks, if the weather is good."

"You are leaving? How will I see you?"

He turned to me with a look so piercing that I caught my breath.

"I would take you with me if I could, Mary."

He drew me close and kissed me. This is what I had been afraid of, but when it happened, I was not frightened. I will always remember that his kiss felt shockingly exquisite, yet at the same time, warm and safe. It was as if I had slid into a warm river and been swept away. In that short moment, I floated, amazed, against his soft and full searching lips. His arms went around me to keep me from falling.

"No, Mary! No!" It was Hannah, yelling my name.

We startled. His lips left mine. His hands went to either side of my face and held me as I pulled away. "Mary, I had better get you home. Hannah, you did not keep your sister safe from me. Tell your Father to be prepared. I am in love with his daughter," said Joseph, speaking to us both.

Hannah saw nothing amusing about his comments. We could end up in the pillory if the ministers learned of this. It was a long walk back, and she stomped the ground with her feet indignantly every step of the way to the house. Hannah glared at me as she told on me to Mother. Joseph nodded at her that it was true. Mother put her hand on my shoulder and led me away from Joseph, shaking her head at him before she closed a door between us. For me, what had happened ended all doubt. I was unremorseful about my feelings for Joseph. Mother and Father's knowledge of our transgression only made me feel more closely tied to Joseph, even though our relationship was new and so much about him unknown. In response to their admonishments, I stood straight and firm, contrite outside but smiling within at what I was remembering.

When Joseph next visited, Father was ready for him. He surprised him at the door with a six-foot long, hollowed out wooden tube, flared into a bell on each end. It was a courting horn, intended to allow men and women to talk to each other privately, but at a distance, while under the supervision of their family. I had seen such a thing before, but Father had kept it hidden until Joseph came. I think Father had borrowed it from a neighbor.

"If you are courting my daughter, you will kindly address her through this, Goodman Parsons. I expect you to act with respect and restraint. I cannot have my other children party to your affections."

Joseph took the tube in hand. He laughed. "I am glad to see you are ready for me, Goodman Bliss. I am happy that you have taken my intentions seriously."

I was buzzing with thoughts of him. Every time I saw him, I learned new things about him that were fascinating. I was no good for anything that required focus, but I had tremendous energy. He came and went as often as he could that summer. There was never enough time to say all that we had saved for each other, and we were always under close watch. In the evenings when we sat with my family, the courting horn offered us our only privacy. Our whisperings in private conversation made the family laugh, and I think the use of the horn created some kind of shared amusement between Joseph and Father.

The thought of Joseph's touch sent me spinning. I dreamed of having a moment alone with him, but that proved impossible, and it was wrong of me to want it. I dared to imagine a life together, even though I saw that several other women seemed to know him well and sought his attention. I felt their hard eyes evaluating me as a dangerous rival to their hopes. I anguished whether he could be pulled away from me. I knew that I had dared to fall in love with him and that I wanted him all to myself.

My family liked Joseph, although that did not keep them from an increased vigilance in chaperoning our visits. Mother and Joseph loved to spar with humorous words. She doted on him, offering food and drink. Father and Joseph had lively discussions together. Joseph knew everything that was going on in politics and commerce because of his close friendship with William Pynchon. Father eagerly prevailed upon Joseph for news about happenings in the colonies and the civil war in England. Before Joseph came, Father had begun to be preoccupied with our land at Hartford. Joseph opened Father to the world. Watching Joseph with my parents, I liked what I saw. I wondered how he could be so patient with them while I felt such urgency to have all his attention.

One night in particular I grew very annoyed with Father. It had been over a week since I had seen Joseph, but Father met him at the door and took up my entire visit with Joseph, keeping him talking about the increasing resistance to the King of England. I had not had a chance to speak with Joseph the entire precious evening. Even though Joseph turned his head to me many times, his smiles and his deeply moving glances only frustrated me the more. I began to feel angry with the both of them and sick with longing for just a few words from Joseph to fill the pain I felt in loving him. Finally, I could bear the gulf of modest civility no more. I felt pouty and unseemly, wounded by a visit that hardly included me. Just as I was thinking about how to excuse myself to go to bed and leave those two lovers to each other, Joseph broke off the conversation with Father.

"One moment, please, Sir. I have thoughts I would like to express to your daughter."

Joseph picked up the horn and whispered to me through it.

"Wait for me by my horse. I need to speak to you tonight. Forgive me that it has gotten so late. I must speak to you. It is urgent."

When I arose, my parents seemed not to see me go. I was invisible when Joseph was present.

I waited for him in the shadow of the barn. I heard his footsteps coming in the darkness. My heart began to pound with a sudden jolt. He must have heard my breathing. He reached out and his fingertips found me. He pulled me toward him. Suddenly I was in his arms, his lips on mine, his firm kisses sweet to the bottom of my soul. One of his hands at my waist slid to my breast. I could not press close enough to fill the completeness of my love for him. My breast swelled into his palm, betraying my secret feelings.

"Joseph, I am lonely for you," I cried through our kisses, my mouth moving against his, as if his tongue were saying my words.

"Then marry me. I want you…to be my wife," he breathed into me. His powerful hands stroked my back and bottom through my clothes. He pushed me hard up against the whole length of his body. His warm mouth inhaled me. It was all so sudden, but it felt as if I had always waited for this without knowing that I did. I gave myself to the swirling sweet goodness of being in his embrace.

"Mary?" My father had stepped out of the door and into the yard and was speaking to us.

We pulled apart, painfully. "I'm here, Father." I was gasping. I spoke only out of habit and wondered that my mouth could form words.

"I know you are. Let not the Devil behold you!" I heard amusement and worry in my father's voice.

"Sir, then watch over us, by all that is good and holy. I ask a moment more with your daughter." Joseph responded to my father, still holding me in his arms in the darkness.

"Be quick, sir, I am waiting" retorted Father, firmly now.

"Mary, I came here with the intention of asking you a most important question. Forgive me if it seems I ask you now in haste. There is nothing of more importance to me than your answer. Mary, I love you. If you feel the same, say you will be my wife. Will you marry me? Will you be my wife, Mary?"

I knew what my answer had to be. My ears heard his question, but emotion filled me too fully to speak. My breath would not cooperate with my voice. Every day I wanted only to be with him, but crossing over to him was of roaring enormity.

"Mary?"

"Yes…yes, I love you." I heard my voice, and suddenly I was calm, focused, alive, standing willingly against him as he held me, the only place I wanted to be. My mouth had spoken unbidden, the decision made in a moment by the truth of my heart's desire pouring out of me. It was my rational self that rallied and told him, "Yes, Joseph, I will marry you and be your wife."

"Ah. I am glad." He embraced me. My face pressed into his shoulder. His glorious warmth and smell surrounded me, reassuring and wonderful. I let myself feel all the closeness of him. The joy of releasing my love to him was peaceful. My father began to cough awkwardly and to make shuffling noises in the doorway, showing his impatience with waiting for us.

"May I tell your father?" Joseph asked.

"Yes."

"Sir, I have asked your daughter to be my wife and she has agreed! With your permission, I will be your son-in-law!"

"What is said in the darkness must come into the light. Come in! Margaret, come here, Joseph has something to say." Father stepped aside so that we could enter the house. Mother came to his side, curious.

"Goodwife Bliss, I have asked Mary to be my wife," Joseph told her.

"Mary, is it true?"

"Yes, Mother. I have agreed."

Joseph spoke to my parents. "May I visit you tomorrow? I know I have surprised you. When I come tomorrow, I hope you will have an answer, that you will give your permission for Mary and me to wed."

My Father spoke, gravely. "Margaret and I must speak to Mary. We will see you at midday."

Upstairs, I could hear my brothers and sisters whispering. It would not be right for them to come down now, but they had heard, and in the morning, they would tell their friends.

How could I be apart from Joseph any longer? It was late. Why did it have to be so late? Could it not be morning, so that we could talk?

As if hearing my thoughts, Joseph said to me, "Mary, I wish it were tomorrow. I am a most happy man. I will spend the night looking forward to what the day will bring. I have arranged to stay with friends. I must leave now before it grows later. I do not want to be a trouble to them. Goodnight to you all until tomorrow. God bless you."

Surely, we needed Your blessing for our love, because I do not think we could receive it for our thoughts. Even now, I am moved and shaken by the passion that melded me to Joseph. We began to tell each other what we knew You saw in our hearts. Joseph whispered things to me through the courting horn that left me limp and blushing in front of my parents. We caressed each other with words and glances until it was almost unbearable.

One night Joseph visited so late that my parents invited him to stay. As was common, our few visitors shared our beds with us, usually at the foot of my parents' bed or with my brothers. To my surprise, Father affixed a "bundling board" to the largest of the trundle beds and allowed that, since Joseph was my betrothed, he could spend the night with me, as long as he stayed on the other side of the divide. When Joseph came to my bed, we were each on our own side of the long board between us. All the family lay in their beds nearby. I could hear Joseph breathing deeply close to my ear. When we thought the family had fallen asleep, we succumbed to the overwhelming temptation of our nearness. By twisting and sitting up, we could reach the top part of each other, and that we did. Our muscles were tortured by the awkward confines that both limited and allowed contact with each other. We struggled to be quiet, and struggled to be saintly, but he left moaning in the middle of the night, leaving me breathless, my lips and breasts polished and swollen from his kisses and his hands.

We tried bundling several more times, but although it was delicious to be so close, it was excruciating to be held apart. Ever under the watchful eye of my parents and our Puritan brethren, our only hope to be together fully, to enjoy each other in freedom, lay within the bounds of covenanted marriage. With the vision of being able to come into each other's arms pulling at us, we prepared our way to the wedding bed.

Delight Yourself in the Lord; and He shall give You Thine hearts desire. Psalm 37:4

Chapter 10

The Spell

Hartford, October 1646

My Lord, I have rejoiced in the fullness of Your blessings. I remember. I have not forgotten. In this battle against despair, I grip these memories like a shield. If I lose them, I will be overcome.

It seems so long ago that Joseph and I struggled with the urgency of sanctifying the longings in our bodies to the needs of our souls according to Your covenant. I remember the Saturday night that Joseph carefully lettered our wedding announcement, our "banns," as I sat at his elbow watching. That very night he went out to post it upon the front wall of the meetinghouse so that the next morning's sun would rise to find it among the necessary public notices, according to our duty. When we went to worship on Sabbath morn our intent to marry was there for all to see. I blushed with excitement when I saw people reading and discussing our announcement with interest. All that long day people regarded me with curiosity. I prayed and sang with excitement, hoping for a sign of Your favor. Friends of my father and mother came up to congratulate them. Walking home in the evening, the sun's long rays reflecting against the bright colors of the autumn leaves made a golden halo over all, manifesting the glory of Your creation and the certainty of Your blessing upon Joseph and me as a couple.

We had to wait to see if anyone would object to our marriage before we could proceed. This was an important custom in order to avoid being punished for a disorderly marriage. It was my responsibility to make certain that the announcement or its copy remained nailed to the wall for three lecture days, which was two Sabbaths, and one bi-weekly worship service. Over the next week, I walked to the meetinghouse every day to see to the condition of our declaration notice, making certain that it remained in place for the time required. I watched how it fluttered amidst all the other public notices, some official and others not. I remember being amused at knowing that our banns were nailed between notices for the sale of hay, a brood of pigs, and a litter of puppies. Our future was posted alongside such commonplace things as these.

When it became clear that the community had accepted our notice without complaint, Joseph and I visited with the church deacon to discuss our "coming out." As the intended bride, I had the great honor of selecting the Bible text upon which The Reverend Hooker would base his Sabbath sermon. I knew with certainty that my selection would be a chapter that Father had read to me many times when he needed reassurance about the uncertainties of the future. The Deacon wrote down our Bible selection and we set the date for the Sabbath when we would stand before the community so that they might witness our contraction to each other.

It was an exciting time, except that a week and a half before the ceremony something happened that tainted everything I believed about my community. One afternoon the Deacon came unexpectedly to visit, not my parents, but me. He seemed troubled and stuttered awkwardly about the nature of his call. Finally, he stated that he had come to request that I change my Bible selection. He was loathe to offer an explanation why he asked this, but finally, when pressed, it came out that another girl had just selected by coincidence the very same chapter that I had chosen. Even though I had selected first he had accepted her choice. The Deacon apologized but he insisted that I change my Bible text. I was stunned.

"Deacon, Isaiah is what I have chosen. They are words very dear to me. You agreed to read that chapter at our contraction. Would you go back on your own promise?"

"Miss Parsons, this girl comes from a very prosperous family. Her family has been part of the development of this plantation from its beginnings. Surely, under the circumstances you will not be prideful or incorrigible in this delicate matter. I am sure that if you could think with a reasonable mind you would come to your senses and defer to such people of wealth and stature as these. Perhaps you should speak to your intended husband about this and take his counsel. I am sure he will be more gracious."

"Deacon, can she read?"

"Why, yes, of course, why do you ask?"

"She can select another chapter."

"Mary, I have given the selection of her choice to her. It is an honor her family most deserves."

"Deacon, did our Lord and Savior deserve to be born in a manger because his family was not of wealth?"

"That blasphemy ends our conversation. I can see I have made the right choice. The other girl is very pious. You have five days to select your text. You must give The Reverend Hooker time to prepare a sermon. That is the end of the matter."

The Deacon turned on his heel and left in great agitation. A darkness and terrible dread overcame me. It seemed a bad way to start our marriage. I could not look at my parents as they stood questioningly by the door. I did not want to admit to them that the Deacon thought so little of our importance to the congregation. Joseph was away in Springfield preparing his home for me, his soon-to-be wife. I wished that he were here. I went outside but there was no place to go that would give me comfort, and no one I trusted to give counsel. I felt anxious. Impulsively I began to run. I ran and ran, not knowing which way I went, possessed by the blindness of despair. In a while, I woke up on the ground, not knowing where I was. Two children were poking me with a stick.

"Is she dead?"

"Poke her again, see if she is dead."

The stick hit me smartly in the cheek, just below my eye.

"Stop that," I yelled at them.

"Ahee! Watch out! It is alive. I would have liked it better if it were dead. Now it's just ordinary," said the tallest child.

"I feel a little dead," I said, feeling sick and dizzy.

"Oh, she is dead! She is a deadie, a dead, dead, deadie!" They marched around me thrashing their sticks.

"Shoo! Get away from me. Bite your tongues!" I said rising to sit.

When I moved, the boys gasped and then began to scream. The littlest one froze. I saw that he wet his pants as he stared at me in horror.

"The deadie is coming after us! Run!" The oldest boy shouted as he suddenly turned to flee. The littlest one tried to follow. Perhaps his wet pants bound him for immediately he fell flat on his face. At first he was silent and then he began to howl shrilly. From out of nowhere a woman appeared, running toward us, yelling.

"Boys! Boys! What is going on?" She intercepted the oldest boy. He grabbed her around the knees.

Pointing at me, he sobbed, "Mother, a deadie is chasing us!"

"What are you doing to my boys?" she screamed.

The littlest boy stood up, yowling, his mouth a bloody hole.

"Oh, my God! What have you done to him?"

"She told us to bite our tongues, Mother! She said it. She said it. She made him bite his tongue off!" The oldest boy danced around his mother, hopping up and down in fear.

"Let me see you," she said to the little one, whose howls were now gurgling. "Your tongue is bleeding. You have a cut in your tongue! Oh, my poor, poor darling. Oh, my little poor darling." Putting her apron into his mouth to soak up the blood she held him to her, glaring at me over his small head.

"I did not chase them. I am so sorry this has happened," I remember telling her. "How can I help? What can I do?"

"Get away from my boys! You, get away from here! I will find out what you did. I know who you are, you, you… Bliss girl. Get away! Leave us alone!"

I turned and walked toward home, my head roaring. What was happening to me, I wondered? In shock, choking and trying not to sob, the welted cut under my eye throbbing and oozing blood, I stumbled into our house. My mother turned to me as I slumped into a chair and put my head in my arms on top of the table. It was a while before I could describe what had happened and still she could not explain the story to my father when he came in from outside. I was of no help for I went to bed. In the morning, Mother sat down beside me on the bed and began to question me carefully about the events of the previous day. I told her everything, leaving out that the Deacon had said the other girl came from a more worthy family. When I said the girl's name, I think my mother understood the reason for the Deacon's decision without my telling her. She offered no suggestions, patted me through the blankets, and left me, to my relief. I could hear her talking to Father, her whispers carrying through the house. I paid no attention; my emotions were too strong to concentrate on what they said. When I heard Joseph's voice, I came alert and frantic. What would he think of me? Would this change everything between us? Straining, I listened carefully.

"Yes, I know about the tongue-biting gossip. I heard the men talking about it at the wharf. They make it sound as if Mary put a curse on the boy. Of course it is nonsense."

I could not hear my parents' response. They were talking about me without me there, as if I were a child or a thing. I went rigid with indignation.

"Mary? May I talk to you?" Joseph called up to me.

"Just a moment, I will get up." I would not have them hovering over me.

I straightened myself up as best I could and came down the ladder from the sleeping loft. I had no apologies to offer and no explanation for what had happened. I had done nothing wrong, but clearly, there were dizzying forces at work, swirling me like a leaf in an eddy. I was awash in feelings. I remembered feeling this frightened and insignificant as a child in England when the King's men had tried to crush us without paying attention to what kind of people we were. In a rush, I also remembered the shame of presenting myself to the awful gossips aboard ship. Sometimes the world seemed not to care for the beauty of life. I so dreaded the familiar presence of the senseless power of scorn, and now I stood dripping in it as I stood numbly before my family and the man I loved.

Joseph convinced me to go that very day with my mother to visit the aggrieved family and to bring a generous gift of candy to their household. Joseph laid a heavy bag of hard sugar candy before me on the table. He swayed me with his argument that even with a swollen tongue the boy would be able to suck the sweet sugar, giving sustenance to the child, relief to the parents, and perhaps some forgiveness for me. My parents agreed with Joseph that I should go to the family to pay my respects. The day was drizzly and windy, but my mother and I put on our cloaks, drew up our hoods, and set out for the house.

I hung back while my mother knocked on their door. The boys' mother barely opened the door wide enough to see us. She did not seem to recognize our shrouded figures. When my mother introduced us, she began to withdraw, but before she could, a man came up behind her and opened the door wider. He stepped out onto the doorstep and said his name. We came to understand that he was the father. I began to apologize to him for frightening his children on the road. I ventured that I hoped their little one was feeling better and offered the candy to the mother. The wife would not touch the bag but the husband took it.

"You gave our little ones a scare and our youngest is hurt and cannot eat. We have called the physician, who has given him a poultice for his swollen tongue, which is bitten half through, but now he drools, cries and cannot be comforted. He has just fallen asleep, finally."

"I feel badly that this has happened and hope that you will accept my regrets at this bad turn of events. I was sick myself and fainted and when I roused it affrighted the boys."

"My children tell that you cast a spell over them. You understand that we are wary of what happened and will watch how you have to do with our children in the future. However, this is not a good day to be about outside. We thank you for the candy for our boy. Go home before you catch a chill. Leave us to our children."

"We shall pray for the good health of your family." My mother was most sincere in her few words.

"Thank you, Goodwife." The man closed the door, and we turned for home.

Joseph and my father were waiting for us when we returned. Joseph was pleased that they had at least accepted the candy and thought that a good sign. I felt grateful to be by the warm hearth with my wise Joseph beside me, the confrontation over.

At the next Sabbath worship, my father rose up and spoke on my behalf to confess publicly my remorse for my actions that had caused the boys fright. Through Father I was able to ritually unsay the words that had hurt them. I would have preferred to repent for myself, but it was not our custom. Father cautioned me to refrain from such a sinful thought.

> *Let your women keep silence in the churches: for it is not permitted unto them to speak; but they are commanded to be under obedience as also saith the law. And if they will learn anything, let them ask their husbands at home: for it is a shame for women to speak in church. Corinthians 14:34-35*

Mother must have thought it a time to surround me with womanly ministrations. Mother's friends began a steady business of taking me under their wing in a way that was at times amusing. One by one, they took me aside to prepare me with advice regarding the duties of a covenanted wife. Most of the information they shared had nothing to do with baking bread or knitting socks. Some of the tales they told about their first night of marriage left me wondering that babies were still being made. There seemed to be a strange array of natural truth among women. I was not certain what the duties of being a wife would be like for me but I knew with amazement that my secret parts blossomed in sweet warmth for Joseph. Low in my belly a heavy yearning waited for his touch, churning whenever a thought of him entered my mind. I prayed to You that You would bestow upon us Your gifts that emanated from Your perfect love.

Father escorted Joseph and me back to the Deacon before the five days were up with a new Gospel selection for The Reverend Hooker to read in honor or our upcoming marriage. The Deacon wrote down what we had chosen as if we were speaking to him for the first time about our wishes. We chose from The Epistle of Paul, Chapter IV, One Body, One Spirit. Joseph did all the arranging for the employment of The Reverend Hooker and for the date of the coming out sermon. I thought that the worst was over as I walked back home between the two men I loved most in the world, my father and my future husband.

Within a few days we suffered a great tempest, the like of which I had never seen. My family huddled inside our house as the winds howled and rains poured in sheets upon our roof. There was a fearsome racket as things banged and thumped against our walls. We hoped the animals were safe in the barn and were grateful that most of our crops had been harvested. When the wind grew quiet and it was safe to venture outside again we saw debris everywhere. Chunks of roof and bits of things littered our yard and were caught in fences. Fields and trees were flattened alike.

The storm distracted people from thinking about me, but forever after, the mother of the children I had frightened kept her brood away from me when she saw me, giving me ugly little sideward warning glances. Sometimes in the market place, I would catch other women, perhaps the woman's friends, staring at me with looks that made me feel uncomfortable. I could only attribute their cold glares to having something to do with the tongue–bite incident. As for the hurt child, he seemed to mend well. Now that I knew what the two brothers looked like I noticed them many times. Truthfully, I was happy to stay apart from them. Where the children had poked me with a stick remained a scar.

Let not them that are mine enemies wrongfully rejoyce over me, neither let them winke with the eye that hate me without a cause. Psalm 35:19

Chapter 11

A Wedded Bliss

Hartford, November 1646

Lord, forgive me that the Sabbath of our "coming out" is not a memory that I offer to You.

Our intention to be married was dutifully made known before the congregation by the minister's announcement prior to the sermon. It seemed too late to accept the recognition as either a gift or an honor. The Reverend Hooker's sermon was good, and it was momentous in importance to my family, but no matter how well said, I realized that they were the words of a man. I felt as prim and spiritually unmoved as the deacon's profile. It is a sin to be stiff-necked in Your house of prayer, but You know that I am humble before You. The church service declaration of our coming out did serve to bring closer the day when we would be wed.

The memory of our wedding I do offer to You in its full glowing beauty. It is a polished memory that is my treasure. Our wedding took place November 26, at the home of my parents at Hartford. In keeping with the Puritan tradition, which rejected the proud pomposity of papist weddings, ours was a simple civil ceremony before the magistrate, without vows or rings. The magistrate asked us if we freely entered into the bonds of marriage, to which we each answered yes. With that, the ceremony was over. We walked to the home of the town clerk and signed the civil book, registering our marriage, a bride and a groom bound to our duties.

We had walked together this rapidly once before. My skirt had snapped in the same way against my legs. On that day, we had found ourselves together, and we had kissed. Now we could kiss except for the urgency to return to our family and friends, who awaited us.

We came into the house where I lived with my family. Rich smells of food greeted us. Father bade us to sit down and enjoy the wedding dinner. My mother and our family friend Goody Bartlett stood smiling over the simple feast they had prepared for us, with the help of my sisters. Hands reached out for us, and Joseph and I were passed from relative to friend until we were congratulated all around by the small group. Goodman Bartlett embarrassed me by exclaiming over my appearance. As the Bartletts lived just across the road, they were more used to seeing me toiling in the garden, smudged and sweating or at meeting, somber and subdued.

It was my wedding day. I was dressed better than any other day in my life. A fresh white linen cap covered my hair. I wore a new flax blossom-colored bodice with buttons all the way up the front. The sleeves were brightened by thin blue ribbons Joseph had brought to me as a gift. The blue matched the light blue wool skirt I had made myself for the wedding. I felt beautiful, and hoped this was not vanity, but joy.

I took a moment to gaze at Joseph as he talked with my family and friends. I did not care if anyone noticed me watching him. He was my husband now. I admired how he presented himself with such ease. He wore a square-collared cream-colored linen shirt; a close-fitting russet-colored wool doublet with silver buttons, belted at the waist; brown kersey breeches; white hose; black leather shoes; and a black, low-crowned beaver hat with a round brim. His dark hair curled loosely at his shoulders. I wanted to touch him and to have him turn toward me.

Seated at the table with my family and our dearest friends, Joseph looked handsome and happy. He constantly found me with his eyes as we ate our meal. In all my excitement, I do not remember much of the meal, except for the dainty wedding cake brought out to us with great joy, and the deliciously intoxicatingly sac posset, a hot mixture of sweetened milk and spiced wine, which quickly went to my head. We had just sung a psalm together when Father rose, turned toward me, smiled, threw back his head, and bellowed triumphantly.

Why sayest You, O Jacob, and speakest, O Israel,

*My way is hid from the LORD, and my judgment is passed over by
my God.*
*Hast You not known? Hast You not heard, that the everlasting
God, the LORD,*
*The Creator of the ends of the earth, fainteth not, neither is
weary?*
There is no searching of his understanding.
But he giveth strength unto him that fainteth,
And unto him that hath no strength,
He increaseth power. Even the youths shall faint and be weary,
And the young men shall utterly fall:
But they that wait upon the Lord shall renew their strength:
They shall lift up the wings as the eagles:
They shall run, and not be weary,
And they shall walk, and not faint. Amen, and amen.

The room was quiet as everyone watched Father to see if he was
finished. He still stood.

"Mary, the final words of Isaiah 40, verses 27-31 for your
wedding." Father's voice had softened.

Tears sprung to my eyes. The words rang in my ears as a tender
surprise.

I did not mind that the verses my Father had chosen to call out
were an amusing poke at my unfortunate fainting spell. It was all too
true that I had fought and lost the attempt to have words precious to
my father said from the pulpit in honor or my wedding, and that I had
faltered because of it. At last, here in my father's house was the
blessing I desired, said with love by my father's own voice.

There was no time to dwell or reflect upon it. The sun was near to
setting. The crowd was excited to bring Joseph and me to the marriage
bed. Robert and Ann Bartlett had graciously offered the use of their
house so that Joseph and I might spend the night alone. The Bartletts'
and their daughter, Abigail, were good naturedly crowding in with my
parents.

Everyone pulled away from the table and the entire party escorted
us across the road to Robert Bartlett's house, trooping inside with us.
The men took Joseph. The women took me, and we were parted. The

women were giggling as they led me to the bedchamber. They helped me into a pretty gown that Mother and my sisters had secretly made for my wedding night. Mother patted my hair.

More in awkward humor than in seriousness, I whispered Mother's favorite words. She joined me earnestly. "The Holy Spirit illumines the heart."

She surprised me by embracing me, then she pushed me away to arms length.

"I wish you well in your marriage," she said. She watched as my sisters and friends tucked me under the bedclothes, then she left.

Joseph was brought to me, dressed in nightclothes, escorted noisily by the men folk. He was put to bed beside me with much ribald jesting. The women tittered and shushed their men, and began to push them out. The door was quickly closed upon us. Everyone remained just outside the door singing, and clapping and laughing. We knew it would be like this. It was a tradition from old England. I had participated myself as a wedding celebrant many times, making noise, and enjoying the hilarity. Now I was the bride, lying next to my groom. The raucous nearness of the crowd made me nervous. I froze in my finery. Joseph, lying on his back stiff as a man in his coffin, abruptly began to laugh. He shifted and turned to me, and threw his arm across my chest to lay his hand against my cheek. As he moved, a loud clanging rang out from beneath us.

"Oh no, cow bells. They have tied them to the bed ropes," he said.

The bells rang loudly with the motion of his rolling to get out of bed. Outside the door, there were hoots and cheers. Joseph unhooked the leather straps and the bells fell to the floor with muffled clunks.

He got into the bed beside me saying, "You know that no one will come in here."

"My mother and father are out there."

"No, they are not."

"Yes. They are."

"No, they are not. They have gone home satisfied," Joseph said. "The only ones left out there now are the ones wishing they were us. Everyone out there knows what will happen next. Everyone who has someone has gone home to do what we will do. Mary, turn toward me. I want to look into your eyes. Mary, my Mary."

As soon as I turned to him, I no longer heard the noise. Looking into his eyes. I went into them. He was everything I wanted. He put his warm hands over my ears, his thumbs pressed my eyes, and his mouth covered my lips. I melted into rapture. There was only him, only Joseph. His hands caressed me. Every place he touched yearned toward him. He touched me where I had never been touched before. He stroked me, and drew the line of my body into his soul. Pressing against him in the fullness of my pounding blood, I molded myself to his body. The fabric that separated us lifted away. I held him, he held me.

Outside it had grown quiet. In the peace of it, we explored each other, he more boldly, and then we loved. We moved together in a dream of only each other. He drew himself against me and a part of him pushed until he was inside. There was one moment of sharp, ripping pain that swirled away on my gasp as I released myself to a wondrous ecstasy. When I came back to myself, I lay in Joseph's arms in complete satisfied safety. I dozed for a time. Each time we stirred that night we lazily and slowly found each other again until at last we could do nothing but hold each other. His man-part was soft within me and made us one. When it slipped from me to lie dearly upon my thigh, a love I had never known filled the empty place he left. Our bones, flesh, and spirit melded. Under his head that lay heavy upon my bosom, I truly felt my heart illumined, and I whispered into the warm peace of it, "Amen."

When I woke in the morning, cradled in Joseph's arms, I saw beside me on the floor the gown my mother had made for me to wear for this night. It had a covered slit in its front to allow my husband's secret parts to find mine. I would never tell anyone that Joseph had no use for such modesties. The gown lay crumpled and abandoned in a shaft of the morning sun and we lay together in utter serenity. I wished never to rise away from him, only wanting to stay there forever as we were, but we could hear sounds from outside. Someone downstairs was putting logs on the fire, and we could hear men's voices outside.

Reluctantly we pulled away from each other to dress. I did not watch him, but I knew he watched me, and it felt much different from dressing before my sisters. Nothing was ordinary any more, not even the feel of my clothes against my skin. I was keenly aware of him when he came to me to put his arms around me from behind.

"Ah, my beautiful wife, did you sleep well?"

"A little, my handsome husband. Did you?"

"No, Wife, my dreams came to life, and I was all the night encharmed."

"I, too."

"My wife?"

"My husband."

From outside, Nathaniel called to us. "Mary. Joseph. Get up. Mother is making breakfast. Come and enjoy!"

"It is only you I wish to enjoy," Joseph said.

"When we go to your home in Springfield we will be alone. We will have each other to ourselves. That is what I will enjoy."

"Yes, Mary. I am bringing you home this very day."

It would have been usual to remain for a time to visit friends and people in the community but Joseph had made it known that we would be returning to Springfield at once. I had no objections. It was my mother who would have enjoyed taking us around to her friends, but she understood.

As we walked across the road, I could see that someone had tied Joseph's horse to the fence. His light cart stood ready nearby, all the harness oiled. In the kitchen, Mother had indeed made a large breakfast for us all, which Joseph and I enjoyed together with Robert and Anne Bartlett and all my family. Mother packed food into a lunch basket for us to take. My sisters gave one last look around the house for anything I might have forgotten before I closed up my trunk full of wearing-clothes and items I had assembled or been given to set up housekeeping. My father saw to it that my brothers hitched the cart and loaded my trunk into the back of it. The family walked with us to where the horse stood in harness. Joseph helped me climb into the cart. When I looked down, my family was smiling up at me. I remember their ring of faces, each so precious. My throat stiffened in pain and almost choked me as I gasped at the depth of my love for them. To climb down and embrace them, as occurred to me, would have been awkward because it was not our way. Joseph clucked to the horse and suddenly we were moving.

Turning my back on my family to face ahead with Joseph, my head roared with the fullness of the moment. I pushed my mitted hand under Joseph's arm that held the reins. He squeezed my hand against his ribs in reply. As we passed through town, people along the roads hailed us. Joseph was jovial in his return waves; I nodded and smiled. I felt proud to be sitting next to Joseph as his bride. Watching him raise his arm high to all he saw made me laugh. Joseph teased me by turning onto every road in town so that everyone could see us. The carthorse began to prance with a more lively air. Joseph decided to make several short stops to shake hands with men important to him, to introduce me as his wife. I was surprised when Joseph hitched our horse before some of the largest and finest homes in Hartford. When we were let inside, Joseph was greeted with warmth and respect, all of which was extended to me as well. I learned more about Joseph and felt more bonded to him that day than at any other time in our courtship.

Our visiting was informal and quick because it was understood that we had far to go. It was mid-morning when we crossed the Great River north of Hartford at the ford near Warehouse Point. The way north to Springfield from Hartford was not quite thirty miles, but even if the horse stepped smartly along, we would not be in Springfield before nightfall. Joseph had brought bedding so that we could camp along the way. The day was dry but cold and a north wind whipped at our cloaks in the open cart. We pulled our large brimmed black hats low over our eyes and ears, and tucked furs tightly around our legs and feet. As we leaned into the wind, we swayed against each other, sometimes talking and sometimes silent.

We made camp early at the edge of a little brook in a flat place under the shelter of a tall hemlock. Joseph kicked out a circle in the duff of pine needles, scraping out a shallow fire pit with his boot. He lined the edge with stones from the streambed. I went to gather sticks. I hoped there would be good wood. Even though I had gathered wood all my life, I was not a woodsman like him, and I wanted to please him with this first task. There was no need to worry. Within hardly twenty steps, there was a fallen maple with dry limbs easy to collect. He must have already seen it when he decided to stop in this place. I dropped an armload of wood by his feet and watched him crumble dry twigs and bark scraps between his fingers. Into the tinder he lay a smoldering ember, which he carried embedded in a hard hoof-like fungus. He gently blew on the spark until it glowed and flared within its little teepee of twigs. As the fire began to crackle and rise, he reached for the wood I had brought and began to lay small sticks upon the fire. I quickly went to gather more wood, and he joined me. When we had a large enough pile to last the night, he chopped the large pieces with his axe while I broke what I could over my knee.

The wind had died as the sun lowered in the sky, so the fire rose upright without a choking cloud of enshrouding smoke. We sat together by the fire and looked into it, and then at each other. I laughed at the growling I heard in his belly. Joseph told me where he had packed his kettle, and I fetched it, and filled it from the brook. He propped a long green forked stick at an angle between two rocks at the edge of the fire pit so that the kettle hung over the middle of the fire. While we waited for the water to boil, Joseph broke off pine boughs and laid them thickly under the wagon, and spread the furs in two layers upon them. I unwrapped some of the food Mother had packed for us.

That evening we had hot tea and bread, and we ate already cooked meat, warming it on the heated rocks. We cleaned up well so as not to create a scent of food that would draw beasts, and then we crawled under the furs together, fully dressed against the cold air and the dangers of wild animals and Indians. Joseph's gun was nearby, dry and protected, but ready to be fired if anything came for us in the night.

It was not long before our little nest grew warm. We could not resist parting the clothes that held us apart. Keeping our heads under the furs, the heat we made together was stronger than any cold that lay outside. I smiled to this day in memory of that night which You gave us to enjoy, alone except for the eyes of Joseph's horse.

Before first light the next morning, we got underway without taking time to make tea. It was cold, but we did not rekindle the fire.

We pulled out some biscuits to eat as we rode. We still had far to go, and it was not safe to linger in the wilderness.

"Mr. Pynchon has invited us to take a meal with him, no matter how late we arrive. He is the only one I invited to our wedding, but he had other business. He is most eager to meet you, although of course he knows who you are."

"I will look terrible from traveling. That is how you want me to meet him?"

"Mr. Pynchon will only just be returning home himself. Mrs. Pynchon will have gotten up a meal for him whether we come or not. She made me promise that I accept her invitation to make our first day comfortable. She very much wants to meet you. We have to eat, Mary. They will not expect us to stay. If we go, I would not be surprised if while we are at sup, Mr. Pynchon has his men unload your trunk into my house. I suspect we will find my house all ready, warm, and waiting, and the horse in the barn, unhitched and fed. Let the Pynchons welcome us, Mary. Mr. Pynchon is like my father, and I am certain that you will enjoy his wife, Frances. This is important to me."

"All right, Joseph. I want to meet them. I am up to it, and it is what you want."

"I am bringing my wife home! Ha! The horse seems to know my urgency and has kept a good pace. I want to arrive in Springfield in broad daylight so that everyone can watch when we come down the road. 'What a pretty one Joseph Parsons has married' they will be saying."

"Oh, Joseph. I do not care what they say. I am so happy to be with you. I am eager to have the door of your house closed behind us."

"A house that will be blessed with my children?"

"Lots of children, God willing."

Our journey went as Joseph planned. We came to Springfield at my favorite time of day when the lowering sun bestows upon the world a last golden glow of glory. There were people who saw our arrival, as Joseph had hoped. They turned toward us and stopped whatever they were doing. They hailed Joseph with a wave of their arms and a shouted welcome to me. Joseph had a comment for each person he passed along the road. We were both in high spirits.

The settlement of Springfield was much smaller than Hartford, as were the houses. It looked odd to me that most of the houses were only on one side of the road. The front doors all faced the road in the usual way, with glimpses of the Great River visible behind each one. The community was a narrow ribbon between road and river.

Joseph pointed to an unremarkable house and said, "There it is, the first house I have built here, but not the last. There is no smoke from the chimney. We will go on to Mr. Pynchon's. I am hungry."

The Pynchon home was larger than the others were, and busy. Several men recognized Joseph as soon as he turned the horse into the yard. They were upon us immediately. A smiling stranger helped me down from the wagon. Another man took Joseph's horse by the bridle and held it without hitching it to the post.

"We will take care of your horse and wagon. Go in. Mr. Pynchon is waiting for you."

A smiling older man of strong body and bold gaze, Mr. Pynchon himself, greeted us at the door. That evening Mr. Pynchon and Goodwife Frances, who I liked as soon as we were introduced, made us welcome. They brought us immediately to the table. The moment we sat down with the Pynchons, hot and familiar food was set down before us. I soon relaxed under the warm comfortable way they treated me. The Pynchons were interested in our wedding and our trip, and they asked about my family. They already knew my brother, Nathanial. After dinner was finished and we were satisfied, we were admonished to go home to take up married life. We were escorted to the door with well wishes. Mr. Pynchon had one of his men take us home in Mr. Pynchon's wagon. We were told ours was in Joseph's barn, the horse unbridled, brushed, and fed. My trunks had been brought into Joseph's house.

Joseph let me into his house, and, tired as we were, we made the bed warm with our loving. It was a good beginning.

Let the Saints be joyful with glorie; let them sing loude upon their beddes. Psalm 149:5

Chapter 12

A Bended Ear

Springfield, Winter 1646 – Winter 1647

With You before me as the cloud that guided Moses and the children of Israel to a new land, I began my life in Springfield as a married woman.

My visions of the life a daughter of Zion should build were clear. I attempted to create the routines I had grown up with, adapting them to my own home, expecting that life with Joseph would be like the relationship my parents had, with Father coming in from the fields all during the day for breaks and for his meal. This was not to be so.

Joseph was very busy with his various properties and enterprises, even in those early days of our marriage. In addition, he, like every man, trained with the militia and contributed work hours to the town. At a town meeting earlier in the spring, before our wedding, Joseph had been appointed to the position of highway surveyor to complete a road and bridge from the Mill River at the south end of town to the long meadow. Because of all his responsibilities, it was not uncommon for Joseph to be gone from morning until just before dark. When he went out trapping, he was gone for many days and nights, sometimes for weeks at a time. I missed him keenly when he was away. When he was in town, I begged him to come home instead of having me wrap up food for him to take for his midday meal. I told him that I enjoyed watching him take delight in the food I prepared especially to his liking. Joseph promised that he would come home when he could, but he asked that I try to be more understanding. The first time he asked that, I felt hurt. After he left, I went out to hang up the laundry and wept in loneliness, as I smelled his scent in the shirt I hung to dry.

I thought I heard my mother calling my name, "Mary, Mary."

"Mother," I called back. Her voice was insistent and forlorn, innocent of the distance between us. I missed my home. My heart ached for my family. Under the huge blue depth of the immense sky, I felt small and remote. I forced myself to do my work, but I listened from time to time for the voice of my mother, afraid to hear her again and be unable to go to her.

That night Joseph came home early.

"Joseph, I am feeling sad. I miss you when you are away, and then I begin to miss my family."

He patted my cheek and asked what I had made that smelled so delicious. I turned my attention to the iron pot that bubbled lightly as it hung from the hook over the fire. We ate together until he was sated. He leaned back in his chair and smoked his long stemmed pipe, the smoke curling around him. When my work was finished for the evening, I came to the hearth to sit near him. Joseph reached out for me and pulled me onto his lap. I lay across him by the warmth and light of the fire. He stroked my body as he talked to me about his plans and accomplishments. He had no apologies that his business took him from me. I knew he expected me to understand. I wanted to be a good wife, but I did look forward to the evenings when he sat down with me and told me about his days. I loved to hear his voice in my ear grow husky, and grew to expect that his stories would end when his hands began to seek me under my clothes. After our lovemaking, he would fall asleep, and I would nuzzle him with all my love until I fell asleep against him, naked, as he preferred. In my upbringing, a person was considered undressed when wearing a shift, but Joseph stripped me of this undergarment every night we lay together. Nothing that bothered our lives ever seemed to cross into those private times between us.

The marriage we were making was not like that of my parents. As the months went by, I resolved to accept that I could only change myself, not him. His interests took him away from the house, and that is the way it would be.

Joseph sometimes brought guests home with him. I could see his satisfaction when the two of us offered the hospitality of his home and hearth to his friends. The circle of his friends' wives immersed me into a social life of my own. When my brothers dropped by, and my parents and my younger sisters came to visit, I was proud for them to see the wife I had become.

In those early days, we spent many an evening with the Pynchon family: Mr. Pynchon and his wife Frances and their four children. Their only son, John, was a little younger than Joseph, but the two of them could have been brothers. I felt comfortable with John's wife, Amy. The conversation was always lively, especially when there were other invited guests. The Reverend George Moxon and his wife often were present. Elizur Holyoke was one of my favorite guests, always full of stories and adventures that went beyond the usual theological expoundings. Sometimes Mr. Pynchon received important guests from Boston. I made a new skirt and embroidered my best blouses in order to appear more dignified in the company of the town's proprietors.

I began to accept Springfield as a wonderful place to live. William Pynchon had chosen the site for Springfield at a location on the river favorable for fur trading. The settlement was built on a strip of dry ground that lay between the east bank of the Great River and the edge of a hassocky marsh. The houses were laid out on the brow of a small hill, closely spaced in a single row along one center roadway. The rutted wheel track ran roughly north and south, paralleling the margins of the waters that defined our town.

Our house lot, like most of the others, was a narrow, four-acre strip that stretched between road and river. On the marshy side of the road, there was little land suitable for building. Our house looked out over the wetlands where tiny brushy islands and tufted tall grasses poked up through shallow pond water that drained in from several small rivulets out of the hillside beyond. Long stilt-legged herons stalked the edges of the marsh and small birds flitted and sang in the bushes. I could see the forested hillside slope where each landed man had his assigned woodlot.

Our crops were grown in the fertile soil on the west side of the Great River and our pasturage was at the long meadow south of our village. Joseph said the first settlers had built their homes across the river where our fields were. They had named the place Agawam, because of the Indian tribe there, but the Indians had warned that in some years the land flooded in the spring. When Mr. Pynchon arrived, he sited his new town on the east side of the river.

We lived on a lot two houses down from Nathaniel's. Our home was one room with a sleeping loft under the peak, made of rough timber felled from Joseph's woodlot and cut in the town saw pit. The walls were wattle and daub, the clay clapboarded over on the outside. Joseph had replaced the thatched roof with wood shingles. Joseph was especially pleased with the chimney, made of solid brick, an improvement over the older style English chimney of round sticks daubed with clay, which had been prone to catching fire. There was no stepping-stone at our front door because at Springfield there was almost no stone to be had, except for some poor quality red rock that was hauled up from the Mill River south of town. Our house was small, but I liked it.

I was surprised and overjoyed when Mother bought the lot next to ours. When old Grandfather Hulins had died in England after we departed, he left Mother with a monetary inheritance that she had refused to use until the time was right. Although it was unusual for a woman to be able to buy land, Mother used this money to buy several large pieces at Springfield on her own. She believed that Springfield would prosper, and thought it would be wise for the family to own land there. The comfort of having my brothers nearby overseeing Mother's land was immeasurable.

Spiritually we were immersed in Mr. Pynchon's world of deep religious ponderings. Joseph was impressed that Mr. Pynchon was so adept at proposing intricate layers of religious scholarship. Joseph told me that Mr. Pynchon read the Bible in the tongue of Hebrew in order that he might better understand the truer meanings of the ancient words. Because Joseph was clever, Mr. Pynchon and The Reverend Moxon welcomed Joseph into their discussions, responding to his wry comments and questions with amusement and patience. Mr. Pynchon particularly seemed to enjoy refining his lofty ideas into plainer explanations for Joseph. Mr. Pynchon was writing some kind of theological tract that questioned and enlarged upon the scope of God's forgiveness. Women were not included in their weighty discussions about sin and salvation, which did not seem to bother the wives, who were thoroughly occupied with other conversations among themselves. Since most of the talk among the women was about their children, I had little to offer. When I could, I quietly listened in on the men. I was very curious, finding their thinking very different from the simpler emotional worship of my father.

Those evenings as I watched Joseph, my impressions of him were confirmed. I noticed that my husband was generally well received by other men, whether they were educated or of the trades. Joseph was a personable man whose common sense and zest seemed to cause other men to feel capable, comfortable, and masculine. In Joseph's presence, the women also brightened. I thought that some women warmed to me in especially kindly ways to cover the depth of their fascination with my husband's charms.

At the beginning of March, 1647, I began to suspect that You had inclined Your eye to me. During one of mother's visits, I confided with her about the changes in my body. She listened and then rejoiced, confirming my hope with her experience. Joseph gathered me into his arms and held me close when I told him I thought that he soon would be a father.

My mother's visit was bittersweet. She bore her own news, which offset our joy. She told me that she worried about Father. For a man of 56 years, he seemed unnaturally tired and his feet were swelling, she said. Often she saw him leaning against his fences unable to catch his breath. She complained that he was becoming very forgetful in his fatigue. She said that often my brothers Lawrence and John had to finish his work, but Father did not seem to notice. Other times, Mother said, he blustered his frustration until something in his chest began to flutter, forcing him to sit until his body quieted. Mother had tried every herb she knew and had consulted the physician, but Father grew weaker rather than stronger.

We talked about Father's illness with Joseph that evening. Joseph listened carefully and then sat, thinking. To my surprise, when he spoke again, he had made up his mind that the best thing for me would be to go with my mother to be with her during my pregnancy and to help her with Father.

"Joseph, I cannot live without you by my side!"

"Mary, it is not my intent to leave you. I will come with you. Your Father will do better with my help."

"But what of your land, your fields, your responsibilities to the town?"

"Merrick and I are nearly finished with the road to the long meadow. As soon as it is done, I will be able to go with you. As for planting, there are plenty of men who will do it for me in trade for some of the harvest."

In May, back we went to Hartford for an extended stay. As the baby within me grew, my father doted on me, a justifiable reason for him to linger about the house. Indeed, I could see that he was not well. My younger brothers who still lived on the farm had taken over most of Father's chores and obligations, and my sisters fussed over him as well. That spring, Father failed to train with the town militia, a duty of all men from the age of sixteen to sixty. For this lapse, Father was called to appear before the court, reprimanded, and fined. Father might have defended himself by admitting his failing health, but he refused to do so.

In July of that year, a terrible illness came to the settlement at Hartford. Many were ill. On July 7, our beloved Reverend Thomas Hooker was taken from us by the sickness. It was the Sabbath. On that day I had noticed that he seemed to have a cold and that he wheezed and coughed into a handkerchief throughout the meeting. His assistant, Rev. Stone, being absent, Reverend Hooker gave both the sermon and the sacrament of the Lords supper in the morning, and then performed a baptism in the afternoon. After the meeting, we heard that he grew weak and went to bed. It was there he died, all of a sudden. It was a devastating blow to my father, to the town, to the entire colony.

Under the circumstances, Joseph and I decided to prolong our stay in Hartford. Being in Hartford, close to Windsor, was of profit to Joseph because the docks there were great centers of trade, a link to the great coastal wharves at the river mouth where seagoing ships loaded and unloaded goods being shipped to a recovering England. On a good wind, smaller ships could sail all the way up the deep tidal channel of the Great River to the rapids at Windsor. Some river trade was poled up the rapids by flat boat, but that took the efforts of at least twelve strong men.

Mr. Pynchon had warehouses just below the fast water at Warehouse Point.

The great bounty of the colony's inland harvests waited there for shipment: wood, furs, peas, corn, flax, wheat, barley, and more. The warehouses also received incoming supplies, which were off-loaded for distribution and trade, or were carried overland the fourteen miles from Windsor to Springfield.

Joseph was a good trader and bargainer. He often did business at Mr. Pynchon's docks and warehouses. There was money to be made with England for men who had motivation and ability to satisfy the needs of their markets, and my Joseph had both. A few times Joseph brought me with him to wait together until whatever man he had arranged with arrived; be it Indian, planter, or trapper. While he talked, I watched all the activities going on around me. Joseph had more ventures going all over the valley than he could tell me about. The high regard and good recommendation that Mr. Pynchon had for Joseph was advantageous and helped Joseph to prosper where ever he laid his hand.

My Joseph was remarkable in his eye for opportunity. It did not matter in what town Joseph lived; he saw possibilities for business where other men did not. By the time others began to imitate and compete with him, he was on to something else. I saw that Father took energy from Joseph's strength, which Joseph gave willingly.

That summer there was a great infestation of caterpillars. Many wondered and worried about this sign. Caterpillars crawled up the walls of every house and barn. The leaves of the shade trees in our yard became chewed with holes. The branches were filled with ugly web nests containing dark wiggling bodies. Joseph said that in the woods, caterpillar droppings fell like rain. One night he poured little pellets out of his pants for me to see. He said the droppings had rolled off his hat, down his collar, and into his clothing. In the fall, the leaves were already brown when they fell away. The caterpillars disappeared, to the relief of everyone.

Our baby was born November 1, 1647 at Hartford. When I realized my time had come, I was fearful but relieved in a way, until waves of pain began to rip me apart, carrying me beyond sensibility. Women murmured over me. I grasped at the midwife. She tried to comfort me as she could, but she could not save me from the power larger than us all that swept over me and took me. I nearly lost hope that it would ever be over, and then amazingly it was. They pressed a small weight into my arms. I opened my eyes and looked into the tiny face of my child. It was a boy, a perfect little boy. Joseph came next to me. As I handed the little babe to my husband, I whispered my choice for our son's name, Joseph. You had answered my prayers.

Hearken unto my voice, O Lord, when I crye, have mercy also upon me and heare me. Psalm 35:19

Chapter 13

Certain Shadows

Springfield, 1649

Oh, My Lord, our lives were filled with laughter as we watched Little Joseph, our Joey, grow strong under the watch of my family at Hartford. The memories of those days are my sweet offering to You.

My first babe was a miracle to me. What I lacked in experience, I made up in love. The next spring I realized that we had again been blessed. I was carrying another child. Our second son was born to us January 22nd, 1649. He was a beautiful infant. We named him Benjamin, after Joseph's brother. Benjamin looked just like me. The second child was easier for me than the first because I was more confident. I raised my two boys in great delight. It was late spring of 1649 when we decided to return with our children to Springfield. Joseph had become increasingly eager to move back. It was hard on my father for us to leave him, but my sisters promised that they would take good care of Father. Mother wished us "God speed."

Upon our return to Springfield, I realized with comfortable resolution that, although Springfield was not as large as Hartford, it was a fine place to grow our family. I was glad to be in Joseph's home. Besides the occasionally missing tool, the local Agawam Indians gave us little worry. The wilds were yielding to our presence. The wolves' chilling howls in the night grew quiet as their numbers grew less. The prowling catamounts were seldom seen any more. Although our town still had less than fifty free men, our meetinghouse was the first built west of Boston in the Massachusetts colony.

I would never have imagined that You would test the measure of our love by taking our second lamb, Benjamin. The day was June 22nd, 1649, exactly five months to the day of his birth. I still remember how I lay the babe down for a nap in his cradle by the hearth. I watched him fall asleep, saw his lashes drop to his plump little cheeks, never knowing it would be for the last time. When Benjamin did not rouse to nurse, I went to wake him, only to find that there was no breath in him. I screamed. I pleaded with You. My brother found me this way and went to get Joseph. Joseph returned home to find me sobbing, rocking the lifeless baby, trying to fill him with warmth again. I vaguely knew that poor Joey was clinging to me in fear. Joseph lifted his limp infant son from my arms to look at him. I remember how Joseph slowly sagged to his knees when he realized that our Benjamin was gone. He began to roll with the child pressed to him, moaning. I will never forget the sight and the sound of it. The grief in it pierces my heart and my memory forever.

We buried Benjamin that same day. Joseph and my brothers dug the grave. We lay our child into the hole in the ground, wrapped in a blanket my mother had made for him. I remember that yellow butterflies fluttered over the meadow, rising around us as we lingered silently around the small mound of fresh earth in the meadow.

A great darkness descended around me. Each time I went to the cradle and found it empty, a little more of me drained away. My heart hurt and my arms were strangely heavy as if they had taken on the weight of the missing child, but my eyes could not weep. I did not have the energy to sustain sorrow. I stepped out of myself and tried to meet my tender, precious child in the mists where he had gone. I heard people telling me that I still had little Joseph and that I would have more children. It was no comfort. Their words drove me deeper into a lonely blackness. They did not understand that the loss of Benjamin grew more real and more terrible each day. Benjamin, Benjamin, I could not do anything else but yearn for him. He so much needed his mother's thoughts surrounding him. He was so small, too tiny to be away from me.

Joseph asked women to come and sit with me and watch after Joey. My neighbors seemed bent upon distracting me from my sadness. For weeks I was surrounded by the unpleasantness of their loud voices. They patted my hands and they brushed my hair. They cooed over Joey, spoiling him. I would have rather had them quit me and go away. It would have been too difficult to shoo them away, so I withdrew further into my darkness. They stayed on. At last, they turned away from me and began to talk among themselves. It was not long before they began to argue.

I tried to shut out the annoying sounds except that I could not ignore the sound of my name on their lips. My ears heard their ugly story unfold. One of the parties in their tale bore my name, Mary Parsons. I realized that the Mary Parsons of whom they spoke was the Welshwoman, a Catholic papist who lived near us, who had my same name. She was Mary Lewis, married to Hugh Parsons, the brick maker. They were not believers. They lived as impious strangers among us, she going to meeting once a year, he even less, although Joseph said that the word at Pynchon's store was that Goodman Parsons was liked by the other men.

Something had happened between Goody Parsons and Widow Marshfield that had caused them to have words between each other. The women who gathered at my house gossiped about how Goody Parsons said this, and how she said that, and how she went about afterward accusing Widow Marshfield of being a witch. The Widow Marshfield visited me almost daily because she was tending to our neighbor Goody Bedortha during the last days of her pregnancy. She and her friends chewed on and on about the outrage of the slur against her. The Widow pressed upon me. It was important to her that each of her friends shows her support of her because nearly everyone in the town was taking sides. She was gleeful when Mr. Pynchon finally put an end to the quarreling.

Mr. Pynchon called Goody Lewis Parsons to appear before him, as he was the Magistrate. After hearing the case, he judged her guilty of slander. The poor soul was sentenced to pay a fine or be whipped twenty lashes. Hugh Parsons paid his wife's fine with 24 bushel of corn, a severe blow for a man of his means. It was a bad thing and hearing about it was upsetting. My mind felt heavy and rotten as a blackened peach covered in mold. The ugly stories around me buzzed like fruit flies in a cloud of doom.

I complained to Joseph about the disturbing gossip. Joseph did not approve of his house being used as a gathering place for such talk. Joseph liked Hugh. He had employed him several times. Hugh had daubed our walls with plaster and built our chimney and fireplace.

The next day Joseph stayed home long enough to thank the women for coming to care for Joey and me, and then he sent them away, saying that I needed my rest. My sister, Hannah, came to stay with me. She patiently urged me to get out of bed. As I stared into the fire, it seemed that the other Parsons' pain and mine mingled at the hearth where the cradle had stood.

I brooded. Sometimes Joseph came to sit beside me but there was nothing to say. Our sorrow was the same but we could not share it nor reach across it to help each other through it. Our sorrow became a deep silence between us. Sometimes Joseph talked about things that he did, things that he could fix and make better. He told me about his work, what went on at town meeting, and his dealings with other people. He mentioned that Hugh Parsons had begun to be quarrelsome, causing trouble with some of the other men. Joseph said Hugh was making accusations and causing suspicion. All of the turmoil in the surrounding houses seemed part of the bleakness inside me.

The sadness that filled our house must have made it feel very small. Joseph began to talk of building a new house at the long meadow south of Springfield, as many of our neighbors were doing. With the bridge that he had been working on for the town completed, the roadway there was open. Joseph began to occupy his evening hours with his plans.

One day about the last of September, Joseph came home early from training with the militia. He bore dreadful news. Hugh and Goody Parsons' little boy, Samuel, their third child, barely more than a year old was dead. Joseph sat by me for a time, and we watched our young Joey playing out in the yard, innocent of our pain. In a while, Joseph left to see if he could help the Parsons bury their child.

Tears that had not been shed for my child fell from my eyes. Joey watched me. He was quiet. He had stopped asking anything of me.

I tried to reassure him, "Mother is here, Joey. Mother is here." He did not believe me, I could see it in his eyes.

One remarkable day, unexpectedly, You saw fit to deliver me from the awful weight of gloom. It happened oddly. I was sitting in the outhouse. A bleed was upon me. Usually I was either nursing or pregnant and did not have to bother with the bleeding that troubled virgins and childless women every month. Rather than bleed into my clothes, I went to the outhouse to wait out the worst of it. I had opened the door a bit because of the heat. Chickens were scratching in the yard. One poor hen was being chased and pecked by all the others. It seemed to me that if only the battered bird would shake of her terror and stop running, the others would stop their chase. I needed to rescue her.

I closed the door. In the dim light of the little toilet house, I cleaned myself and made ready to go catch the bird. I scooped up the stupid, pecked-over chicken and dropped her into a closed stall in the barn. I filled a basin with water for her, and gave her food. I vowed I would take care of her until she recovered her confidence enough to return to her flock. As I stood looking at the chicken, a yellow butterfly took me by surprise by landing on my hand. It seemed like I was being given a tiny reward for helping the hurt chicken. Its small companionship reminded me of the day we buried Benjamin, how the yellow butterflies had filled the air around us. As soon as I had that thought, the butterfly rose up with its impossibly delicate wings and circled my head, brushing my cheek before it sailed away. I had a strange feeling that I had been visited and given a sign. My Benjamin was safe. I did not have to worry about him any more.

The color of the sky was a brighter blue than it had been. I had not noticed the fluffy towering clouds. A slight breeze came up, cooling my skin refreshingly.

I turned and went into the house. I embraced my surviving child. I began to tend to all the many things I had neglected. How uncharacteristically patient my husband must have been with me over the past months as he waited for me. I turned to Joseph and began to feel my need for him. He accepted me back into his arms. We held each other in the night, rediscovering the warmth and textures of our skin. We resumed our marital covenanted duties. The joy we created together healed the rifts and sealed a pact. Flushed and sated after our pleasures, my head upon his beating heart, a warm safety encompassed me within the soft temple of our blanketed sanctuary. In the quiet hush of our breathing, I offered silent praise for Thy gifts of splendor.

My few dear friends had gotten out of the habit of visiting me so I went to visit them, joining them around their quilting frames or spinning wheels, enjoying conversation. Joseph wanted me to see the beginnings of the new house on his fields at the long meadow. One day we harnessed the horses to the wagon, bundled up Joey, and drove out to view it. I saw again that the land was beautiful and that the future house was rising strongly upon it. We talked lightly about when we might move in.

Talking about the community reminded Joseph to tell me that the book that William Pynchon had been writing was finished and that the manuscript had been sent by ship to England to be printed. It would be many months before the bound books arrived. He also told me that he had heard that Hugh and Goody Parsons were expecting a baby.

"Joseph, I don't have a good feeling about that. Is she well?"

"Obviously well enough," said Joseph with a laugh, making a little joke with me.

My husband and my son seemed so happy. Joey chatted endlessly, pointing at things, asking a hundred questions, which Joseph answered even while giving me little squeezes. Living could be so sweet.

Soon there were signs that a new child grew within me. Winter closed in, worked its fury upon us, and then broke. As the spring came on, my belly swelled like the bud of a dandelion, showing that there would be a babe come summer.

My God, I trust in You;
let me not be confounded. Psalm 31:1

Chapter 14

Sin, Disobedience, and Words Ill Taken

The Long Meadow at Springfield, 1650

One morning late in June I woke up feeling as if there was something special about the day. As large as I was with child, I felt light and full of purpose. All morning I had the feeling that something important had happened. My mother was visiting from Hartford. I questioned her about the day, wondering if I had forgotten something.

"Mother, I feel such a beautiful radiance filling this house. I am so excited and happy, but I cannot remember what is special about today. Can you?"

She looked at me.

"Mary, today is the day that Benjamin died."

"Oh. Oh. Yes. Of course. It has been a year. Ah, Mother. I do not understand then. What I am feeling is as if a heaviness has lifted from me. How could that possibly be, today of all days?"

"Perhaps it is because today you know in your heart of hearts that Benjamin has made his way to God."

"Mother, you hurt me. How can you say that? We will not know that until Judgment Day!"

"There are many who believe that God in His mercy elects all for paradise."

"Oh, Mother. Stop it. Does your 'many' include people like Anne Hutchinson? You know what happened to her. It does not matter what you think. She, Adam, Eve, and all humankind are barred from paradise unless elected by God. Moreover, we will never know until we get there who was chosen. You know that. The only ones we know will not be in paradise are those who already believe that heaven is their destiny. So be careful."

"I once believed that same way, Mary. I used to, but not anymore. God chooses us all."

"Chooses us all! In spite of our sin? You do not believe that we are all born in sin; that to live is to live in sin?

"No, Mary, I do not. God is Mercy. God is Love. God has closed the gates of hell. Hell is empty. We are loved."

"Mother, you talk such heresy! You might get away with saying that here in Springfield, but never in Hartford. You best watch out how you speak when you go home, and you should not try to convert me to something I am not ready for."

"Tell me that what you feel is not the peace of your child in paradise! Are you not describing yourself the spirit of grace of a child who is with God?"

"I wish you were right. I wish Benjamin were with God, but I cannot know. We can't know."

"I think we can, Mary. We can know that we are redeemed when our spirit becomes illuminated by grace. I think you feel the spirit of grace illuminating Benjamin, and that is the source of your happiness today."

Mother went to the door and opened it. She began waving her hands around in a funny way. She looked so odd that I had to laugh.

"Mother! What are you doing?"

"Oh, there is a yellow butterfly beating itself against the window. I am letting it out. See it? There. There it goes."

"There is no use arguing with you, Mother. Now you even have the butterflies on your side."

"Yes. That is the first clever thing you have said today. I'm glad you recognize that there is no use arguing with me." Mother seemed amused.

"I have been noticing many butterflies. Have you? Do you remember all the butterflies the day we buried Benjamin?" I asked.

"I suppose it is the time of year for them," she said, distractedly.

Mother did not seem to be interested in making observations about butterflies. Since I had accidentally managed to end the conversation about her favorite topic of redemption, I decided to let it go. I busied myself with cooking, and she helped me. I ruminated upon my own thoughts and kept them to myself.

In the days that followed the anniversary of Benjamin's death, I did notice one change. Grief that had been so painful had become familiar. In a way, I began to treasure the times when I was filled with moist, deep sorrow because it was all I had left of feeling near to Benjamin. I took yellow butterflies to be a peaceful reminder of Benjamin, something I could see. I went to Benjamin's grave several times to watch the butterflies.

One night as Joseph and I lay in bed, I tried to explain to him what I was thinking. Drowsily he listened. His hand was cupped over my belly. He liked to feel the strong bumping of the new baby growing within. Joseph mumbled a response and fell asleep before I could finish my thoughts. I stared into the darkness, my thoughts running in endless circles as I sought to see a way through the mysteries that enshroud Your grace.

By Your blessing, our third son was born to us August 14, 1650. I poured out my heart to You that no harm would come upon him. We called the boy John, both the name of my brother and of our family friend, John Pynchon. Soon after, we moved into the new house on the Long Meadow, with the help of my brothers and sisters. We lit the fire in the new hearth and made a joyous meal. Joey continued to flourish, and baby John grew robustly. I watched both children closely, scarcely daring to take my eyes from them. I loved them with all my heart and felt full of satisfaction at being their mother. I ran the house well around them. You filled each day with small delights and little moments of perfect grace, which I acknowledged gratefully by accepting my duty to take notice of every gift by giving to You the thanks You art due.

Joseph kept himself busy all the time. Both as Mr. Pynchon's fur agent and in his own ventures, Joseph was enterprising in the way he made partnerships with various men in the community. Mr. Pynchon owned almost all the businesses, but Joseph always kept his eye toward anticipating work that Mr. Pynchon might need done, or the goods Mr. Pynchon might require for his ventures. Joseph was first in line to take over business that Mr. Pynchon was planning to sell off. In his shrewdness, Joseph was never short of ideas about what to do. Our life was full of men and plans. I was happy for the evenings when I had him to myself, for the times when we could talk alone, for the quiet times when he took up his pipe and mused aloud as the smoke from the tobacco rose in curls. It was on such a night, as I sat beside him nursing the baby, that he presented me with a small book.

"Look, Mary. Mr. Pynchon has been waiting in Boston to meet the ship from London. Here is one of the first copies ever to be read. He has only just arrived from Boston today and he gave this to me himself. I think you would like to hear what he says. I will read it aloud to you if you wish."

Joseph sat down and read Mr. Pynchon's book to me that evening by lamplight. The words melded into me as I sat stroking the precious softness of my sleeping baby's warm cheek. The book was titled *The Meritorious Price of Our Redemption*. I admit that I found much of Mr. Pynchon's book ponderous and theological, but when the reading of the book was done, a part of me filled with an immense resonating relief to think that the way to paradise could be achievable through obedience to Your law.

It did worry me greatly that Mr. Pynchon ranted dangerously against the teachings of the church, which he said "makes God the Father more rigid in the price of our Redemption than ever a Turkish Tyrant was, and to be a harder Creditor in the point of satisfaction than ever any rigid Creditor was among men." Many of his thoughts would make our ministers angry. I feared for our friend, Mr. Pynchon. Our ministers allowed one interpretation of the Bible. We had traveled far to be free to proclaim that one truth.

Joseph was not alarmed. He had been part of long discussions with Mr. Pynchon and The Reverend Moxon. Joseph had been flattered that two such educated men had used a workingman like himself to test their ability to explain their theology. Joseph reassured me that Mr. Pynchon was so powerful and so respected throughout the colony that his ideas would be seen for their wisdom and scholarship.

Joseph was wrong. Not a day had passed when official word was sent to Springfield from the General Court sitting in Boston notifying Mr. Pynchon that his shipment of books had been seized immediately after delivery from England and condemned as heresy by the Boston ministers and the General Court. Every copy that could be found had been confiscated and thrown into a pyre at the Market Place in Boston and burned by the Common Executioner. William Pynchon himself was demanded to present himself at the next convening of the General Court of Election on the very first day of their sitting to admit ownership of the book and to offer satisfactory retraction of its contents. A day of "Fasting and Humiliation" was ordered for every inhabitant of the Massachusetts Bay Colony to atone for the growth of Satan's influence among us.

For us in Springfield and Long Meadow this judgment against William Pynchon was as if lightning had struck down our town, our church, and everything we believed in. Our loyalties were divided. Our trust was dishonored. Even our relationship with You seemed in question.

On the morning of the Sabbath of Fasting and Humiliation, the beat of the drum going up the street summoned us to meeting with demanding insistence. Quickly we threw on our cloaks to join those already walking toward the meetinghouse. The quiet creak of leather boots shuffled against the packed dirt of the roadway in steady rhythm with the drum. I thought that the guns and Bibles we carried must weigh less than the dread in our hearts. We had heard that a minister had been sent to Springfield especially to admonish our congregation.

Somehow, I was surprised that our meetinghouse looked as it always did. The bell tower and the watchtower upon the steep roof still rose to point the way to heaven, where I directed my gaze in hope. When I looked down, I was startled by my attention to the heads of the wolves that were always nailed by bounty hunters to the side of the meetinghouse. I had never noticed how their blood ran down the boards of the meetinghouse in dark streams, staining the wood to the ground. I shuddered before their faces of sunken-eyed death and gaped-mouthed barbarity.

Men went in one door, women into another, as usual. Inside the benches awaited us, and we all sat down in our habitual places. The mood of the congregation was grim. No one spoke. No eyes met. Only the large enormous eye painted on the pulpit looked upon us, a reminder to us of our transgressions before the Lord.

The Reverend Moxon was in his seat, the guest minister who was to be announced was beside him. Mr. Pynchon was absent; some whispered that he was ill. That Sabbath was indeed a humiliation to us directly and personally.

The day seemed to be never-ending. I felt for myself what the flock of Moses gathered at the foot of Mount Sinai must have felt when they suffered the despair of punishment. Any belief by the community in Mr. Pynchon's book was presented to us as like unto a celebration of the Golden Calf. The berating and lecturing went long into the afternoon. When we returned home for a shortened break between services, our fires were burnt to feeble embers. There was no food, neither were there answers.

In the chaos that followed the storm of shame, it was not long before strange things began to occur. One morning Hannah Lankton opened her pudding bag and found the pudding within slashed from end to end. She was frightened and had no explanation for it. Right after the same thing happened a second time, she opened her door to find Hugh Parsons standing at her doorstep with no excuse for his presence. Goody Lankton came to me, as she did to all the neighbors, to warn us to beware of Hugh Parsons.

She said, "The spirit that bewitched the pudding brought Hugh Parsons to my door. Be careful if he should come to yours."

I thanked her for the caution and tried not to worry whenever a knock came upon my door. It seemed certain that the Devil's hand was in this place when in another household an ox tongue disappeared from a kettle fully at boil. Joseph said that various farmers were telling of their cows acting strangely. I asked him if he thought it true that an evil spirit had been unleashed in Springfield.

Joseph said, "There is such a contagion of rumors everywhere about the town that we would do well to guard our thoughts and actions. We must be certain to offer our ardors only unto the God of Heaven, and pray for His fondness. There may be some who have fallen into the Devil's dunghill that has been laid here by the insults to Mr. Pynchon, but it is only because some people have allowed themselves to be distracted from remembering and trusting that our community has prospered righteously until now under the good and knowledgeable leadership of Mr. Pynchon. It would not help us to pay too close attention to stories of evil. I will not let the fears that have spread from Boston taint our home."

I saw that Joseph burned with fury in defense of Mr. Pynchon. He told me that although everyone was on watch, it was not true that everyone was taking all the gossip about strange occurrences seriously. He said that the men who worked cutting lumber with Hugh Parsons continued to defend him against the gossip.

What Joseph said about the woodcutters who worked with Goodman Parsons was true, until the day they saw what happened to Thomas Miller when he teased Hugh about the slashed pudding. Even Joseph had to admit that all the men who were there said the same thing about what happened.

"The way I heard it, the men were working in the woods as usual and took a break at noon to eat their meal. Thomas Miller opened his sack and started waving around his meat pudding, saying, 'Look here! My wife has cut my pudding too thick. How is a man supposed to get his mouth around this? Hugh, see if you can use your powers to slice this thing.' They said that when all the men started to laugh and joke about Hugh bewitching the pudding, Hugh began to curse Goodman Miller, saying he would get even. They returned to work and had only been at it a few minutes when Thomas Miller suffered a great gash upon his leg."

After that, the men listened more carefully to what their wives were saying about Hugh. The menfolk began to spread their own stories.

William Branch told of a dream he had concerning Hugh Parsons. "There was a light all over the chamber like fire, and there came a thing upon me like a little boy, with a face as red as fire…and I felt something like scalding water on my back, and then I heard a voice saying 'it is done, it is done.' "

Jonathon Taylor complained that one evening he found himself unable to loosen the tap on a cask of beer to fill the cups of his thirsty friends. Even though he used all his considerable strength, he succeeded only in drawing his own blood, but no beer. All around they laughed at him, especially when his wife declared that she could withdraw it with her little finger, and did.

Those present declared, "It could not be so except it were bewitched."

Griffin Jones could not understand the failing that had caused him to lose three house-knives, only to have them suddenly reappear, "which made me blush." He was shamed by the incident and swore it was Hugh Parsons' doing.

At least a dozen persons had complaints of Devilish arts being practiced upon them. Included most loudly among them was Hugh Parsons' own wife. With no apparent restraint, Goody Parsons went about the town regaling anyone who would listen with descriptions of her husband's mysterious absences from home, of the torments that he inflicted upon her, and of the threats he made against anyone who came against him. I tried to stay away from her, but I noticed that a new babe lay cradled in her arms. It had been born almost unnoticed in the excitement that surrounded the book burning. It bothered me that within inches of the little ears of the infant named Joshua, Goody Parsons mouth confided loudly and to all the most hideous tales of the ways the babe's father made show of being a witch.

We visited the Pynchon home to stand by William Pynchon in support and to try to console his wife Frances. The scene there was most upsetting. Mr. Pynchon was sequestered in his library with The Reverend Moxon. The Reverend Moxon knew with certainty that his own career was deeply threatened by his association and collaboration with Mr. Pynchon. Frances Pynchon told me that she was in shock that her husband's former colleagues were speaking and writing letters against him. Frances poured out her outrage at the betrayal.

"The culmination of my husband's entire life study is in ashes, but he will never recant his beliefs. He is convinced that the Calvinists have become too harsh in their thinking. This all just proves to him how right he is about that! Why are the ministers not willing to open their eyes and see the wisdom of William's interpretations? After one quick reading, the General Court summarily threw away the opportunity to understand more deeply God's message of redemption. It is a disgrace. It is a disgrace and a pity. To think that these men were friends of William! These men have fashioned themselves as our only permissible authorities. Except as they must bow to the King of England, they would have us believe that here in the colonies they alone define God and God's laws. Are they blind? I do not know how my William can exist in such a climate. I truly fear for his well-being. William is the kind of man who will stand firm because he believes that what he has written is sound theology. He wrote as a labor of love. What will they do to him when he goes before the court? It could go very badly. I know he will never recant! We could lose everything. People have been hung for less."

In anxiety, I listened to Frances Pynchon. Any thoughts of how to reassure her seemed hollow in the face of such a genuine assessment of danger. It went no better in Mr. Pynchon's study because whatever discussions Joseph was party to there caused him to return home as if from a house of tragic mourning. Afterwards he paced angrily, alternately throwing up his hands or clasping them together in a gesture of pleading. Incredulously, he repeatedly asked the same questions of me, but he never waited for me to answer what I could not.

"How can this be happening? How could this happen to Mr. Pynchon? He is the upholder of civil and judicial law in our community. He is the most influential man in our valley. He is such a learned man, such a good man. How can this be happening to a man who labored so long to bring reason and light into religious thinking? He is a genius, not a heretic! How can the ministers of Boston not see the brilliance of his conclusions?"

I could do nothing but listen as he ranted and grew bitter at an unfairness he could not change.

"It is impossible to call such a man a criminal! They call him a blasphemer. He was educated at Oxford. He built our church! It was because of his influence that our pulpit has a minister in it at all! He employs almost every person in this plantation. There would be no town if not for him! Not one of us would be here if not for him."

Joseph knew what had been here before William Pynchon. He was only a young man of seventeen years when he stood by Mr. Pynchon's side in 1636 to witness the bargain Pynchon made with the Indians to deed over the land that was to become Springfield for the price of eighteen fathoms of wampum, eighteen coats, eighteen hatchets, eighteen hoes, and eighteen knives.

"Why eighteen of everything?" I had asked Joseph. "Is it because there were eighteen chiefs?"

"No. I told you, Mr. Pynchon reads the Bible in its old tongue of Hebrew. In that language, eighteen stands for both a number as well as the word for life. For Mr. Pynchon, the payment was symbolic of his hope for a blessing upon the deal. It was his way of showing honor to the tribes and to the land. He had a vision that the businesses he planted here would find roots and grow, which is why he gave this place its name of Springfield, after his beloved home in England."

Mr. Pynchon had founded our town as a successful fur trade center with Joseph as one of his fur agents. It was Mr. Pynchon who had brought settlers to come and build homes here along the banks of the Connecticut River. As Mr. Pynchon had prospered, so had my Joseph.

Joseph could not bear to watch the undoing of the man he so admired. Now in the full power of his manhood, Joseph could do nothing to defend his benefactor, nor protect him, nor stand by him in any way to lessen the blows that the Massachusetts Bay Colony cast upon anyone who diverged from lawful belief and behavior. As Joseph had stayed by me through my dark days, I so resolved to stand by him. I would not fail him.

The sorrows of my heart are enlarged: draw me out of my troubles. Psalm 25:17

Chapter 15

Evil Overwhelming

Springfield and Long Meadow, 1651

Your mercy must ever be inclined to me for the remorse I feel at being overwhelmed by the terrible iniquities that besieged our community in those days.

The early days of January were often bleak and cold and I grew more irritable. Joey and baby John gave me great delight, but even their clever cuteness could not calm my restlessness. I fell back upon my old soothing habit of walking, bundling up my two boys to take them with me across fields of white frozen snow, seldom with a direction in mind. The boys were fascinated when I showed them the tiny glinting rainbow colors that shined out from single snow crystals, a reminder of Your pure miracles. Usually I came home feeling much better, more focused.

One sunny day when the snow was firm enough to walk upon without sinking in too far, I took the boys for a walk out across the windblown meadows. We came upon the blind man of Springfield sledding with his daughter down a small hill at the edge of the woods. Suddenly their sled swerved right toward us. I yelled a warning, but Joey was struck, and he fell down hard. I scolded the man soundly, scooped up my boys, and left the blind man to pursue his careless folly. I thought nothing particularly of it until Joseph came home and asked me what had happened. Since Joey was not harmed, the whole thing seemed of little consequence. I described the incident to Joseph without looking up from my weaving. I did not see until too late that Joseph's eyes were flashing.

"Did you not know that you hurt that man with your words? Did you not see that his child took a sounding fit and went into a faint? The poor man put his daughter on his sled to bring her home but he could not find his way. His girl acts as his eyes. He has only just been found.

Both of them were shivering and near to die of cold. What got into you, Mary, that you would cause such offense?"

I tensed under a feeling of ominous danger. My Lord, I prayed for You to keep me in Your ways, but the path seemed to grow ever narrower, and a pit of cold, uncaring darkness seemed to yawn at the edge of my footsteps. The buzzing of evil became audible, pecking at the edges of my thoughts like bothersome insects unless I drowned out the sound by chanting the holy psalms of David. I tried to look unaffected for the sake of my family.

That February the people of Springfield and Long Meadow huddled in knots in their houses and on the streets, speaking to each other endlessly and inescapably about the threats upon us, until a few of the most aggrieved rallied in strength to stand against the evil they believed had come to dwell among us. At least a dozen townspeople, including the Moxons, brought formal charges of witchcraft against Hugh and Mary Parsons. Because both Parsons blamed each other of witchcraft, each stood accused. The trial was to begin February 27, with Mr. William Pynchon presiding as Magistrate. We waited for the date in anticipation. Around us, the claws of bared twigs reached out from naked tree branches to scratch at the icy gray horizons of our plantation. Close to the town, the snow was unclean, and dogs sniffed where invisible foul things lay.

Before the trial was to start, word came from Mother that she needed me in Hartford. Father was ailing. Mother had to call all her children home.

In a panic, I loaded Joey and baby John into the wagon and hired a man to take me to my parents at once, going ahead of Joseph. The way was cold and uncomfortable. The wind pushed against our progress, holding us back, fighting against us. The hooves of the steaming oxen alternately slipped or caught in the ruts of the frozen road.

I reached my parents' home to find Father very ill and taken to the bed. It was apparent that he was in his final days. I sat at Father's bedside willing him to breathe, trying to fill his chest with my breaths, struggling to push death away. Even as he gasped with the effort of speaking, his caring for us was his last thought as he spoke his final words to my mother. He knew he was dying when he whispered his last wishes unto her care. My father took his final breath on February 14, 1651. My dear, dear Father was gone. Joseph was not able to come in time to say his farewell.

We could not bury Father because the ground was frozen. He had to be left in a rock and dirt crypt until spring. He looked so alive when we closed the doors upon him. I worried we had been mistaken about his death. I suffered with this thought, imagining Father stirring feebly, alone and abandoned in the dark and cold, and crying out for us. I asked Joseph to go check on him to make certain that he lay in peace. Joseph assured me that Father was safely at rest and could no longer feel the cold. It made no difference what anyone said. Every time I thought of Father, my breath caught and my heart toppled painfully in my chest.

Joseph stayed on with me in Hartford through all this. He was very kind to Mother and understanding of me. I was touched that he stood calmly by me as my refuge. Mother appreciated that Joseph was there, but I think she took her greatest comfort in the company of her younger children and little grandsons. In the days that followed Father's death, Mother began to talk of leaving Hartford and moving to Springfield. At the beginning of March, a few unseasonably warm days thawed the ground enough so that it yielded to the shovel, finally allowing us to lay my father to rest.

Joseph and I returned home to Springfield soon after. It was an arduous and nearly impossible trip because the roads had turned to deep mud and crossing the Great River was treacherous at that time of year. We left in the evening and traveled all night to take advantage of the short time when the road would be refrozen. Even so, sometimes in the dim fluttering light of our torches we broke through the thinly frozen mud. When dawn came, a wind came up and the temperature dropped. The ground never thawed, so we traveled all day without rest. It was hard on the children. We were exhausted when we arrived home after dark. How grateful we were that my brother Nathaniel had built a fire to warm the house. My sisters had hung a pot of stew over it to simmer. We all slept late that morning and did not rise until the sun was already high in the sky. All day I felt weary and slow as I put our things away, and I was very glad when it was time to get back into bed again. Late that night I was awakened from a deep sleep by a loud commotion outside. Someone was banging on our door, calling for Joseph.

"Murder! Murder! Joseph, come help us. Joseph! Joseph Parsons! Come help us! There has been a murder. Come quickly. Joseph!"

Joseph jumped up and began to throw on clothes over the nightshirt he wore in the winter. "Mary, you stay here with the children. I'll go see what has happened," he said as he pulled on his boots.

I went to the window and saw Joseph join several other men whom I did not recognize because their features were indistinguishable under their great coats and black hats. They stood together for just a moment and then they went to the road and headed south.

Because of the angle of the road, I soon lost sight of them. I checked that our children were safe, and then I got back under the quilts to wait. Fretting over what could have happened and worrying about who had been stricken, I counted off all the families who lived in the direction they had gone. They had not turned into any of our neighbors' yards, the Sewell's, Taylor's, or Matthews' so they were all right. Beyond them were the Branch's, George Colton, and Griffith Jones. I sensed that they were also all right. Next to them were the Dorchester's, then Reice Bedortha. Could they have gone to the Bedortha's? Blanche had been having some troubles with unusual cutting pains after the recent birth of her child. She had been blaming Hugh Parsons for it because the pains started after she had a disagreement with him. Could it be that his curse had killed her? Next to them were only Benjamin Cooley, Hugh Parsons, and last, John Lombard. Goodman Cooley was too steadfast to have anything unusual happen to his household, and John Lombard the same. I guessed the trouble to be either at the Parsons or at Bedortha's. Murder? Had they really said murder?

It seemed a long time before I heard our door latch click and heard Joseph's steps below. He did not light the candlewood lamp when he came into the room; he just undressed in the dark and came to bed, chilled and weary. He lay down with a groan, and then sighing, began to tell me what had happened.

"It was the Parsons. Their baby died tonight. When I got there, the mother was screaming in a corner, swaying, holding the baby, and sobbing out that Hugh had killed it by his witchcraft. We had to pry the baby away from her to see if there was anything that could be done for it, but it was dead. She became like a wild thing then, pulling at herself and at us. For a time we had to hold her down to prevent any harm. As it is right now, the constable has ordered that Benjamin Cooley and Anthony Dorchester watch her overnight, and Goody Cooley is with them. Hugh has disappeared; we are not certain where he has gone. Probably he is hiding in his barn."

"Was the child murdered, Joseph?"

"Sarah Cooley said that the child was strangely taken. We do not know what happened, Mary. It is impossible to make any sense of Goody Parsons' ravings. We only know what Benjamin said that in the middle of the night Hugh ran to their house and pounded on their door. When Benjamin let him in, Parsons was half crazed, dressed only in his nightshirt, barefooted and barelegged. He was crying and begging hysterically that Goody Cooley come help his wife with their baby because it was choking. When the Cooleys got there, it was already too late. Goody Parsons fought them off when they tried to see the baby. That is when Goodman Cooley went to Goodman Bedortha for help. They came to get me."

"Is anyone looking for Hugh?"

"No, Mary. What could we do for him tonight? There are only a few hours until daylight. In the morning we will look for him."

"Don't you think he is a danger? Shouldn't he be captured?"

"The man has just lost his child, and his wife clearly has gone mad. Let the poor man be, Mary. The inquiry about him is still in process. Mr. Pynchon will decide what to do. No more questions. I am tired. We will take care of it in the morning. There is nothing to do now. I need to sleep."

Joseph turned away from me and soon dozed off heavily. I lay beside him thinking and must have fallen asleep myself, because in the morning I awoke with a start. Was last night a bad dream? Joseph's place beside me was rumpled and cold. He was gone from the house. Shining through the window, the morning sun was high, lighting the sky a soft blue. I looked long into the heavens, knowing that the sun brought a new day that little Joshua Parsons would never see. After the death of my child and then of my father, I had many times been amazed that over all beauty could continue to exist before my eyes with not a single blemish to show that a dear person was missing and that life had gone awry. I looked for signs from Your creation to show that living under Your wing offered peace and caring for the single soul.

The gentle rays of sun brought the perfect blue of the sky through my window, offering light but no guidance. I felt an odd kindred sympathy for the fragility of the other Mary Parsons, who had lost her child and her mind. I wondered if our shared name was Your warning to me to ever have my mind held against the madness, or whether it was a mocking joke of the Devil.

I did not go out to see for myself what was happening down the road. Joseph returned in a few hours to gather up some things that he needed for the day.

"Mary, you will be relieved to know that Hugh Parsons has turned up. He came to George Colton's house about eight o'clock this morning to beg some tobacco to cut for his pipe before he went home. It was very strange, because apparently he had not even known that the child had died. Hugh told Goodman Colton that he had only learned of the death from Jonathan Burt earlier in the morning. Goodman Colton was struck by how lightly he seemed to be taking the news. I heard all this from Benjamin Cooley and Goodman Colton when I went over to Goodman Cooley's this morning. Hugh went to Goodman Cooley's house after visiting the Colton's, puffing on his pipe. He came apparently to invite the Cooleys to the child's burial. Goodman Cooley was struck by Hugh's seeming lack of emotion. The Cooleys both sat with Goody Parsons all night. Goodman Cooley says Goody Parsons ranted the whole night long about Hugh and all the things that he has done that make her believe he is a witch. There is no evidence except what his wife says that it was Hugh who hurt the child, or even that the babe was murdered. I need to go now to help with the burial. We have been able to break through the frost line and have dug a grave. Hugh went home. We will bury the child as soon as Goody Parsons is able to go. Mary, I ask that you do not go to the burial. It would be too upsetting for you right now. It would not be good for you."

The next few days were stunning. Those who watched over Goody Parsons said that she remained in a mania of accusation against her husband, shouting out against him all manner of examples of his threats and curses and vile ways that led her to believe him to be a witch. Her certainty that Hugh had killed their child so that she would be free to help her husband with his work convinced us all that it was murder, although we wondered that she seemed increasingly to be losing her mind. Everyone was astounded when Goody Parsons began to reverse herself, sometimes telling Mr. Pynchon that she had killed the child herself, and sometimes that it was she who tormented the Moxon children, but sometimes denying it all.

Thomas Cooper went about with a report of something he overheard her say while in one of her erratic rants. He said that while she was telling about a night when she was with her husband, Goodwife Merrick, and Bessie Sewell in Goodman Stebbin's lot, he heard her say in her own words that "we were sometimes like cats, and sometimes in our own shape, and we were a-plotting for some good cheer; and they made me go barefoot and make the fires because I had declared so much at Mr. Pynchon's."

The town was in a frenzy of suspicion and fear. I sorely regretted that Joseph had to leave us at this time to return to Hartford so soon after we had just left. Richard Sexton of Windsor had brought charges against Joseph pertaining to some damages he perceived Joseph had caused, and Joseph had been called to appear before the court. While Joseph was away, Goody Parsons made a full confession to Mr. Pynchon about her witchcraft. Mr. Pynchon stopped her examination immediately, as well as all the other depositions being taken from townspeople. Murder and witchcraft being capital crimes, Mr. Pynchon turned the matter over to General Court at Boston.

Joseph returned from Hartford. He was disgruntled that he had lost his case and had been ordered to pay a fine of five pounds. I was just glad that he was back, and thanked You that nothing worse was being visited upon us, given what was occurring around Goody Parsons. She had been arrested and put into the town jail, to be held there until the weather would allow her to be taken away to prison in Boston to stand trial both for the murder of her son and for witchcraft. Hugh Parsons remained free while the case against him was examined. Mr. Pynchon, in his duty as Magistrate, found reason to believe that Goodman Parsons should be taken to the court at Boston to answer to charges of murder laid against him by his wife. With both parents in prison, their four year-old daughter Sarah, the only child left alive, became almost an orphan. Her fostering, feeding, and Christian conversion became a burden for all to share. The mark of evil that lay upon Springfield was invisible, but everyone felt its consequences.

I wondered at the awful calamities that had descended upon our community in such a short time. William Pynchon's work and possibly his reputation lay in ruins. The Moxon family had endured mysterious torments. In the Parsons family, one child was dead and murdered, another abandoned, the mother imprisoned in the madness of unfathomable sin and Devilry, and the father cast out and suspect. Many families were waiting to testify as to the afflictions brought upon them by vengeful curses. Two other women, Sarah Merrick and Bessie Sewell, were being accused of having taken part in the strange doings.

Springfield reminded me of the woods after a burn. All the landmarks of life seemed like tree trunks left standing scorched and blackened after a fire. Great pieces of our lives had been destroyed in the flames, reduced to unrecognizable ash. The sooty residue and lingering stench left its taint upon anyone who came near. Life would begin again, but I did not know what would be strong and what would have died forever. Thine anger was upon us, and the Devil came forth to delight in the working of devious wonders.

I asked Joseph if he still loved me.

"You are not asking the right question, Mary. I chose you as my wife, and I do not regret that, but I am worried. The question is how do we get through this? If someone as powerful as Mr. Pynchon can be brought down, who is next? I need to be able to depend upon you to behave, as a wife should. If you fail, some will think it is because I am not man enough to control my wife. Weakness brings danger."

In the Lord put I my trust:how say You to my soul, flee as a bird to Your mountain? For, lo, the wicked bend their bow; they make ready their arrow upon the string that they may privily shoot at the upright in heart. If the foundations be destroyed, what can the righteous do? Psalm 11:1-3

Chapter 16

Disturbances and Trials

Springfield and Long Meadow, Spring 1651

I took heed when The Reverend Moxon found his voice, and it thundered upon us.

Let Your work appear unto Your servants,
And Your glory unto their children.
And let the beauty of the Lord our God be upon us:
And establish You the work of our hands upon us:
Yea the work of our hands establish You it. Psalm 90:16-17

I thought The Reverend's words profound. The words pointed to a direction I should take, at a time when I found the way elusive. It was a reminder to busy myself with my work. I took heart that the work of our hands was righteous, and that because of the work of his hands, Mr. Pynchon would surely be vindicated. I went home desirous that Your glory be shown to my children, that Your beauty might be upon us in our troubles.

The next Sabbath, as The Reverend George Moxon again stood before us offering his solemn sermon, the sounds of crying rose from the women's benches. Looking from the sides of my eyes past the row of my sisters, I saw that The Reverend Moxon's own daughters were weeping softly. Their mother reached over discretely to quiet them, but the girls pulled away and abruptly stood up from their bench. First Martha Moxon and then her sister Rebecca opened their mouths wide and began to wail inconsolably. Their voices pierced the sudden stillness of the meeting. The unholy chorus of the girls' cries chilled me with a rush of fear. Apparently unconcerned with the spectacle they made, they began to twist and turn and shake. With shrieks as if in pain, both girls suddenly fell to the ground in the throes of some kind of fit. As everyone rose in horror, another voice began to scream into the din. Before I fainted away, I realized that the voice was my own.

When I awoke, I felt as if my head was full of heavy wool tufts. It was hard to think clearly. My limbs felt twitchy. To my surprise, I was in my own bed. I became aware of the voice of Goodman Simon Beamon in my house. By the responses, I knew he was speaking to Joseph. So, Joseph had returned from his hunting trip. He had not come home in time for the Sabbath, as he had expected. I had been worried, as I always did when he was delayed. Relieved to know that Joseph was safe, I listened blurrily to what Simon was saying to him.

"As the Moxon's children acted, so did Mary, just all one. I could discern no difference in their fits. I carried her to the Warriner's house, from whence I took to carry her here. I carried her behind me and could hardly hold her up upon the horse. I discerned that she did not understand herself where she was, and she would often cry out of the witches. She called out that the witches might creep under Goodwife Warriner's bed and kill them."

I heard Joseph and Goodman Beamon speaking together in lowered voices, and then I heard the outside door close. Joseph came to stand over our bed, looking down at me. I did not open my eyes because I could feel the heat of his disapproval. I hated it that Joseph was annoyed with me because of this embarrassing incident. As the days went by his stony annoyance did not subside. Because of the coldness of his persistent disappointment with me, I found it difficult to come back to myself.

"You acted as a child," he said. "It is unseemly for a grown woman to act like a hysterical child. People are not sympathetic to you, do you know that?"

I wondered what people he was talking about, and who had turned against me. Joseph never told me. I dared not ask him.

I began to realize something about Joseph. At the first opportunity, I told him what I was thinking.

"My value in life is that it be lived right, but for you it matters more that things look right."

"No, wife. You are mistaken. It matters to me that I live so as not to be controlled by any man. It matters to me that my home and family are safe. I am trying to protect you from bringing humiliation upon yourself."

His eyes glittered as brightly as the keen edge of a sharpened axe. I felt a wedge driven between us. I resolved to let him see that I carried myself with dignity in resistance to the tests of Satan. My promise proved difficult to maintain.

I heard that the Moxon children were growing worse afflicted. That upset me. The girls had stopped coming to meeting. A woman who worked in the Moxon household told me that sometimes something would seem to rise up in the girls' throats that stopped their breath. I, too, had felt this! Although this very same thing had happened to me, I did not interrupt my friend's story to mention it. She said that at times the girls were better, but when the fits returned upon them, they were overwhelmed violently by something no one else could see. She told me that she believed the cause of it all was a curse upon the Moxons by Hugh Parsons. Only the week before their torments began, The Reverend Moxon had words with Goodman Parsons over his dissatisfaction with the chimney Parsons was building for him. She had heard with her own ears when Hugh Parsons threatened The Reverend that he would get even with him. She insisted that the girls suffered the malignant effects of Hugh Parsons' curse. I wondered if somehow I suffered from a curse without knowing it. Inside my body I felt alone and nervous, troubled about something faceless and unknown. It took everything I had to hold back the threat.

My long walks with the children offered my only means to calm myself of anxiety. Sometimes Mother walked with me, other times I walked alone. As I passed homes and fields, I noticed how visible the lives of others were, much less private than I am sure they imagined. Overheard snatches of conversations carried worlds of meaning never intended to be revealed. The sighting of a horse hitched secretively hinted at forbidden visits. The posture of bodies told of feelings unsaid. Our small plantation offered little privacy. When I walked, eyes followed me.

One day I began to realize that several men always seemed to be near at hand to me when I went out. They kept a distance, but they watched. A few times, I even saw one of them lingering near the bushes around our house. When I told Joseph, he scowled.

"Do you not know that men are as prone to gossip as women? Some people glean their best stories by snooping. It does not matter to people how information is gathered, only that it be true. People know everything you do, Mary, of that have no doubt."

I did not reveal the name of the neighbor men who spied upon me. Instead, I began to change my habits, taking to the fields to walk the margins of the river. I did not want people to see that sometimes I had spells. Ever since the trouble at Springfield started, a restless anxiety sometimes came over me so powerfully that even the most common of sensations grew loud to my ears and chattered against my body until my palms felt twitchy and full of independent life. At such times, I felt a need to flee to where I could be alone, away from everyone who might judge me. Something very peculiar was happening to me. Several times I awoke lying on the ground. I had no idea where I was or how I had gotten there. I could only remember running before it happened. This torment was of no business to anyone but me. I had no way to explain it. I hoped no one saw, but they did. My own brother Samuel caught me in one of my fits. He went to Joseph with his worries about me and Joseph was wild with worry and jealousy when he told me what my brother had said.

"These are the words of your own brother: 'Something is not right with Mary. I saw her today in a state like the one she fell into at the meeting. I was herding a flock of sheep when I recognized her running down into the meadow in the strangest flight. She appeared so stricken that I went for help. I was not able to go to her myself on account of my sheep. I went to the house of Goodman Colton as fast as the flock would let me. Fortunately, I found him at supper with Goodman Sykes. I asked Goody Colton to go fetch my mother. The two men easily overtook Mary because she had fallen down. They said it was as if she had fallen asleep, but they could not rouse her. They had to carry her here in their arms. They lay her upon your bed, but they dared not leave her until she awoke. When she opened her eyes, she looked at them in fear. She then bowed her head, as do the Moxon girls. They did not think that she recognized them or knew where she was. They left her when my mother came.' That is what your brother said!"

After Joseph repeated what my brother had told him, he began to rant at me. "Men have to carry you home! How do they touch you when they carry you? Do you even know? Mary, this is a thing not fit. Why do you not stop it? It is bad enough that you do this at all, but I cannot have it known that men are touching my wife behind my back!"

I was frightened at the degree of Joseph's anger against me. I had no defense. It embarrassed me that I could not answer his questions about the men. I never could remember what happened to me. I worried that I did not know myself how men treated me when there was no one around to witness. I did not say it. I knew that at least once, I awoke fighting and scratching a man who held me, but I did not know why.

"Joseph, I try to stop these fits from happening, but I cannot seem to be able to prevent them from coming over me. I never know when it will happen. I am sorry. Joseph, believe me, I am sorry. I wish I could make it go away."

"You must find a way to stop these fits, or at least not let yourself be seen having them. If you do not, I will. You cannot be allowed to bring our family to disgrace."

In his ugly mood, Joseph began to keep himself distant from me. I explained this to myself as being a part of his frustration at living amidst the ill effects of so many events he could not control. To make matters worse, Joseph's brother Benjamin had recently settled in Springfield. I strongly suspected that Benjamin did not entirely approve of me. This was a concern because I had seen that Joseph did not do well when his loyalties were divided. I tried to get along with Benjamin, for the sake of Joseph and our marriage. Benjamin continued to be stiff with me.

As the rest of the world grew more unsafe around me, providing the routines of care for my young sons became my only assurance that life was sane and manageable. May 13, 1651 loomed heavily upon us as the date set for the beginning of the trials of Mary Lewis Parsons for murder and witchcraft, and of Mr. William Pynchon for blasphemy.

Hectic overwrought surges plagued me. I fretted in anxiety about Joseph's concerns for Mr. Pynchon. During the day, I had the children and the many tasks of housekeeping to distract me, but the nights were the worst. In bed, Joseph was restless. He turned first this way and then that, sighing deeply in his sleep. All our married lives, except when disrupted by the final days of pregnancy, we slept together on our sides, both facing in the same direction, one of our front sides cupped around the other's back. When we woke up we were always still in each other's embrace. Even in our bad times, we slept pressed together. Now, Joseph was so fitful that his feet abruptly kicked out, startling me every time it happened. He had begun to move independently of me, forever shaping and reshaping himself. I could not sleep, and he was not sleeping well. Trying to keep the bed quilts over us, I felt helpless. I could not help him to get comfortable. I had to turn away from him to give him as much room in the bed as possible. It frightened me that everything around us seemed to have changed, even the way we lay in our own bed.

There was a crushing grip in my chest. My temples ached. I was tired, but sleep would not welcome me nor offer me its peace. On more than one night, I got up out of bed and went outside as my family slept so as not to disturb them. The multitudes of stars shimmering in the blackness reassured me of Your presence and lifted the feeling of dread that encumbered me. The cool night air of May would not kill me, and it was something real that I could remedy with just a shawl and by movement.

One brightly moonlit night I found myself walking to keep warm. The grass being damp, I went upon the road. The steady rhythm of walking was satisfying, like a restful dream. After a while I became aware that that I had gone too far. I turned around to go home.

The road glowed gently under the light of the moon. In the quiet, I stopped. I sensed something. There seemed to be a dark shadow upon the roadway. I stepped behind the protection of a nearby bush, keeping my eyes on the shape. It moved. It became the outline of a man. I hoped that I had not been seen. I held my breath and listened. There was a faint crunch of heavy footsteps coming toward me. Slowly I edged into the dense grasses of the swamp, trying to make no noise.

The grasses closed around me. My feet found firm footing upon two hummocks formed by the rootballs of the grasses. I eased into a low crouch, steadying myself with my hands. The footsteps slowed. I squeezed my eyes closed and imagined being nothing but a sodden stump in the marsh.

I thought, "I am just a stump in the marsh" and tried to disappear.

The footsteps did not stop. They passed by and faded away. It was a long time before I dared look up again.

By the light of the moon, I could see that the grass mound on which I stood was flattened at the top. All the mounds were like this. I could step easily from one to the next. The children must have made a game of leaping from hummock to hummock. The root-balls of the grasses grew like small-scattered islands in the knee-high water of the marsh. I realized that I could easily cut through the cover of the marsh to get home. There were places where I had to gather myself to jump over watery breaches, catching myself by grabbing handholds of bushes or bunches of grass. Carefully keeping my balance, I went on.

I had only gone a short distance when I thought I heard a crash. There was a loud rustling. Someone or something was behind me. I had just come to a place where the watery void was too wide to jump. I could not go back. I threw my pale knitted shawl across the water to catch the branches of bushes that grew there and was able to pull myself across to them. My shawl fluttered in the moonlight. Large green moths took flight with my passing.

At last, I reached the road across from my house. I cautiously came out of the marsh and crossed into our yard. As I softly pulled at the string to raise the door latch to go in, I sensed movement by a bush near our fence. My breath caught. I could see that a person stood there. In one quick motion I opened the door just enough to slip inside and then closed it securely behind me, barring it against the man. With my back pressed against the door, I prayed. "Oh, Lord, be with me."

I had been seen. I was being watched. Now I knew.

The man might not know I had seen him, but I had recognized his face. I knew who he was. I had seen my neighbor, George Colton. He had followed me. He had chased me in the night.

That morning I nearly went several times to confront Goodman Colton and insist that he leave me alone. A woman could not do such a thing, but I felt angry. I decided to wait and think carefully about what I should to do. As long as he did not know I had recognized him, I had time.

People liked George Colton, and Joseph owned land with him. Clearly, I was liked less well. With all the threats around us, if people knew that I accused George of spying, they might believe he was right to watch me if he told them I was where I should not be.

When my boys went down for a nap, I dozed off beside them. I woke up some time later with a start, confused as to the time and day. My mouth was dry, my body heavy. The boys were still sleeping but I knew that Joseph was there. Had I slept through making dinner for him or was it morning?

"Mary, what is this about you walking around in your shift last night? Goodman Colton has it all over town that he saw you and that he followed you. He said that you went out with another woman, a spirit in white, and that you led him through the swamp on a merry chase. He says you walk on water and never get wet, and yet he was wet to his knees when he followed you."

Joseph's voice was shaking.

"Have you done this before? He says you have."

"Joseph. Wait. Let me wake up. What are you saying?"

"I am saying, what are you doing walking around half naked at night?"

"Joseph, let me explain. I could not sleep. Things have been so terrible. I was restless. I wrapped up in my large white shawl and went outside for air. It was a beautiful moonlit night. I was so tired that I started to dream. I guess that I began to walk. When I realized what had happened, I hid myself in the swamp and made my way home. It is easy to walk on the hummocks. No one was…"

"What do I have to do to keep you from making a laughing stock of me? Mary, no more walks. No more walks, not anywhere. You stay home. If you need something, I will get it. I want no trouble. Do you understand me?"

His statement sounded more like a threat than a question. I did not answer. My head hurt so much that I did not have the energy to talk. I just sat and let him go on until he was finished. How could I make this end? When would he turn back into the man I loved? When would he love me again? Why did we have to fight when I knew we needed each other so much?

The children woke up and began to cry. Joseph left, but I could hear him banging around in the barn. I comforted the children and started our meal, hurting from the inside out.

When Joseph came back in, he said, "Don't fix any food for me. I am going to eat with my brother. I need to talk with him. I do not know what to do about you. I just do not know what to do."

Joseph did not come back all evening. When it got dark, I put the children to bed and went to bed myself. I lay awake, fitful, until I felt him slip into bed beside me. That night I had dreadful nightmares. I dreamed I was in the swamp and there were men chasing me through the darkness. The flickering of their torches glittered like evil eyes behind me. I jumped from hummock to hummock with no place to hide. I feared they would hear my gasping breaths and my rustling in the grasses. The men came onward, without shouts or murmurs, steadily pursuing. I willed my escape. My feet lifted and I rose above the tops of the grasses. For a moment, I soared. It was exhilarating until I lost my balance and toppled into dizzying swoops. The men caught sight of me. They began howling. I could hear them panting. Like wolves, they snapped at my feet. I could just barely keep above the grasses. They slogged on through the swamp, leaping up towards me, grasping at me, pulling at my shift. I heard ripping and felt absolute terror. I lifted up and flew into my yard. I dreamed I walked into the house and got back under the covers and pulled the safety of their weight over me.

In the morning when I awoke from my dreaming, Joseph was beside me. I lay there, hoping the day would be better. As I slid out of bed, I noticed that my feet were gritty and there was a tear in my shift.

Joseph was quiet after he got up. He waited for me at the table while I dressed the children. We had breakfast in silence. Afterwards,

while the boys played on the floor beside us, Joseph told me
something I could not believe.

"I am going to lock you in the house when I leave. It is for your
own good. I think you are wandering. My brother suggested it. I think
we should try it. People will not have to know."

"Joseph, I am not wandering. Just that once. Just once, Joseph,
that is all it was. I will not do it again. I know you do not like it."

"Other men say they have seen you. You have fits. You cannot
remember what you do."

"No. That is not true. I have had fits, but I only went out the one
time."

"I don't know what to believe. You have been acting so strangely.
I do not know what you will do when you are in those fits of yours.
You run and you do not even know yourself what you are doing. I
have to be sure you are safe, so I am going to lock you in; that way I
will know where you are. When this all stops, we can go back to the
way we were, but I cannot have my wife running around behaving this
way!"

"Joseph, don't do this to me!"

"Mary, I am sorry. You are not safe and I will not let you hurt
yourself. This is the way it is going to be. I have to leave now, so I am
going to lock the door. Do not make a fuss about this."

"How long will you be? How long are you going to keep me
locked up?"

"I will come home at noon. You can make a meal for me. That
would be nice. I know how much you like that."

When Joseph left, he locked the door. I watched him through the
small leaded glass window. He looked like a stranger. His horse
looked the same, his hat looked the same, but the man I married was
not him. I stared for a long time at the place where I had last seen him,
with the children chattering and laughing behind me in their play.

Joey came to me and asked, "Momma, can we go outside now?"

"No, Joey, we are staying inside today."

"But, Momma, I want to go outside. Can't we collect the eggs
now?"

"No, Joey, Poppa wants us to stay inside today."

"It's not raining out, Momma. Come, Momma. Let's go outside." He pulled at the door but it would not open. "Open it, Momma."

"It's locked. I do not have the key. Poppa took it. We have to be inside until he comes home."

"You don't have a key?" Joey looked at me, his head tipped to the side.

"No, Joey. I do not have a key."

My two boys looked up at me, their little eyes round like buttons on the face of a poppet. I needed to squeeze them in my arms, to feel the reassurance of their warmth, the normalcy of their affection. I lifted Joey and baby John up and hugged them both so hard that my arms began to shake. I could not press enough love into me. I wanted more.

"Ow, Momma. Let me go." They both began to struggle.

"No. We are playing a game." I began to whirl around with the two of them until their legs flared out around me. They screamed and giggled. We turned in circles until I became dizzy and fell on the floor with them in a heap on top of me.

"Momma, that was fun. Do it again."

We whirled, twirled, and played chase until it started to feel rough. I stopped. I did not want to do it anymore. The walls were too close. The children smelled sour. I felt dreadfully wrong. All around me, the air had a stinging sound. My neck felt stiff, and my hands were twitchy. It was all I could do to keep from becoming very cross with my children.

Joseph must have gone to get my mother. I heard the key turn in the door, and saw that he was letting her in. Seeing her was an immense relief. Mother and Joseph sat down at the table and we talked for a while, but as I knew would be the case, Mother did not fully take my side.

"Mary, Joseph is worried that you are not yourself, and I have heard that you are walking outside at night. Is something wrong, dear?"

"Mother! Everything is wrong! Look around at our town! I am nervous and worried, just like everyone else. I cannot sleep. One night I foolishly took a walk to clear my mind, and all of a sudden, people are making something strange of it. George Colton has taken to following me. He is making up stories about me, which everyone believes, even Joseph. Today Joseph locked me in with the children, Mother! He locked me in!"

"Mary, Joseph knows from other people that, in your fits, sometimes you run until you fall down, and that you are taking walks at night in only your underclothes. They say that a woman no one knows comes for you and keeps you company. You do not seem to remember any of it. We are both worried. The town is talking about it. Do you know that William Branch has gone to Mr. Pynchon and complained of you?"

"What has Goodman Branch to do with me?"

Joseph responded, "Apparently he was reporting what George Colton told him."

"Ah, and everyone believes Goodman Colton, a man who hides behind bushes watching me? Something is the matter with him, not me."

"George Colton and I own a lot of land together at Mr. Pynchon's old mill. Why do you think it strange he would be visiting here to talk to me at my house?" In apparent exasperation, Joseph stopped talking after that, but his pained expression told me everything I needed to know.

I knew it was an unforgivable shame upon Joseph to have Mr. Pynchon made aware that a business partner was saying that his wife was afflicted by torments. I knew that was exactly what Joseph was thinking. I despaired that there was no way I could make things right.

Mother went on as if I had not replied to her, determined to make her points.

"Obviously, we need to know that you are safe, Mary. I am going to take the boys home with me so that you can lie down and take a rest. You are acting like a person overwrought. Do not worry about supper. I will cook for you tonight. When you wake up, come straight away to my house and we will have a nice visit. All right, dear?"

She gathered up the boys. They left with her, happy to be going out.

Joseph did not look upon me as he demanded firmly, "Go to bed. I will come back this evening to get you. You must not leave the house."

"All right, but do not lock the door, Joseph."

Joseph made no move to come close to me. He shook his head. Before he turned away, I saw a look of deep sadness. He opened the door to go out. When he closed it, he locked it behind him, leaving me standing there alone.

"No! No! This is wrong! Joseph! Come back! Please! I love you!"

I went to the nail where Joseph kept the house key. It was gone. There were two keys. Joseph kept one in his pocket. I searched the house for the second key. I moved every thing we owned. The key was nowhere to be found.

I admit that I flew into a frenzy. I had to get out. I shook the skin windows, but I did not want to rip them. That seemed very important. Do not rip the windows or break the glass one. That would show that everything was wrong. The only way out was the lock. What did I have that could open it? I began to look for something else that would fit into the keyhole, something strong enough that would open the lock. I could hear myself moaning. My head felt thick and fuzzy, but I forced myself to think, to make an idea that would open the door and let me out into the free air. My eyes fell again on everything we owned, trying to see what I might have missed before. I picked up the flax comb, noticing immediately as I held it in my hand that its teeth were long and slender but very strong. With a little bit of effort I managed to break a tine free. Pulling up a stool, I sat down with the lock at eye level and began to poke inside it, pushing on each little surface, hoping to feel something move. After a long time, with the smallest of sounds, the lock opened.

The door opened. I stepped out. I breathed in the scents of trees and grass, animals and soil. I began to run. I ran all the way down to the river, took off my shoes, and entered the shallow water at the river's edge fully clothed. Floating and cold, I felt the stickiness of my mind and the foulness of dread wash away. I pulled myself out of the water and up the riverbank. I knew what I had to do. After wringing out my skirt and my shift underneath it, I put my shoes on and marched home as quickly as I could, chilled. I put on fresh clothes, combed my hair, and picked a bouquet of wildflowers from the edge of our hedgerow. Leaving the door wide open, I cleaned the house thoroughly, wiping and sweeping. When Joseph returned, I was weeding the garden.

He examined the door. I had been careful to leave no marks.

"How did you find the key?" he said.

I raised myself up to face him, imagining that everything could be all right now, if I made it so. My love for him would touch him and he would remember how much we cared for each other.

"I said, how did you find the key?" he demanded.

"Joseph, let's not worry about any of that anymore. Please. We will make things all right. Do not turn away from me. I need you. I love you. I can be a good wife, remember?"

"I forgot to lock the door. I must have forgotten to lock the door."

"Joseph, stop fretting. You do not have to worry about locking me in anymore. Let us go to Mother's and have supper. I will walk with you. Are you ready? I have already fed the animals. You must be hungry. I am ready to go."

On the way to Mother's, I asked if he had heard any news that day about Mr. Pynchon. Joseph said no, nothing today. He did not pick up the conversation. I wanted to reach out and touch him, but I did not try.

Mother had cooked a wonderful meal of fish, beet greens, and bread. She had already fed the boys. Mother and Joseph seemed careful in their conversation. They discussed light gossip that had no consequence. They were babying me as if I might not be able to take hearing about the troubles our plantation faced. I hoped I acted bright and cheerful, although in truth I felt self-conscious. Joseph offered me some strong hard cider, instead of the diluted beer that women and children drink. It was never my habit to take strong beer or wine, but I enjoyed the sweet vaporous brew that night. It made me feel pleasantly relaxed. I hardly remember going home.

In the middle of the night I gasped and came awake, hoping as I felt around that I would find myself in bed. I reached out, felt Joseph next to me, and relaxed. I counted Joseph's breathing, then, enveloped in his warmth, I counted the flicking of my toes against the covers. I thought of everything that would fill my mind and lull me to sleep. Lying awake, I imagined doing laundry, carding wool, shelling beans, anything to keep me from sliding my feet out of bed and walking out into the moonlight. It was hot inside the house and mosquitoes hummed. I wanted to see the moon casting shadows on our lawn, to bathe in the fresh night air, to feel hope and promise. When I tried the door, it was locked.

I went back to bed and was still awake when Joseph got up in the morning. He took the boys with him and locked the door. His decision put me into dazed shock. The outrages that affected our community seemed to have swallowed up every normal bit of our lives. In the sweaty stillness of confinement, I prayed. Shreds of verses and psalms interlaced in torn incompleteness. I could not find You.

I picked at the lock with the small metal tine of my flax comb until it gave way. I went out into the yard and sat down. I watched the clouds and noticed the color of leaves. I lay back and pressed my body against the earth. I believe I napped.

After a while, I got up. I managed to do a few necessary chores. I put meat and root vegetables into the pot over the fire to simmer so that it would be cooked when Joseph came home. My eyes fell upon a pile of soiled clothes in the corner. I gathered them up to take to the stream to wash. Leaving the yard for this reason was justified.

There was a still pool in the little stream near our house that was a perfect place to wash our clothes. A slow eddy had carved out a quiet curve where I could put the clothes in to soak, and right above it there was a little run of swift water where I could rinse the clothes just by holding them out into the stream. The bank had a small sandy patch upon which I knelt while I washed.

As I rinsed the clothes, water filled the short legs of my boys' pants and the soap ran from them. Bubbles fled in little rows down the middle of the current, pausing behind rocks until little spouts of current caught them and the bubbles were bobbed away. Their progress was jolly. As I watched the bubbles, I noticed something in the water. Peering closely, I was startled to see faces there. Two little faces grinned up at me, little poppets lost by a child, or spirits, I could not tell which. I thought one had the expression of my lost babe, Benjamin, and the other, the dead child of Hugh and Mary Parsons. I reached to save them but when my hands broke the water, they were gone. Suddenly I did not want to be alone there. I grabbed up my heavy wet laundry and rushed home. The wind wrapped the clothes around me as I tried to hang them to dry. I found myself wrestling the fabric in the most unpleasant way. I was still trying to make order out of the tangled clothes when Joseph came into the yard. The boys were not with him.

"You found the key again. How can you keep finding the key?"

"Joseph, I have work to do. You cannot keep me locked in all the time. I would get nothing done. I only passed through our gate to wash the clothes. And, Joseph, I do not need your key. Do not fret yourself about the key."

Joseph opened the hatch to our earthen cellar and went down into it. I wondered why. Perhaps he went into the coolness to calm down. After a short time, he stepped out and came to me. He put me into his arms and picked me up. All the while he said the soothing words I had been waiting for. We went down into the cellar together. He set me down on blankets. A candle lamp dimly illuminated his face. He turned quickly from me. Before I could get up, he was out and had barred the bulkhead from the outside. Joseph had locked me in the cellar.

You hast kept me alive that I should not go down to the pit. Psalm 30:4

Chapter 17

The Locked Door

Long Meadow, 1651

In my fright, I did not call upon You as I do now.

My circumstance of being locked in the cellar was made worse by the realization that Joseph had prepared for this day. He had brought down a bedstead and blankets. There was a chamber pot, a pail of fresh water, a jug of weak beer, a cup, and a candle lamp with a small supply of candlewood. It frightened me how long he meant to keep me here. I wondered if he meant to starve me. No, he would not do that. But what kind of man would lock his wife and mother of his children away in a cellar? Sitting on the bed in shock, I became enraged. No matter what, my life was worth more than to be treated this way.

Almost immediately, I heard my mother's voice. Was she aware of what Joseph was doing to me? My heart pounded in my chest so hard that my ears rang. My hands clenched into fists and I was ready to fight my way out, but the heavy door would never move for me. I knew that.

"Mary? It's Mother. Mary, do you hear me?"

"Mother, I am down here, in the cellar. Let me out. Please."

"Mary, I know. Joseph has gone to Mr. Pynchon to ask his advice. He sent me here to comfort you. He is frightened, Mary. He does not know what else to do other than this. This is only for a little while."

"This is long enough. Let me out, Mother."

"Mary, I cannot. Not until Joseph has a plan."

"Obviously he has a plan. There are a bed, blankets, and water down here, even a chamber pot. He seems to think he will keep me here for a while. You certainly do not want your daughter down here like this. Mother, let me out."

"Mary, rest for a little while, and when you wake up you will be more ready to put things to right. I will see to it that you do not stay here long. Rest my child, and I will go help Joseph."

"Help Joseph! And leave your child in a cellar? Mother!"

"This is breaking my heart, Mary. This is very hard for us all. We do not know what is happening to you. We love you, but for your own good, you must be contained. I must go. I will be back. We will bring you some food."

"Do not go, Mother. Do not go!"

There was silence above me. It all was too awful to comprehend. I lay still, holding the quilts to me, staring into a darkness. I imagined that I was in a crypt next to my father, waiting to be buried, and that we were both alive and both forgotten. Perhaps I was dreaming, because when I opened my eyes the candle lamp was lit and there was a bowl of hot stew beside me. I heard no sounds from the house. I began to yell, with no answer. Then I heard the scrape of a chair leg and knew Joseph sat above me. His inaccessible nearness angered me. I ate the stew, used the chamber pot, and then sat on the bed. I thought of nothing. I just waited.

In a while, the bar of the bulkhead rumbled. The heavy door swung open. Joseph's silhouette was framed against a gray, darkening sky. I sensed someone was with him.

"Mary, I am coming down. Are you ready?"

"Ready for what?"

"Ready to talk to me, Mary."

"I was never not ready. How long have you kept me down here?"

"I did not expect it would be so long. A day and a half. I hope that is what you needed."

"Who is with you, Joseph?"

"My brother."

"Is he supposed to protect you from me?"

"I thought I might need help, yes."

"Exactly what do you need help with? Do you have some kind of new plan for your wife, besides locking her in the cellar?"

"You are safe from me, Mary. Am I safe from you?"

"You are the one who locks women away." I grabbed the bed staff from its socket and stood ready to defend myself. When Joseph began to descend towards me, I thrashed it in warning. "Don't you touch me."

Joseph's brother lunged through the bulkhead and knocked me down, pinning me to the floor. "We've had enough of your fits!" he said.

Joseph knelt beside me and I tried to kick him. He held my legs.

"Mary, tell us when you are ready to come back to us. Tell us when you are ready to be safe. Until then, I can do nothing but keep you here so that you do not hurt yourself out there. Do not worry. No one knows about this but your mother, my brother, and John Pynchon. When you stop acting bewitched, you can return to the community with no one knowing that all this has been necessary."

"Necessary? This is not necessary! Locking your wife in the cellar is a sin."

"If you will sit on the bed, Mary, we will let you up. Are you ready to be let go?"

"Of course I am." Benjamin let go of my wrists. I glared at him. I sat up, and Joseph touched my hand.

"Mary. Never doubt that I love you."

I spat on the floor at this, but I wanted to hear him say it again and again. The words he said, uttered as he left me in the cellar, cut my heart.

Sometime after they left, the lamp went out. In the darkness, all familiarity vanished. It was no longer the place of ordinary things where I stored vegetables in sweet straw. I began to hear a ringing in my ears that sounded like faint voices. I could not make out the words. As I strained to see, I made out the shape of two little glowing faces, the same little poppets I had seen before in the water. I held out my hand to touch them, but they were at a greater distance than I could reach. At first, I thought that the poppet was the spirit of my lost child come to comfort me. I opened my arms to him, but when I looked into his eyes, I saw the reflection of a million faces. I screamed in fear when I saw that it was not my boy at all, but a demon wearing his face. The two poppets began to torment me with their distorting features. In their loveliness, they were spirits that showed me people who were gone, lost people who I wanted to reach out to in love. In their hideousness, they showed me the many faces of cruelty. I tried to drive away the visions by hurling pillows and then bedclothes at them, but their faces did not retreat. I whimpered as I witnessed that which no one should have to see alone. I heard a feeble sound repeating over and over, "…help me…help me." It was my own voice, the only thing that I could trust to be real. I began to chant psalms there in the cellar to comfort myself. At the sound of Your name, the faces faded.

I gathered up the bedclothes and made order in the darkness. Defiance filled me. Although I could not make things right, I did know what was wrong. The wrong was not within me, it was outside of me. It was wrong to be watched for the purpose of gossip, wrong to be accused falsely and wrong to be locked by my husband in the cellar. I vowed that I would never be quiet about wrongs again. With my new clarity, I realized that despite Joseph's opinion otherwise, clearly our plantation was under attack by the Devil. Why else would I have had to do battle and push demons away? Having nearly been lost, now I knew it was possible to put up a resistance against a horror so much greater than myself. In my great need, I looked to You to give me strength, and You caused me to be released.

By the turn of Your hand, Joseph's effort to save face by locking me away became the reason I was let back out again. I remember sitting on the bed in the cellar, vigilant against further onslaughts. There was not a sound to be heard from above. Joseph was gone, the children probably taken to Mother.

Abruptly, a horseman came into the yard. Soon there were scraping sounds of metal upon wood. I guessed who was out there when I remembered that Joseph had been waiting in the previous week for the local cooper, John Matthews, to come and make barrels for him. I listened, wondering how to call the man over without frightening him away. Just as I was ready to begin to shout, I heard Joseph's voice talking to the man. Shortly, footsteps came toward the house, and the door to the cellar was raised open.

"Mary, come out. Come, quickly and quietly."

"Joseph, what is it? Could it be that you do not want anyone to know that you keep your wife locked in the cellar?"

"Quiet! Do not make this a cause for argument, woman. Come out and go into the house. Be quick."

"Or what? You cannot keep me here in the cellar with your hired man standing so close. He will see, and you would not want that. Offer me a promise that if I return to the house quietly I shall remain there in freedom, to come and go as I need."

"Please, Mary. It is you that causes me to have to protect you. I have responsibilities for your safety. I can make no promises until I see how it is with you."

"How it is with me is that you lock me into vile confinement with only the company of spirits. I had to beat them back with the bed staff, with bedclothes and pillows, and still you left me here. Did you not hear me fighting? I might have been consumed by the Devil!"

"Mary, you are led by an evil spirit. That is the company you have chosen to keep."

Our voices were raised. Both Joseph and I noticed at the same time that the cooper had come to stand at the barn door to watch. I did not know for how long he had been there. Although I was out, perhaps so was our story. Joseph turned away from me. Flashing a look of exasperation, he mounted his horse and rode away, leaving me outside with the cooper, who was looking at me questioningly.

I apologized to Goodman Matthews. His response was polite and his manner caring. Because he asked me about the spirits, I felt I had to tell him what I had seen. I regret that I did.

For You desireth no sacrifice, though I would give it. You delight not in burnt offerings. Psalm 51:18

Chapter 18

The Way Wherein I Have Walked

Boston Jail, Massachusetts, April 1657

Lord of all creation, this is my prayer. Look upon me in this prison and place me under Your wing for I am in need.

Recalling being locked in the cellar has caused something to happen to me. I had feared that thinking back upon that time would do me no good, but instead of causing me to come apart in confinement, as I did then, I feel as if I have witnessed a revelation as momentous in my life as the separation of night from day!

I have realized suddenly that I did not understand then the meaning of what was happening to me. You were showing me signs! Into the darkness You shined upon me the faces of my guardian angels. You offered Your help and I rejected it in my fright and anger.

After all this time, I have come to know that the demons I saw—my dead child and the murdered child, the face of my father in his crypt, Anne Hutchinson scalped and dying, the smallpox-scabbed Indian, the child with a stick—they were all Thine angels sent to protect me. I was given what I needed to understand, but I did not understand. Because I divided the world between angels and demons, I missed the voices of all Your messengers.

It was not the Devil who came for me in the cellar, it was Your Holy Spirit. I see that now. I survived my fits by vowing to be whole and by vowing to fight wrongs, but I used my anger as a tool and a weapon. Oh, could it be that my own anger has brought me to this cell? Has it been my anger all along that has frightened my brethren? Ah, my Lord, my Protector, have I put myself here by my own stiff-necked haughtiness? For so long I have divided the world between right and wrong that I might walk Your path of righteousness, but I did not heed Your voice of loving kindness along the way. Thinking of myself all the while as a daughter of Zion, I have entered into judgment of Your servants; I have not been humble. I have made a prison for myself of anger. I have let fear of the strange infirmity of my fits cloud my thoughts. I turn to You to help me open my soul, to free myself from darkness. I feel remorse for the way wherein I have walked.

I pray that I may turn myself toward forgiveness. Your gifts of mercy are infinite. Amen.

Chapter 19

My High Horse

Springfield and Long Meadow, 1651 – 1652

Yes, Lord, I see now that when I was let out of the cellar, I emerged as if upon one of my father's matching grey steeds, riding hard to right misdoings.

When I was freed, I did take a new path, but the road I took was not the one You had intended to show to me. I had the bit in my mouth, and sourness in my stomach. The very next day being Sunday, I went to meeting with my small brood and took my usual seat among the women. In answer to their stares, I glared. I remember that as they slid away from me on the bench a small space opened between them and me. When we disassembled, people kept a polite distance away from me as I passed through them. No one bothered me with any questions. At the time, I was relieved not to have the weight of the other women and their broods pressing upon me, but now I rue that the distance created between us opened a hole that was taken up and filled by the invisible presence of the Devil.

I learned that while I had been locked in the cellar, the trials had begun at Boston. Mr. Pynchon had been called to testify in the witch case while at the same time standing for trial himself. It was expected that Mr. Pynchon would be gone a fortnight or more at least. The many witnesses in the trial against Mary Lewis Parsons left in groups to attend to their duty at court, facing a long and difficult trip to Boston. Among them there was no one who could speak in defense of Mr. Pynchon. The words of his book would be his witness. Joseph asked to accompany Mr. Pynchon to Boston but Mr. Pynchon said that he would prefer it if Joseph remained behind to help his son, John.

With the trials of Mary Parsons for a witch and Mr. Pynchon for a heretic underway, composing myself under the sight of others, including my family, became even more exhausting. It took all my vigilance to prevent my nerves from coming under attack. I tried to be well, but sudden sounds or unexpected surprises of motion caused my heart to pound in my ears.

One afternoon when I was in the yard helping John Matthews put away his tools before an impending storm blew in, a loud clap of thunder and a crackle of lightning split the sky. In an instant I fell to the ground in a faint, right before his eyes. There were these small lapses, but for the most part, as much as anyone would cooperate with me, I did get along.

Provocative news from Boston began to arrive almost daily as the people who had testified in the trials of Mary Lewis Parsons returned home. They told that the day when Mr. Pynchon would testify in the matter had been moved up to a closer date because Goody Parsons had become dangerously ill while in jail. Joseph said he had heard that there was concern that she might not live to complete the trial.

The days went by. News came to us, but nothing that we heard eased our community's distress. The Moxon girls continued to suffer unearthly afflictions and were seldom seen outside their house. Joseph came and went according to his business, not saying when he would return. I kept to the house with the children. A hush came over our lives as we waited for the verdicts.

Late one afternoon Joseph suddenly appeared in the house and began to change out of his work clothes into his better shirt and coat, as fast as he could.

"I must go to the Pynchons'! I hear that Mr. Pynchon has returned from Boston."

He rushed out, leaving me to wonder what had happened. I hoped the news was good, for all of our sakes. Could the world come apart any worse?

I fed the children and waited for Joseph. When at last he came home, he began talking as soon as he came through the door.

"Mr. Pynchon refused to retract his book! He did agree to make a few minor changes, just enough to satisfy the clergy and make them look victorious. His book will be reprinted with the changes, but Mr. Pynchon says he was not repentant enough for the court to be satisfied. The court allowed Mr. Pynchon to return to Springfield because of troubles at home. Goody Pynchon has become ill with worry, and has not been eating. Mr. Pynchon does not know what penalty the Court will exact. For now, he will remain with his wife and wait. The judges told him his sin is unpardonable. He has to appear for the next session of the Court, which is not to be held until October 14. Mr. Pynchon told me that he feels too old and saddened by all of this to fight any more. He fears that the Commonwealth will confiscate all his property. Both Mr. Pynchon and The Reverend Moxon are talking of returning to England. Mr. Pynchon says that with King Charles thrown over, and the new thinking of Oliver Cromwell on the rise, there is more religious freedom in England than there is here. I think we are about to lose both Mr. Pynchon and The Reverend Moxon! The Commonwealth will have nothing to take from him if Mr. Pynchon leaves all his lands and business interests to his son. Mr. Pynchon told me that he has to decide immediately what he will do with his property before any fines are laid against him."

Joseph sat down at the table. I went to the beer barrel and drew a cup for him. As he sipped distractedly, staring at nothing, I stepped behind the chair where he sat and began to stroke his temples and rub his neck, as I had many times before. I felt him relax under my hands. I wondered that the length of a woman's arms could span the great distance between us. My hands began to cramp and stiffen with the dread of all that could not be repaired. I withdrew from him, holding my breath as I pulled away. The moment stretched long. A log fell heavily in the hearth and sparks flew into the room with a crackling sound as the fire flared. Joseph did not turn to me. We had no words to share.

Finally, word came to assemble at the meetinghouse to hear the verdict against Mary Lewis Parsons. While I waited on the grass amongst the crowd to hear the official reading, I strained my ears to listen to two townsmen who had been there. They were describing to their friends what they had seen.

"The day Goody Parsons was brought from the prison to the Court to make her pleas the court was full of people. We had already heard all the testimony against her. I was curious to see how she would answer and what she would do. A door opened, and I made out that she was being carried in. It was hard to see her, but when I did, I was surprised to see that she had broken down completely, that she had become a wretch—unwholesome, and very old."

The other man said, "That's right. It took two men to hold her up before the Court. She was only a wisp. Her legs were buckling under her. I could see that it did not matter what sentence was given—she was a dead woman. It made me angry that justice would not be served, although I suppose I should be satisfied at God's judgment. I confess I came to see the witch pay, to watch her hang from the gallows for what she has done."

The first man continued, "The charges against her were read. When they read the charge of murder, she began to weep. I heard her admit her guilt with my own ears. I heard it and I know it is true."

I was shocked. I had still held out the hope that her child had died of illness. The two men stopped their reports because, upon hearing what they said, the people gathered around began to grumble and make loud angry comments about a mother who would kill her own child.

Finally the Goodman was able to continue, "When the Court gave its verdict we were surprised to hear that not enough evidence had been presented to prove her a witch."

"What? They found her not a witch?" People were loud in their indignancy until they began to realize that in their shouting they were drowning out the official announcement of the final verdict.

There were cries of "Shush! Shush!" It became possible to hear the verdict, read in the same words as were said to Goody Parsons.

> *"Mary Parsons: You are here before the General Court, charged in the name of the Commonwealth, that not having the feare of God before your eyes nor in your harte, being seduced by the divill, and yielding to his instigations and the wickedness of your own harte about the beginning of March last, in Springfield, in or near your own house, did willfully and most wickedly murder your own child, against the word of God, and the laws of this jurisdiction long since made and published...."*

Because of the crowd's angry murmuring, I could not hear the entire verdict but was able to make out the judgment.

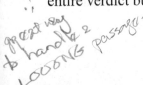

188

...You shall be carried from this place to the place from whence you came, and from thence to the place of execution, and there hang till you be dead. "

At that, the commotion became unmanageable and the reader's voice disappeared into all of the crowd's agitated noisemaking. Once it was clear that all the news had been heard, I returned home with my children amidst the stream of townspeople and the babbling of their conversations.

"Is she to be hung here, from whence she came?"

"No, in Boston, from the jail to the gallows."

"If she lives that long. You heard what was said."

"It will be a lot longer than her child had."

"The Devil take her."

I was glad when I could get my children inside and close the door upon the ugly words.

In the days that followed and all that summer, Mr. Pynchon was not much seen about town. Joseph said he stayed in his study talking with his family and friends. In September, about two weeks before the Court was to meet, he conveyed all he owned to his son, John; all his businesses, all his land holdings, all his mills, buildings, and warehouses. When the Court met on October 14, Mr. Pynchon failed to appear. He chose to remain in Springfield among his supporters. I was proud of his non-cooperation, but nervous about the consequences of it.

The much-awaited verdict of the Court appeared about two weeks later. A man rode into town on horseback and nailed a paper to the meetinghouse wall. All day long people came to discover what news had come. The written words were constantly being read aloud by those who could read to those who could not.

The Court doth judge it meete and is willing, that all patience be exercised toward Mr. William Pynchon, that, if it be possible he may be reduced into the way of truth and that he might renounce the errors and heresies published in his book, and for that end, doe give him time to the next Generall Court, in May, more thoroughly to consider of the said errors and heresies in his said book, and well to weigh the judicious answer of Mr. John Norton, and that he may give full satisfaction for his offence, which they more desire than to proceed to so great a censure as his offence deserves. In case he should not give good satisfaction, the Court doth therefore order, that the judgment of the cawse be suspended till the honorable Court in May next, and that Mr. William Pynchon be enjoyned under the penalty of one hundred pounds to make his personall appearance at and before the next Generall Court, to give full answer to satisfaction if it may be, or otherwise to stand to the judgment and censure of the Court.

I heard many people express their loyalty to Mr. William Pynchon, and recognized in their voices the secret thrill that defiance gives. Alas, by the time the Court next met, Mr. and Mrs. Pynchon and the entire Moxon family were gone from Springfield forever, having sailed away in hopes of finding a better life in England. Left behind, our community mourned.

Not surprisingly, Joseph, with his usual energy, rallied behind John Pynchon to help him assume the enterprises left to him by his father. Aiding young Pynchon brought out the best in Joseph. Things went much better between us once Joseph began to come home happy and excited, rather than upset and angry. His trade with the Indians began to exceed anything he had ever accomplished. The men working for him were reliable, prices with England were up, there was an uneasy peace among the tribes, and the fall harvest had been good. As the winter came on, Joseph told me that the quality of beaver skins he was seeing was excellent. He was hopeful that it would be a good season for trapping.

The nervous dread around us began to lift. As for myself, I dared hope that the fits that had tormented me had passed. Joseph and I talked about ordinary things as we lay together in the dark. The feel of him was warm and safe. The sound of his lowered voice, the sensation of his breath upon my neck, his hands upon me, that simple goodness was all that I wanted. Our love became like a night blooming flower. We opened to each other in the quiet moonlight.

There was no great notice when Hugh Parsons was tried for witchcraft. With his wife dead and gone, people were almost glad

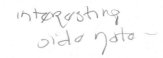
interesting side note —

when they heard that he was acquitted and that the matter was done and over. No one seemed to care that he did not return to Springfield after the trial. In fact, we never heard of him again.

The officially published answer to Mr. Pynchon's "damnable heresies" did become available, prepared under Court appointment by The Rev. John Norton, a foremost clergyman of Ipswich. No one that I knew read it. We also heard that Mr. Pynchon, upon his arrival in England, had bought a small estate in a small town called Wraysbury. It gave Joseph some measure of solace to know that his friend would at last be able to study theology and to write in peace, surrounded by his wife, his daughter, and her family.

We turned the corner of the seasons into a new year, 1652. The beaver trade was strong, which gave Joseph money to build new businesses. Everything he touched thrived. He was buying more land for pasturage and farming and began to look farther for more.

By the vote of Town Meeting, Joseph was voted a freeman. He had the right to vote and all privileges of respect. As his wife, I felt pleased, which helped me whenever I felt unwelcome eyes looking at me curiously.

One day I had the satisfaction of putting George Colton in his place. I remember that it was a Wednesday, because it was a market day. I was on the way to the common early in the morning when I realized that someone was behind me, whispering. If I had been by myself, I might have just walked faster and ignored them, but that day I was with my little son, John. His short legs could not take up a more rapid pace. I looked back and saw that George Colton, Goodman Branch, and several of his friends were following us. A swell of indignancy came over me. I thought that men should protect a woman walking alone with a toddler, not harass her in front of her child. On impulse, I decided to confront them about their behavior. I turned right around, took a breath, and waited for the men to catch up to me. I looked Goodman Colton directly in the eyes, daring him to come closer. The other men hesitated, tittering and nudging each other. For the sake of my child, this was no joke, and I was determined to end it.

"Good day, Goodman Colton. Good day, goodmen." I spoke with civility, I thought.

"Good day, Goody Parsons." They greeted me all around, smirking.

"Goodman Colton. I believe you have lost something which I would like to return."

"Have I, now?"

"Yes, I believe you have."

"And what would that be, Goodwife?" The men accompanying Colton sputtered as they held back from chuckling at the sight of the two of us speaking together there on the road, I supposed.

"Well, I know that what is lost does not belong to me, because I keep my own very close, so it must be yours. I believe I might be the best one to return it to you. You have lost nine and ten."

"Nine and ten? I've lost nothing so much as that!"

"Yes, indeed you have. You have lost your commandments nine and ten. Nine, in case you have forgotten, is you shalt not bear false witness against your neighbor. Ten is you shalt not covet; not your neighbors house, nor wife, nor manservant, nor maid, nor ox, nor ass, nor anything that is your neighbor's. My husband is Joseph Parsons, and he is your neighbor, and I am his wife. Now do you understand?"

I noticed that the commandments are satisfyingly well-said when spoken vehemently.

At first, the men standing with Goodman Colton stepped back and roared. Their laughter was turned toward him. He did not answer me. His eyes dropped from my face and he looked quite shocked. The men stopped laughing. The silence of discomfort came heavily upon them.

I made the decision not to be the first one to move. Clumsily, they brushed by me. I let them pass quietly by. Their heads were leaned forward upon their necks, which bowed their shoulders. They walked away quite fast. I could not see if they said a word amongst themselves, at least until they got well away from me.

John looked up at me and asked, "Mama?"

"Everything is fine, John. Let us go on to market."

I knew for certain that You had planted the seed of a new child for Joseph within me. I wanted no more foolishness from the likes of Colton. Nothing ever got back to me about the incident. I surely did not mention it to Joseph. Having stated my mind that day felt amazingly good. Goodman Colton did not follow me again.

That fall, Town Meeting elected Joseph to serve the town as selectman, a high office of great honor. He was one of seven men responsible for ordering the affairs of the town and for the distribution of land. It galled me a little that one of the men elected to the same office was George Colton, but Joseph also served with five other men, all of whom I admired: John Pynchon, Sam Chapin, Henry Burt, Benjamin Cooley, and Thomas Stebbins. The duties of the office took time and consideration, but Joseph seemed to enjoy it. Given his disposition for keeping many things in mind at once, I hardly noticed a difference in Joseph.

Around me, the townspeople seemed to be freeing themselves from the anguish that had befallen Springfield. I hoped that their households, like ours, were healing and prospering. Beneath all his plans for the future, I could tell that Joseph still regretted what had happened to his friend, Mr. Pynchon. Joseph missed him. He told me that he felt betrayed by the church elite and the laws of the colony that had been enacted to ensure that no one could rise in contest against them.

"As God is my Father, I never thought I would see the day when we here would allow ministers to think of themselves as king and let them sit in the pulpit like a throne," he said.

Although Joseph was moved sometimes to speak like this, still, for his own reasons, he humbly took his seat in the meetinghouse twice a week without fail. At home, he did have a prayer for the ministers and the courts when they annoyed him.

"Shut up this army and let them be confounded with their power, and with their horsemen," I heard him say.

In December, on the ninth day, a great star with a long blazing tail to the east appeared across the sky. It hung there, terrible and awful, all the night through. It remained there every night, less and less, until it disappeared on the twenty-second day. We learned later that the very next night, the great minister at Boston, the witch finder and scholarly exorcist of the devil, the Reverend John Cotton Mather, passed from this earth. I wondered how the splendor of Thine heavens could so

comet

vividly declare Your judgment and yet leave men unable to explain the meaning of Thine unfathomable mysteries.

Chapter 20

Worldly Considerations

Springfield, 1653

My Lord, who causes the passing of time, with the turning of another year, the troubles that had filled my mind so vividly and painfully began to grow distant as the new child within me grew.

My family was healthy, and I offered daily thanks for every day that You blessed the Parsons home. Each morning that I woke up with Joseph beside me, I felt gratitude. The life we made together had been beset by tempests, but it had endured. I had endured, and I vowed never to let the demons of fear work their ways in my mind again. I filled my dark places only with love for my Joseph, my children, my mother, my brothers and sisters, their wives and children, and my friends. I could see that Joseph trusted me again. He filled his arms with me, and he looked into my eyes when he told me stories of his days. He was glad to be with me, and I with him.

Our babe was delivered unto us January 23 with no great difficulty to me. Joseph's desire for sons must have been in his seed, for I bore him another beautiful boy. We named the child Samuel. He was a healthy child, and the robustness of him brought me great joy. It had been a long time since I had been filled with only complete gladness! As my breasts swelled with milk, so did my heart fill with the sweetness of affection. My first born, Joey, was seven, a big boy; and John, two and a half. In the evenings, Joseph and I delighted in watching our two older sons play with the infant. The boys tried to make the baby smile at their antics, which made us all laugh.

Before I put the boys to bed each night, Joseph liked to tell the boys simple stories about the things that happened to him during his days, and about the plans he was making. Listening, I learned much about what Joseph was thinking. His words revealed restlessness, wanderlust for new places. I had seen the same thing in my father. I knew that there would be no standing in his way once Joseph turned to the open possibilities offered just beyond his grasp. By now it was a familiar story to me that men dream of unclaimed forests and meadows, and plentitudes of game. The wilderness lay waiting for Joseph. When the time came, I knew he would go.

Joseph told me late in April that John Pynchon had become aware that twenty-four men of Hartford were preparing to petition the General Court of Massachusetts to grant them the rights to "plant, possess, and inhabit" the place known as Nonotuck. Upon hearing that, John Pynchon gathered with Deacon Samuel Chapin and Elizur Holyoke, and together they wrote their own petition in the interest of the men of Springfield. Their petition was delivered by hand to the Court and read on the same day as the one from Hartford. On May 18, after much consideration, the petition from our three most prominent townsmen was granted over the competing one of the twenty-four Hartford planters.

I asked Joseph, "Did the Hartford men lose out entirely?"

Joseph said, "No, in fact, while the Hartford petition favored only the Hartford petitioners, the one accepted on behalf of Mr. Pynchon favored all the neighboring plantations, which is better for everyone, I dare say."

When I heard the news, I looked around me at the house and all of Joseph's fields and meadows. I knew then that one day we would be leaving all of this. In some ways, even as I pondered the losses, I realized that I would be glad for a clean new start. I would miss having my mother, all my brothers and sisters and nephews and nieces all around me, but there would also be many at this plantation that I would not miss.

I went to my mother to ask her advice about settling in Nonotuck. With no hesitation, she whole-heartedly encouraged me to go. "The great men of Springfield have opened the way to Nonotuck, but their interests are already established here. They will not leave. Joseph has special relationships with these men. By his own initiative, he can establish a ready supply of goods and furs to the markets they have built. They will be his allies, not his competition. He sees this, and he is the one who can do it."

"What about you, Mother?" I asked.

"I am finished with moving into the wilderness, child. I am happy here. When roads are built to Nonotuck, I will come to visit my children and grandchildren. I believe some of your brothers will also be going, but I will not. Springfield is my home. This is a good place for me."

"What if I need you, Mother?"

"I will come."

"You know I had those fits. What if they return?"

"If the weakness comes again, I will help you find a way past it. You are fine now. Trust me, daughter, you are a woman of strong will. We could not break you of it when you were young. Now you are old enough to understand your mind. You will never be broken. You have always been sensitive and nervous at times, but you understand yourself now. Age has a way of tempering us to finer strength."

On May 18 in the spring of 1653, the General Court appointed Mr. John Pynchon, Mr. Elizur Holyoke, and Samuel Chapin as Commissioners responsible for dividing the land at Nonotuck. Joseph took me to the meetinghouse to read the posting on the wall, when it came.

> *In answer to the petition of several inhabitants of Springfield &c, craving liberty &authority to erect a new plantation and township at Nonotuck, &c, it is ordered that Mr. John Pynchon, Mr. Elizur Holyoke, and Samuel Chapin shall be, and hereby are, appointed a committee to divide the land into two plantations, and that the petitioners make choice of one of them, where they shall have liberty to plant themselves, provided they shall not appropriate to any planter above one hundred acres of all sorts of land, whereof not above twenty acre of meadow till twenty inhabitants have planted and settled themselves upon the place, who shall have power to distribute the land, and give out proportions of land to the several inhabitants, according to their estates or eminent qualifications as in other towns of this jurisdiction.*

After Joseph finished reading the posting, he turned to me and said quietly, "I want to be among the first, Wife, have no doubt upon that, but it is important that I know now whether you will be happy to come with me? Will you come?"

His expression was very serious and I was touched. "I like it that you have asked me, Joseph. Yes, I will come."

"Ah, that is good, Mary." He threw his hands outward and began a lilting chant. "I will build you a fine house there, and we will fill it with strong children. Our family will prosper on the rich lands in the curve of the river yonder. You will be glad and think me very wise for this choice. You will see!" He stepped closer and said softly, "I am becoming a prosperous man here, but I can do better there."

"Very well, then we do not need to wait until you build a fine house. I would like to move with you as soon as the children can be made comfortable and safe, so that we can all be together. I do not want it to be like the days when my father left us at Boston Mount and went for whole summers to make ready for us to settle at Hartford. We missed him, and we were too long without him. He worked his heart out for us, and used himself up too early. I want to do this with you."

Joseph nodded at me and smiled. We walked home from the meetinghouse at a brisk pace that day, side by side as we had on our wedding day. I made my skirts snap against my legs in rhythm to the hearty thud of his boots upon the roadway. He smiled at me. I wondered if he was remembering our early days when the rapture of our love surrounded us in all we did. Now there was less time for that. I had his babe in arms and two of his sons bounced ahead of us.

I asked that Joseph include me in all the news related to the new town, and he did. The first task the Commissioners accomplished was to lay out the boundaries of Nonotuck. The land would have to be purchased from the Nonotuck natives. Joseph assured me that no Indian villages lay within the great meadow, nor any burial grounds sacred to them. Seasonally the Indians planted corn and other crops there, fished in the river, and hunted the grasslands and forests, but there would be no difficulty in obtaining title for the land from them. The power of the English had been well-proven, by our soldiers and our money.

In September of the fall of that year, the chiefs and Indian property owners of all the land on the west side of the Great River at

Nonotuck signed a deed that sold unto John Pynchon the grounds, meadows, woods, ponds, and waters of the new town. With their names and signs put down upon the paper, the sachems agreed that they and all their ancestors would, after the next spring, leave the west side of the river forever, beginning at the head of the great falls, northward to the little meadow called Capawonk, and nine miles west from the Connecticut river into the woods. The consideration was one hundred fathom of wampam, ten coats, and some other small gifts.

There was great excitement among our prospective planters. Ten days later meetings began to be held in both Hartford and Springfield for the purpose of writing petitions regarding who would dwell at Nonotuck and how much land they would receive. Joseph attended some meetings, but not all—enough to keep his hand in the goings-on. It was his opinion that most of the men who attended would never set foot in the new town, and that most of the rules and regulations being proposed would never go into effect. Many men like to talk about their dreams, but Joseph did not. Joseph planned, quietly and with direction. He was good at listening to people, and he cared about helping others when he could, but his practicality and energy would not allow him to sit and converse about hopes when he could be doing something.

Joseph told me one night that he had seen Robert Bartlett, his old friend and my childhood neighbor. He said that they had talked for a long time, and that Goodman Bartlett intended to be among the advance party of men leaving in the spring to stake out their claims. Goodman Bartlett would be a good alliance. Whenever Joseph was in Hartford, he made certain to meet with Goodman Bartlett. I was glad of this because Goody Bartlett would be good company for me when we settled at Nonotuck. When I tried to imagine our lives in Nonotuck, it was without knowing what the land would look like, or what our new home would be. Recollection of Goody Bartlett's friendly face greeted me as a pleasant thought for my future.

Chapter 21

To Plant, Possess, and Inhabit

Springfield, Spring 1654

Lord, our prayers went with the small parties of men who first set out to lay their claim upon the lands upriver, beyond the mountains. Our dreams sailed with them upon breezes made of danger and hope.

It was early in May when we heard the news that Robert Bartlett, Edward Elmer, William Holton, and John Webb, all Hartford men, had already left their families behind and had begun the hard journey north. In a week, we heard that four more from Hartford were departed to make their claims: William Miller, Thomas Roote, William James, and William Clarke.

In Springfield, the men making preparations made haste to leave, knowing that others were ahead of them. Joseph's ox cart was ready in the barn with new oak-spoked wheels, the axles greased to reduce the strain. Joseph's best plow was tied down in its bed. The cart sat chocked and blocked just inside the barn door. All around it were orderly piles of farming and building tools, cooking gear, and bags of seeds. The barrels of beer, casks of food, bedding and wearing clothes would be the last to go on. All would have to be packed with an eye toward building a compact and balanced load. Joseph had to finish his town responsibilities as selectman before he could leave.

Unlike most of the other planters who would be staying the season and then coming back when they were ready for their families, it was Joseph's intention to free himself from the grips of any town in order to oversee his expanding trade with the Indians. Joseph had also joined in a contract with four other men—William Holton, Richard and John Lyman, and Edward Elmore, to form a committee responsible for the building of a meetinghouse at Nonotuck. I took great heart that my brother John would also be settling at Nonotuck. The plan was that he would see to the building of our house as well as his own. Joseph hired men to clear the land and break the soil.

The day Joseph left, my excitement and anticipation were high. In the faint early light of morning, the children and I gathered around the cart, waiting to say our farewells. The oxen chewed their cuds placidly as Joseph finished attaching the leather harness to the stout wooden ox bow that had been made to fit over one of these matching oxen's shoulders. Because the way would be narrow and rough, only one animal would be able to pull the cart at a time, while the other would walk behind. The oxen were unaware of what labors lay ahead of them. I gazed into their large, heavily lashed eyes and wondered at the simple steadfast loyalty they had for my husband. They were strong, good-natured animals. I trusted them to pull willingly for their master no matter how hard the way would become. Joseph said a word to the oxen to keep them steady, and then turned to our young sons, who had been standing by with serious expressions. The three of them had lined up side by side, watching their father. Joseph touched each of their heads and admonished them all to do their chores and be helpful to me until he returned. I tucked a cloth-wrapped bundle of biscuits near the wagon wall where Joseph often rested his hand. I found his eyes and nodded. We had made our goodbye earlier, in bed. It would be a while before we would again have each other. The love we had shared would have to be great enough to keep him safe.

My brother turned his team into our dooryard just as the sun touched the horizon. He greeted the children and me. He and Joseph talked for a few minutes as they checked the lashings holding the loads in each wagon. The oxen stood placidly under their yokes, chewing and flicking their tails. There was no great fuss. It was just as if they were driving to market instead of into the remote wilds, but then the time came to part. My heart pounded as I waved farewell.

By that evening, I already wanted news of Joseph, but I could expect none for some time. In the morning, I walked to meeting with eagerness, hoping for word that some Indian or trader might have encountered him, but no one had. Over the next days I wondered where Joseph was, what he was seeing, and what was happening to him, as I always did when he was gone. I was glad that the weather remained fair. There were no storms or cold nights to bother him. The distance was not so far, only about twenty miles. A man on a good horse could easily make twenty miles in a day, but Indian trails were only footpaths, six inches wide, too narrow for a cart. There would be many watery places to ford. I knew that following Indian trails could be confusing, crisscrossing to places for which we English knew no purpose, but my husband had been up the river many times and knew the way. I imagined him walking the meadowlands with my brother, carefully considering the best sites for home lots. I only hoped he chose good neighbors. I wanted a home that was free of vexation at last.

I looked to my little sons with special caring during Joseph's absence. The familiar marks of Joseph were everywhere upon them, in the tip of their chins, the look in their eyes, and the set of their shoulders. It was plain to see that their characters had already been shaped by their father. In size, Joey, John, and Samuel would have made stairsteps, except there was a gap where Benjamin should have been. I desired with all my heart to protect my surviving sons with every bit of my life.

I began to understand that after we left for Nonotuck, I would become a mother in a new way. As long as we were at the Long Meadow in Springfield, the strongest woman in our lives was my mother. She was our family center. Mother was a wise and respected elder to everyone. At Nonotuck, I would be the strong woman. I would rise up to sustain my family using my own senses. I would come into possession of myself as a person, as honestly speaking as Mother. Just as Joseph was at the beginning of inhabiting a new land, so was I at the beginning of inhabiting a new self. More than a new house, I looked forward to living in a new community. I could start right out being known as the able wife of a prospering man, the mother of healthy sons, and the keeper of a righteous home. My purpose was finally about to be fulfilled. Fresh and fertile ground and air clean of petty taints awaited me, or so I believed.

Lord, my heart is not haughty, nor mine eyes lofty; neither do I exercise myself in great matters, or in things too wonderful for me.

Surely I have calmed and quieted myself, as a child that is weaned of his mother; my soul is even as a weaned child. Psalm 131:1-2

Chapter 22

Home Lots and Flowers of the Meadow

Northampton, March 1655

Lord, You must recall my joy when it came time for Joseph to lead us on our sojourn to Your New Jerusalem.

In a year's time, Joseph, with my brother John's help, had managed for there to be enough of a home built to be suitable for his family. He was eager to bring us to it. The land of the Nonotuck Indian was now called Northampton, a proper English name for a plantation that would soon prosper like its namesake in old England.

We planned our departure for as soon as the streams and rills no longer ran high in the freshet of winter melt, when the mud of spring would be firmed enough under our feet to travel safely. We had reason to want to hurry because a child we had conceived in Springfield awaited its birthing. I was swollen and soon would be ungainly, but I wanted my home ready for the new babe, which I expected to come sometime at the last of the May month.

Joseph made many trips between Northampton and Springfield over a year's time. As soon as there was a shelter standing, I started giving him the belongings we would need there. Joseph had so well prepared for or move that our load was relatively light the day we left Springfield to go to our new home. Being large with child, there needed to be room in the cart for me to ride most of the way. The two youngest children rode with me, and Joseph rode double on the horse with Joey. We started at first light in hopes of making Northampton by nightfall. I was grateful that the path had gradually been cut wider. Even so, it was an exhausting and physically harsh trip. We encountered no unfortunate troubles. Joseph guided us across the fords at streams and rivers with such skill that we made it across each time without getting badly wetted. As the day grew late, I began to worry that we might have to camp overnight, but we did succeed in reaching

Northampton in the very last dim light of dusk. Because of the darkness, I could barely see what lay around us. Had it not been for Joseph's familiarity with the road, we would not have found our dooryard. I waited by the cart for Joseph to light a lantern and bring us into the house. Joseph carried in each of the three sleeping boys. I followed, carrying blankets so that I could make the boys' beds.

In the flickering light of the candle lamp, I could not really see how the house was made, but I recognized family belongings. My first thought was to get the boys to bed. Joseph made a fire in the hearth, while I smoothed blankets over mattresses in the loft. Joseph carried up each boy and I covered them. I looked upon them as they slept. We were all safe in this new home.

Joseph went out to unhitch the horse and oxen. Joseph's and my bed was already made because he had been staying in it without me. I could see the hollow on the side where he liked to lay. I eyed the bed with terrible weariness, wanting nothing else but to slide in under its covers. Instead, Joseph and I shared a bit of bread together while we waited for the fire to burn more strongly in the hearth so that there would be embers in the morning. It was too late to start any cooking. We sat together by the crackling warmth of the fire. I dozed against Joseph in delicious sleepiness, only vaguely aware when he helped me to rise up to go to bed.

In the morning, I awoke with a start, knowing at once that I was in a new place. Joseph had already risen, but the children had not yet stirred. I said my morning prayers quickly and with joy. We were living temporarily in what was to be the barn, a stout post and beam hewn frame covered with rough sawn boards, undivided as one open room with a loft. The windows were cut out and covered by oiled cloth. The outer shutters and the thick door looked strong enough to bar against bear and Indian.

Most remarkable of all was what was standing just outside the door—Joseph's new house. Its walls had already been raised and were being planked. It was a substantial size—a long rectangle, one room deep and two stories tall. It was not unusual except for its size. It was much larger than any house we had lived in before. On the bottom floor, I could see openings for two windows on each side of a door.

Upstairs, there were going to be five windows, the middle window centered over the door. The roof came low over the windows on the top floor. Joseph announced to me that all the windows would open. Instead of diamond shaped, fixed leaded glass, they would be casement windows that would slide up and down. The blown glass square panes had been shipped from England. The back and sides of the house would have windows, too. Its large central chimney was completed. I was amazed at the large hearth, fireplace and oven.

The house would soon be clapboarded on the sides. The roof was finished—sealed against the weather by wooden shingles. Joseph wanted me to see that the entire house was built upon a large rock foundation cellar, with hewn log steps leading down. He said he had the house built so large and the stairs so strong because he thought he might want to start a business of keeping a tavern for selling strong spirits in the future.

I told him that I was pleased with what I saw. Joseph's home lot of four acres was right next to my brother's, between a piney plain and the main cart path. They had faced the house south, overlooking a small marshy brook.

I asked Joseph to show me his meadows and fields. Joseph was as eager to show me the new plantation as I was to see it. He hitched the ox to the cart, loaded the boys in, took me by the hand, and set me on the seat beside him.

What I saw made me close the stout door securely behind us when we returned home. I had known that we were moving to the wilderness, and I knew how long we had traveled through it to get to Joseph's new home. The difference is that whenever we had moved to a new plantation before, there had always been people and houses, fences, and an orderly way of life awaiting us. There were not even planks laid across the brooks that crisscrossed this plantation. Several times we had to ford streams to cross over to where other people lived. The houses were clustered upon the places where it was easiest to build. There was no center to the plantation—just a hill with the new meetinghouse perched upon it. We stopped and got down from the wagon to see the meetinghouse that Joseph's committee had helped to build. When we went around one side, I was surprised to see how many wolf heads were nailed to the wall. There were many more than I had ever seen in Springfield. Joseph said that men were paid a good bounty to rid the plantation of them but that there were still dens of wolves in the meadow.

I shuddered with the awful reality of what it meant to be in a place that was only beginning. Your Providence was all around us, I could see that, but I wondered if I was ready to do only with the basics of Your creation to sustain us. I cupped my hands around my belly to protect the babe inside from the enormity of the life that loomed around me.

It turned out that I did not have long to prepare the house and settle the boys. It was only the first day of the May month when the pains of birth came upon me. I had not expected it to be quite so soon. Thanks to You, it was an easy birth. When the midwife laid the babe into my arms, I saw with surprise that Joseph had fathered yet another son. The child was robust and nursed as greedily as a suckling pig. Joseph was doubly proud because his was the first English child born in Northampton. We named the infant Ebenezer, a name that among our English dissenters signified a worshipful place. To us, this child represented Your blessing upon this plantation, which we would make sacred to You.

My brother, John, fetched my mother to assist me during my laying in after the child was born. I needed her help, but her visit also brought its own discomfort. One day as we got to talking about the merits of living in Northampton, she admitted something horrible to me.

"Mary. I am glad that you have settled at Northampton, and that your children will be raised here. They will never have to hear any of that unpleasant talk about you."

My heart beat fast and I startled. "Mother, what kind of unpleasant talk?"

"You know, the suspicions."

"Suspicions? Mother, what suspicions?"

"Oh, Mary I am sorry. I should not have brought it up."

"Mother, you should tell me what you are talking about!"

"Well, the witchcraft gossip…"

"About me?

"You were acting strangely, you know you were. There were those in Springfield who talked about it. But Mary, you are far from that now. You need not bother about it anymore."

I was outraged. Mother and I did not discuss the gossip against me any further. She was clearly sorry she had raised the subject with me.

Soon after, Mother told me that she was satisfied that I was doing well enough for her to return to Springfield. I think she was happy to leave the wilderness plantation for the comfort of her home. When my neighbor Goody Bartlett came to visit me, I mentioned what Mother had said about witch gossip. Goody Bartlett scoffed at such notions.

"You do not have to worry about such things here."

The good weather drew me outside to plant my gardens. Joseph's Irishman had already prepared the soil for me. The hard work done, the rows and hills were seeded by me and patted down earnestly by my boys. When I could, I took all my boys, with baby Ebenezer tied in a shawl sling across my back, to gather spring greens and explore the meadows by the river. A few times Anne Bartlett went with me, which was most enjoyable. We often helped each other at our looms or with sewing. She, being more social than I, knew everything that was happening in the new town and liked to entertain me with her stories and speculations about the other villagers.

It was Goody Bartlett who told me that a new baby boy had been born to James and Sarah Bridgman on the thirtieth of May. She said they had named the child James, Jr. I rejoiced that, as small as our plantation was, it already had two sons born on the land to carry our dreams forward.

Goody Bartlett said, "No, it is too soon to be glad. Both the child and the mother are sickly. As soon as the babe was born he did groan something much. The child has had a looseness in its bowels from the first. Everything that goes in comes out, and now it has a cold. She fears if it continues that it will be the death of her child. She has no nurse to help her, so we women, Hanna Broughton, Hanna Langdon, and I, because we live on either side, are tending her."

The Bridgman's house lot was nearby to me also, but they were people I had never had much to do with in the past. Before Sarah was married to Bridgman, her name was Lyman—one of the Lymans from Hartford. My father had had legal troubles with her father and had to take him to court to make him pay what Father was fairly owed. Father did not hold a grudge against the man because, as he said, the Lymans had suffered a lot in moving to Hartford, and had been among those who lost many of their belongings enroute in the storms. Lyman had never recovered from his losses and had floundered overall in his affairs. In the end, he had fallen into a melancholy and died, with his wife dying soon after, leaving their daughter to fend for herself. My father had forgiven the difficulty he had with Lyman, but I never forgot how it bothered him to have foolishly entered into a bargain that caused him to fall out on the short end and have to rely on the court to save him from it. Sarah and I had always ignored each other. I felt a discomfort toward her. I had been vaguely aware when she married James Bridgman and moved to Springfield. We had never gotten into the habit of having much to do with each other in either Hartford or Springfield.

Now that we were neighbors, I entertained the notion that the time had come to put aside old prejudices and start fresh. That was, after all, one of the reasons why I had looked forward to moving here myself. Since she lived so close, I should surely make her acquaintance. Nevertheless, I resolved aloud that I would keep my children far from the Bridgman house as long as there was sickness afoot.

Anne did not encourage me to help. She gave me a strange look and gave no response at all to my question regarding what I might be able to do to help the family during their time of travail. I should have questioned her at the time about what that look meant. It might have saved me a lot of trouble if I had.

"How sick do you think Goody Bridgman is?" I asked.

Anne said, "I'll tell you, she suddenly looks much older than her years. She suffered greatly during this pregnancy and had to lie abed both before and after she delivered. She has lost too many infants after they were born, and has cause to worry. I pray for the Bridgmans that this baby boy will grow strong. Sarah is frightened by a vision she had. She told me that three days after the birth, as she was lying with the baby in bed, a great blow struck the door to the house. She sent her daughter, Mary, to see who it was, but the girl saw no one there. Goody Bridgman arose herself to look, and saw two women walking by with white clothes over their heads. She is in dread that there is something wicked in this place that is sucking her baby from her arms."

It was about the middle of June when I heard more about how the child was faring. Again, it was Anne Bartlett who told me. Anne came to my door one morning and wanted to talk. She had been there at the Bridgman's helping to watch over the sickly baby when it took a turn for the worse and perished.

"Through the night the baby was limp and cold. I tried to keep him warm by rubbing him. Thanks to God, the looseness had stopped, but I think it was only because he was too weak to nurse and had nothing left in him to pass. He was so frail. For a while, he had been struggling to breathe, gurgling, and wheezing with each breath, pulling so hard at the air that what little flesh he had to cover his bones drew right in between his little ribs. In the end, he just faded away, his breath so faint that it was hard to know when it stopped. When the morning light came he was gone. I put him into her arms. She slept with the babe for a while, her first peaceful sleep in days. When she woke, she knew. We did not have to tell her."

I could not help but be curious to hear what had happened, but it was too hard to listen. The remembrance of losing Benjamin seared through me with a pain too dreadful to share. My eyes grew hot and my throat closed in a choking gasp. Anne stopped talking. She looked at me long and hard.

"Mary." Her voice was sharp. "Mary, I have to tell you that you should watch yourself with Sarah. Because you lost a child you might think you know how she feels, but you do not. It is best if you stay away. You, of all people, can give her no comfort. Your grief could stir up things you know nothing about. Sarah believes the Devil had a hand in beguiling away the spirit of her little babe. She is looking for the reason why. Trust me when I tell you that trying to understand her sorrow will not soothe her. She does not know you as I do. She only knows that you have just had a son, and she has lost hers. You have *everything* that she has lost, and more. Please, Mary, for the sake of mercy, it would be best for the both of you if you kept a distance from her for a time until she is stronger. Do not venture over to her house, even to bring food!"

I raised my eyes to Anne and saw her distress.

She put her hand on my cheek and tucked a wisp of hair under my cap as she said, "Tend to your own house, and take care of your children. The Bridgman's have a child to bury. Yours was the first child to be born here, but theirs is the first among us to go into the ground. It is not the time to crowd around them with your brood."

When my friend left me, I paused in my work to contemplate my marriage, my children, and my home. The words of the psalm about our lives being like flowers of the field, blooming in the day, only to be cut down in the evening, sprang to mind. I prayed to You to ease the losses of the living. I was in sore need of Your protection, but I did not know it that day.

It was winter when I called upon You for help. Without hearing any approaching footsteps, suddenly there were hands beating against the thick wooden door of the house. My baby was nursing sleepily at my breast. The fire in the hearth burned in hot embers, the venison stew simmered. I rose to see who was there. My startled baby wailed. Would I have known then what devious lies sneaked into my house with the opening of that door!

Before me stood Goody Bartlett, frantic. I had never seen her in such a state. Words poured out of her.

"I just left Goody Bridgman's house. I am so frightened. Goody Branch is visiting from Springfield. I was invited to the Bridgman's to welcome her. Of course I was excited to gather to hear news. Oh, Mary, it was all so nice until they rose up a fuss about that awful witch business in Springfield."

"Do not speak of this to me! I do not wish to hear of it. I have put that behind me!"

"Listen to me, Mary Parsons. You must listen to me! Goody Bridgman is very upset and now everyone else is upset. She believes that the trouble in Springfield has followed her here. She told a story about the accident her son had this past summer when he put his knee out of joint in the woods. Do you remember anything about that?"

"Yes, I remember, of course I remember. A doctor had to be sent for to re-set the leg. It was days before he could come."

"Yes, that. Oh, Mary, what she thinks about the whole thing is awful. She told that a strange bird knocked her boy in the head, and when he ran from it, he tripped over two logs and wrenched his knee apart. She says that even after the man set the knee, her boy cried out in pain for a month. One morning at daybreak, he roused the house with his yelling out your name as the cause of it. She said that they came running to his screaming. He told them that you were pulling off his knee and torturing him. He pointed to a shelf to show where you sat, alongside a mouse. Goody Bridgman said that they tried to calm him by saying that they could not see you, but the boy kept screaming in pain until Goodman Bridgman got on top of him to stop his thrashing. Even then, the boy kept pointing you out until he said you left, with a mouse following. Goody Bridgman told us that her son stopped yelling only when he thought you were gone. Goody Hannum stood up after the story was told, and shook her finger in all our faces. She said she was warned against you by people who knew you in Windsor."

"Ah! That is foolishness. What are they talking about! That Goody Branch, what does she really know about me? Nothing. Moreover, you know Goody Hannum is angry with me. She spun thirty-three run of yarn for me and every bit of it wanted for threads. Now I guess that I will have to prove that she is shorting me. I must put a stop to her getting away with it by distracting everyone. The evil is of their own making. Why do people listen to such things?"

"Mary, they are jealous of you and say you are not right. They declared you must be a witch, and most agreed you are that way."

"What! You would tell me this? You sat with them and talked about me, Anne? You?"

"I tried to reason with them and to calm them down, but Goody Bridgman spoke hotly at me for being your friend. All the women were shaking their heads at me and clicking their tongues every time I tried to speak, so I left. And, Mary…, I think I should go now. I came here to let you know to mind your dealings with those women, but I am frightened to be here lest they suspect we are talking about them. I want to go home to my children. Mary, I am sorry to bear this news. I must go."

I watched Goody Bartlett hurry away. My knees felt weak, my face hot. My mind swooned. Oh, my husband would hear of it. My pulse throbbed hot at my temples; my eyes were pounded by searing tears, the walls pressed in upon me.

I felt .....faint. I fell. I fell and fell. Falling turned into flying. Out through the door I soared, free of bone and wood, turning upward, away from people. I raised high over the coolness of the snowy meadow. A giant elm extended its graceful branches to me. At the edge of the river, I could not keep my balance and I dropped. I woke up crying on the floor with my baby, clammy and damp. Goody Bartlett was gone. My husband would be home soon.

I wondered, "How can this be? Why is this happening?" I did not like the feeling of being helpless, and I did not like being blamed for other people's weaknesses and fears. I rose from the floor. I would not be made to weep again. I am only a woman, but I am a good woman. There is no evil in me. I decided then to make certain I never let the Devil look into my soul through other people's eyes. A Bliss, the wife of Joseph Parsons, is not someone whose spirit is easily broken. I gave myself to You for safekeeping.

Ye are blessed of the Lord, which made heaven and earth. Psalm 115:15

Chapter 23

They Were Few in Number and Strangers in It

Northampton, March 1656

Make no friendship with an angrie man,
neither go with the furious man,
lest You learne his wayes, and receive
destruction to Your soule. Proverbs: 22-24

By Your grace, in a year's time, we were well settled in Northampton. By March of 1656, our house was finished and we had moved in to it. The temporary house had become the barn Joseph had intended for his livestock, as well as a storage place for farm implements and grains. Joseph tore down the temporary chimney to make room for more stalls and a tack room to hang harness. Hay filled the loft where the children had slept. Around us, the town had grown to thirty-two families. New settlers had come with skills that made our town better. We no longer had to travel to Springfield for a barrel or brickmaker, for a tanner, a blacksmith, or a sawyer. Town meetings were taking place in the meetinghouse nearly every month to elect officials and enact public business. Joseph was busy with all of that. Our four children were healthy, and Joseph's land holding were enlarging. He had a lively trading business with the other settlers, and he continued to exchange goods with the Indians for the promise of beaver skins, peas, grains, and Indian corn. This was my life, and I tended it carefully.

I chose to ignore any aggravations with the neighbors in hopes of walking an ever-straight path toward the righteousness You desire of Your nation. I grew more careful with whom I associated. I went to meeting every Sunday, sitting on the women's side with the children, as Joseph took his place with the other men. Except for the Sabbath, Joseph never stopped working. His time filled up with the town business, farming and his trading and future planning. Joseph and I were two workers. There was little time to talk, and no time for idleness. Our hands were busy building Zion, for ourselves and our children.

With all of this, Joseph made time for all his children to help him as much as they could. Joseph could be stern with them, but he had a ready laugh when the children amused him. The children rarely saw their father's temper. With them, he was gentle. Joey was eight, old enough for Joseph to take along with him. Joey was proud that he could help his father in his business. John was only five, and Samuel, just two. The young ones stayed home with baby Ebenezer and me. As much as I loved my children, I could not help but realize that our children filled the time that Joseph and I used to have for ourselves. Our time together was at night, when Joseph's hands reached for me, stroking me, and lifting my clothing so that our bare skin could touch. I was used to Joseph's ways. It satisfied me that we shared a passion that was ours alone.

Once we moved into the big house, I asked Joseph if I could hire a girl to help me. He agreed without comment. I thought of Goody Hannum's daughter, who was a good and hard working girl. In March, I went over to inquire as politely as possible about bringing her to live with us. Goody Hannum refused me coldly, with her daughter standing right there. The daughter protested, and told her mother that she was agreeable and that she very much desired to come and work for me. Goodman Hannum came into the kitchen to listen as we talked.

"Girl, be quiet, and listen to your mother," Goodman Hannum scolded. "Your mother has said no, and no it is. She needs you here. Is my home not good enough for you? Would you leave your mother and go off, just because someone else's house is finer? Your duty is here. And you, Goody Parsons, do not try to lure my daughter away. I would thank you to leave my house."

"That is right," said Goody Hannum. "You cannot have my daughter, not even if you offered ten pound a year."

I knew it was because of the gossip that they were refusing me, and because Goody Hannum did not want to admit that she had cheated me. I decided to set things right.

215

"Goody Hannum, you have no cause to be angry with me. I am inviting your daughter into my home despite the fact that you have done me wrong. You shorted me on the yarn you spin. I am willing to forgive it, and will pay a good wage for your daughter."

Goody Hannum fluffed up like an angry chicken, and pushed past me. "You told me about the yarn once before! Show me what you are talking about. It cannot possibly be true," she said.

We marched right out of her house toward mine. I showed her the yarn. She could see that instead of being long and even, it was full of knotted sections. The yarn was thin and lacked for weight. She showed no remorse at all. She only glared at me. She did agree to make it right.

"I have some oakum. I will spin some oakum yarn for you. It will be right."

Nothing changed about being able to hire her daughter. I would have to hire another, but at least I had nipped the tongue of one of the gossipers, or so I thought. The next morning Hannum's cow fell ill. Not long after, I heard it died. I hoped they would not call this out as a sign against me.

Goody Hannum made good on her word to spin the oakum yarn. It proved to be defective in the same way. I used my weights to prove it.

"It was right when I spun it," she said glaring.

She looked at me accusingly. It came to me that she might be thinking that I had undone her work.

She went on, "My daughter has turned sickly since we talked with you, Goody Parsons. She is no good to me. She is listless and cannot work. She is changed…and, my husband's cow is dead!"

She spat her words. She turned and slammed my door behind herself, rudely.

A chill came over me. I had no choice but to go to Joseph and tell him. I knew that I must ask for his patience and for his understanding and help. I prayed to You that my husband would not dismiss me in anger.

That evening, after Joseph ate, he sat down in his chair by the hearth, puffing on his pipe as he usually did. I expected that it would be like most evenings. Usually he sat thinking and planning his next day, mostly unmindful of my presence, until he began to doze by the warmth of the fire. On that night, I watched him as I fed the children and cleaned up. I caught him watching me. I could tell he had something to say. After the children went to bed, and the baby was nursed and put to sleep, Joseph called my name.

"Mary," he said. "People are talking about you." He stopped and looked at me. "Why are they talking about you? What have you done?"

"I have done nothing. It is mean gossip."

"Gossip does not come out of nowhere, Wife. There is a reason for it. What is it? Whatever it is, you must stop it. This gossip threatens my standing."

"There is nothing that I have done, Joseph, I swear. Goody Bartlett says it is because the women are jealous of me."

"This talk is about more than jealousy. They are talking about you not being right, about you being a witch, about you hurting people!" Joseph's voice began to rise.

The words I wanted to say poured from me. "It is because of you, Joseph! They are jealous of you! You do not have to work like their men. You just paid twenty pounds to the town to be freed from any obligation to hold town office this year. You go off buying and trading while their husbands sweat and toil. You hired men to build this house and barn, and made an agreement with my brother John to oversee it all. Your Irishman and his son take care of all the planting of wheat, flax, corn, and hemp; and all your regular chores. Your horses are the best. Your oxen are the best. Your flock of sheep is healthy, and everyone wants to breed to your ram because of its excellent wool. People are always coming to the door to borrow your tools, and I lend whatever they ask for. When they bring your things back, I can see the resentment in their eyes that they have to hand it all back to me. Some of the women, and even some of the men, do not like it that we are no longer like them. You are important here, but I am not. I am just your wife, your woman. If it were not for me, the other women could hope to marry a man like you. I am thirty-one, but I am not all used up, like most of them. My clothes are better. My teeth are better. We have four strong boys. That is all I have done. I have not hurt anyone. I have just had a baby! I keep up your home with good housekeeping. I keep separate from those of lower means so that the children see only good examples of God's rewards for hard work. I have had no time to hurt anyone. I need you to help me! People ARE jealous! Of us! They are the ones who are hurting us, not me! Joseph, help me, you are my husband!"

There was nothing else for me to say. It felt good to have said it all. I hoped Joseph had heard me.

Joseph looked at me, his eyes piercing into mine, and then he looked me up and down. He stood and began to pace.

"You are too critical, and people think you are haughty with them. That is what they say about you, Mary. What are you going to do about that?"

"Do you think I am critical? Do you think I am haughty? What do you think I should do? What would you have me do? When I see a wrong, it is my duty to correct it. I do avoid some people, but even toward them I must be honest. People hear nothing from me but the truth. If they do not like it, it is their sin. "

"I would have you take care of my children, and take care of my house, and leave everyone else to their own business. A woman should keep her tongue quiet."

"Do I not take care of your children to your satisfaction? Do I not take care of your house as you like it?" I asked him.

"Yes, you do. You are a good wife. But something you are doing is causing trouble, and I want you to stop whatever that is, Mary."

"Husband, I will watch myself, but it is too late to change what people say. Will you stand by me in this, or will you shun me, or lock me away?"

"Oh, do not bring that up. Yes, I will stand by you, but this hurts me."

Neither of us talked further. That night we went to bed in silence. My prayers to You were said in silence.

Chapter 24

Murmurs in the Houses

Northampton, March 1656

A day came when our world was ripped apart. It started as a small thing. Young John lost one of his shoes in the house somewhere. We looked everywhere for it, but the shoe eluded us. I put the shape of it in my mind for my eyes to recognize, and imagined finding it, but the shoe would not come to me. I thought that John had hidden it to tease me until I saw how worried John was about telling his father. Rather than have the child wait in shame, I grabbed him up by his little arm and gave him a thrashing on his bottom with the flat of my hand so that he would be scolded before his father returned. He suffered the punishment gravely. No sooner had I let him go then we heard the hoof beats of a horse. Joseph had come home for his midday meal.

John burst out and ran to Joseph, without bowing or any proper manners, crying, "I lost my shoe, Father. I am sorry. I lost my shoe."

"What? Lost your shoe! Those were new shoes. I only just had those shoes brought all the way from Boston. Those were very good shoes! I thought you were a big enough boy to have real shoes, and now you have lost one? No one makes shoes like that in this valley. John, that is carelessness of the worst kind!"

Joseph broke off a switch from the bush outside our door, and in a sort, began to beat the child for the lost shoe. I ran to save John from Joseph's wrath. Our children usually needed their will broken by only a little whipping. Even though the child deserved a punishment, I thought enough had been done.

"Joseph, Joseph, you do not need to do that. I have already beaten the child!" I cried out, but Joseph did not stop.

I pulled at Joseph's arm to stop the downward strike of the switch. With the direction turned, the blow fell upon me. I grabbed at Joseph. We began to wrestle over the switch, and then he began to hit me instead. Something in me broke. I fought him until he overpowered me. It being useless to fight, I went limp. Joseph pushed me to the ground. I rolled away and then got to my feet, overwhelmed but furious, a welt rising across my arm, and a scratch stinging at my cheek.

There was the sound of laughter. I looked around and saw William Hannum and John Webb, our neighbors, standing nearby watching, and making jest of us. I saw nothing funny. I smoothed my skirts, glared at them, and went into the house, closing the door upon them all. Lord, You were my witness to this travesty. I caught my breath and prayed for a sign to show me what to do. If You sent a sign, I was too upset to see it.

Joseph did not come in for his noon meal. He mounted his horse and rode away. In the evening, I waited for him, but he did not come. The next day I went out with the children to look for him. I could not bear the waiting. Just as I started out, I passed by Goodman Hannum and a group of other men at George Webb's. I chose not to ask them if they had seen Joseph and hoped they would not think that I was out looking for him. They said nothing as I went by, but behind my back, I heard a loud voice speak out something revolting. I could only hope that my children did not understand the meaning of the words.

Astonished, I stopped. I clearly recognized the voice. I knew who had laid the insult. Slowly I turned around to face the men.

"Goodman Hannum, was there something you wanted to say to me, or was I not intended to hear what you just said?"

"I said nothing, Goody Parsons!"

"Yes, indeed you did…and it was something that should not be said before a woman or children. Do any of you here wish to take responsibility for what Goodman Hannum said?"

"No. Uh, no, Goody Parsons, we would not say such as that."

The group of men surrounding Goodman Hannum stepped away from him, each denying that they had said the slur.

"Goodman Hannum?" I said.

"Oh, I think it is you who misunderstood a jest" he said. Goodman Hannum shuffled his feet and the rest of the men did not look at him.

I watched as each man looked at Goodman Hannum out of the corner of his eyes. Their expressions confirmed to me that his denial amused them.

Exasperated, I shook my head. I felt a tug upon my skirt, and looked down at my children surrounding me. I decided it would be best if I did not speak another word, so I took their hands and we walked together back into our dooryard, and on into the house. Trying to calm myself, I began to prepare the noonday meal, as if Joseph would be returning to eat it.

The sun was high in the sky when the door opened. It was Joseph. He came into the kitchen and sat down at the table.

Before I could even decide what I might say, he said my name.

"Mary, I regret what I did. I will not trouble you with trying to make any excuses for it. I ask your forgiveness for the wrong I committed in anger." He paused and looked at me.

"I accept your apology, Husband."

Before any more could be said, John rushed into the kitchen holding both his shoes for us to see.

"Father, I found my shoe!"

"You are interrupting, John, but I am glad that you found your shoe. It is good that you did, son. It is evil to be wasteful. I would not want a son of mine to be heedless of the work of our hands, cast as low as a mindless pig in mud. Now go, John, and bring the other children here. I have something to say to all of you."

The boys came quickly to the table, having been waiting for the call to eat.

Joseph spoke to them. "I have asked Mother to forgive me for hurting her yesterday. I do not approve of any man raising a hand against a woman, and do not want you to take my actions as a lesson for how I expect you to behave. Do you understand?"

The boys said in union, "Yes, Father."

"So be it, boys. Do not ever let me hear of you laying a hand upon your wives."

The boys looked at each other out of the corner of their eyes and began to puff up with giggles. "We have no wives, Father!"

"A good man does not beat his dog. Start with minding how you treat your animals, and we will see from there how well you learn to be good men."

When the children were put to bed, Joseph and I spoke of the day.

"I am curious. What was it that Goodman Hannum said to you that was so disturbing, Mary?"

"It was a very strange thing. The men were talking about how you had beaten me and thrust me away, and they were laughing. Goodman Hannum responded by saying, "One of you being his next neighbors must ride.""

"Well…what is the meaning of that? It has an ugly tone, but I do not understand what he was thinking, or why you are bothered by it."

"If you had been there the meaning would have been clear by the motions and grunts the men made in response. It put into my mind the animals of the field. They looked at me was as if I were a beast. They would set their bull upon a heifer with more respect. I was sorely disgusted, not just for me, but for you. Your wife is not such that anyone can ride."

"I am sorry, Mary. I am responsible for making you look bad before the others. I will do everything I can to show my respect to you and to protect you from such ignorance." Joseph looked tired and worried.

He stood up, put his arms around me, and held me. I was always surprised when sometimes he would come to me to hold me like that. How comforting was his surrounding warmth, and his familiar smell. I pushed my face into his shoulder, soaking in his strength, trying to stop the tension of my muscles from hurting in my neck and the pit of my stomach.

There would be no peace. The very next morning a group of men went by our house, all looking for Mr. Hannum's sow and four young pigs that had gone missing. By evening, I heard that the sow was dead. According to Joseph, who had heard the story second hand, Goodman Hannum was claiming that evil forces were at work because his sow had been healthy. Joseph told me that Mr. Hannum was making a great uproar about the loss. He was claiming that it was some kind of a punishment upon him for the harsh words he and I had had the previous day.

Joseph shook his head, rolled his eyes, and sighed when he told me. "I cannot keep these things from you. You must be cautious how you speak to that man. He believes in witches, and will have you being one if you do not take care. It only takes a wrong word. He is not someone you can chide, no matter how wayward you think him to be."

I knew Joseph was right about Hannum, and I vowed to take his warning to heart. It was less than a week later when I had to make a terrible choice about that. Oh, my Father, my Lord, I want to be Your servant and hold fast to You as my help and shield, but sometimes Your ways are not clear. When Goodman Hannum came knocking on our door early one morning, asking to borrow my brother John's young oxen to do some plowing, there was only me to speak to him, both Joseph and John being away. It was not at all unusual to lend oxen in exchange for work, so I told Goodman Hannum that he might use my brother's oxen for the day. I was uncomfortable having to speak to Goodman Hannum, but I was spare of word and civil in manner, and we parted agreeably.

It was about noon when young Joseph came running into the house. "Mother, you must do something. Goodman Hannum is beating Uncle John's oxen something terrible! You know what Father said about how an animal must be treated. I cannot let him do that. Mother, you must do something! Make him stop! Come out and see! He is beating them!"

I followed behind my two older sons, Joseph and John, with Ebenezer in my arms, and Samuel at my heels. We went to the field where Goodman Hannum was breaking up ground. I could see Hannum was at some hard work, the grassy sod being thick and unyielding. He had three pairs of oxen yoked to the plow and all were struggling. Each time the teams floundered, his whip fell upon John's oxen. Blood was running down their sides. Their eyes were rolling wildly, but they were held fast to the work and the whip. Goodman Hannum was yelling, cursing, and sweating through his clothes. He did not see me approach.

I got close so he could see me, and close enough so that I could see well what was happening to John's oxen. They were much smaller than the other two teams, on account of their age. I took a breath and composed myself as I stared at the man. There was a strong smell of blood and sweat, urine and earth, and torn grass.

"Goodman Hannum," I said with a level voice. "Why is it that you have put my brother's oxen in the middle where they are always under the whip?"

"They are young and not very fit to go behind, much less before."

"I fear my brother's team has suffered enough abuse this morning. Please, unyoke them and return them to the barn. Make sure they are watered before you leave them."

"I intend to finish this field before I quit, Goody Parsons. Kindly stand away."

"Goodman Hannum, I cannot lend my brother's oxen to have them treated in this manner. They are my brother's oxen, not mine. I cannot give you permission to use them further."

"I'll be talking to Goodman Bliss about this, don't you worry. Now you move on. I have no time in this day to waste talking with a woman about how a man does his work. You had better stand back lest you accidentally are knocked over. You have no business in this field, stand back!" He shouted to the oxen and the three teams strained on before the plow, the whip cracking upon the backs of the young oxen.

I remembered my promise to Joseph to guard my words with Goodman Hannum. There was nothing to do. I stepped back and let the teams pass. I was angry as I walked away from that field, but I was satisfied that I had not said anything that would cause trouble. I told the boys that Goodman Hannum would take good care of the oxen when he put them away. I asked Joey to be sure to tell his Uncle what he had seen.

My brother was not happy when he saw the condition of his oxen that evening, but he was not as bothered as I thought he should have been. John said calmly, "Hannum is harsher than I like to be with the oxen, but that is the kind of work they are meant for. Their labors make them stronger."

Joseph, on the other hand, was very displeased with the story. "I want you to have nothing to do with that man, Mary. No good can come of it. As your husband, I demand that you stay away from him!"

Three days later, Joseph burst into the house and stormed up to me. "Mary! The damage I warned about is done. You did not heed my words, and another bad thing is the result. As Goodman Hannum was driving his ox and cart to Windsor, his ox was bitten in the tongue by a rattlesnake and it died on the road four miles out of town. Do you know what Hannum is saying of this? He blames you as the cause of all these things. This must stop. Stay home and do not talk to people. I cannot have my wife being the source of such turmoil in this town. Those who are against you are divided against those who support us. I cannot have a conversation or do business without it involving how the man is disposed to thinking about you. What started with Sarah Bridgman is spreading like a sickness in this town. This must stop."

My heart stopped in my chest, and then it began to pound. I thought of something my father used to say.

He shall not be afraid of evil tidings: his heart is fixed, trusting in the Lord. Psalms 112:7.

Chapter 25

Judging Evil

Northampton, Spring, Summer, and Fall of 1656

Let the lying lips be put to silence
which speak grievous things proudly
and contemptuously against the righteous.
Psalm 31:19

After Joseph had words with me, I could see that he began preparing to go somewhere. I went about my household tasks and watched him. The children seemed unaware of the angry silence that separated us. My soul trembled with a terrible loneliness. What had risen up against me was too large to comprehend. My neighbors were against me, and my husband was outraged. My ears roared with a sound I could not hear, my chest was crushed by a weight I could not see. Finally, Joseph talked to me. "I am going to Springfield to speak with John Pynchon about what to do about the gossip and accusations against you."

I did not know when Joseph would return. I kept busy. Everything I did was ordinary. Everything that was wrong was not ordinary. I could only do what a woman needed to do to keep the house right.

Joseph returned with my mother. He helped her down from the wagon, carried in her bags, unharnessed the horse and led it to the barn. I thought he would come into the house and tell me what had happened. Instead, he saddled his riding horse and rode off. He left without a word.

I had no idea what he was thinking or doing. Mother must have seen my concern as I watched him ride away. She was quick to explain that Joseph was taking action on the advice that John Pynchon had suggested. I was curious to hear what that might be.

"Mr. Pynchon talked privately with Joseph and advised him to charge Goody Bridgman for slander for calling you out as a witch. Joseph has already notified the Springfield Commissioners, of which Mr. Pynchon is one, of his intent to bring charges against Sarah Bridgman. Now he has gone to see the Northampton Commissioners for Ending Small Causes to do the same here."

The idea of suing Goody Bridgman for slander felt immediately right! I laughed. I would not have thought of this as a way out from under the heavy weight of ugly talk about me. Suddenly I felt the elation of hope. I had to look at Mother for confirmation that I had understood her correctly.

Mother reassured me. "Joseph has signed his complaint against her in Springfield. She has spoken against you not just here, but there as well. The papers are filed, the ink is dry. There is no going back on what he has started."

Joseph came directly to me when he returned. He told me what he had done. Proceedings for his complaint against Sarah Bridgman for slander were scheduled to begin in June in Northampton before Commissioners William Houlton, Edward Elmer, and Thomas Bascum. The case would go before the Commissioners at Springfield, John Pynchon and Elizur Holyoke, in August. Joseph told me not to talk about the upcoming case with anyone. I detected no irritation in his attitude toward me. Making a decision to take a course of action almost always put Joseph in good spirits.

On June the 10, the testimonies began at Northampton. I went to the meetinghouse where the Commissioners met. Almost every adult was in attendance. Notably, one of the Commissioners, Edward Elmore, was not present; only Commissioners William Holton and Thomas Bascum were there. There was no explanation as to his absence. I would have like Mr. Elmore to be there because he was a solid friend of Joseph's. Perhaps he felt too close to us to be impartial. I did not know. I would have felt better if he was involved in hearing the proceedings.

Sarah Bridgman and all her family and supporters sat together, glaring and angry. My husband, my brother John, and Mother sat close to me. I noticed that my friends were scattered throughout the meetinghouse in their usual seats. I sat straight in dignity. It was time for the slanderer to take responsibility for her words. She would be found out.

The first testimony to be heard was from Robert Bartlett, taken upon his oath.

The commissioners wrote down his words as he spoke, stopping him to clarify what he said, or to give themselves time to dip their quills in ink. Robert was asked how he first became aware of the accusations of witchcraft and who had made the accusations.

Robert spoke clearly for all to hear about the time George Langdon shared with him the gossip Goody Bridgman and Goody Branch were spreading about me being a witch, and about how the woman had said that they had hard thoughts against Anne Bartlett for being my friend. Goody Landon testified to the truth of Goodman Bartlett's story.

"There," I thought. "There it is. Everyone knows now that all of this started when Goody Bridgman gossiped with Hannah Langdon and Goody Branch about me.

No one else was called to testify that day. The next hearing was scheduled for June 20. All the people rose and left the meetinghouse. I did not linger there. I was surprised that so little happened that day after so much fuss.

Joseph told me, "Those who had been saying things about you in secrecy will now have to come out and be held accountable. I have a hint that some people may be beginning to regret that they joined in all the gossip and intrigues. It is not so much what people say that makes me think this, but because of how uncommonly pleasant people are being to me." He laughed wryly.

I watched Joseph's expression carefully every time he mentioned anything about his slander trial against Goody Bridgman, looking for affirmation of his feelings about his very public defense of me. I knew him well enough to know that it pleased him to be able to do something to make things right. He was not a patient man about letting problems remain unfixed. His guarding of me against my persecutors brought me stability, even joy. My life seemed embraced in a pact of trust with my husband. I could clearly feel Joseph's fondness for me. I basked in the closeness and tried to think of as many special things to do for him as I could to make him notice my overflowing affection. With Mother staying with us, I resisted openly touching him, saving that for private.

When June 20 came the meetinghouse was full. Most people had taken up their usual Sabbath seats, except that the men and women were seated together and there were no children present. A small group of Sarah Bridgman's family and friends sat around her. My husband, Mother, and my brothers and sisters sat with me.

Hanna Langdon was called again. The commissioners, William Houlton and Thomas Bascum, with Edward Elmore again being absent, instructed her to testify under her oath that her words would be the truth, which she did. The Commissioners asked her whether she had ever heard Sarah Bridgman state that I, Mary Bliss Parsons, was a witch.

Goody Langdon began to speak, softly and uncomfortably. "Yes, Sarah Bridgman did tell me that her boy, when his knee was sore, cried out the wife of Joseph Parsons, and said that she did hurt him, and that she would pull off his knee."

I prepared myself to hear a recital of all the reasons I was seen as "not right". To my surprise, Goody Landon kept her answer short and ended it with an apology.

She said, "I myself suspected Goody Parsons, but it has pleased God to help me over what they said and I do believe there was no such cause. I am sorry I should have hard thoughts of Goody Parsons upon no better grounds."

With that, Goody Langdon was allowed to take her seat. It was astounding. One of the main gossips against me had apologized publicly. It was only the second day of hearings. I wondered if it might be possible that these indignities of slander might be ended soon.

Sarah Bridgman herself was called up. The Commissioners had her take her oath and then asked her what she had said to Hanna Langdon about her son's injury.

Sarah Bridgman was small and pale, but she had an air of shrill indignancy about her words as she said, "I own that I did tell Hanna Langdon that my boy cried out the name of Joseph Parsons' wife. He said that she would hurt him, and that she would pull off his knee. I thought it was likely to be so because I had heard others say that there were jealousies of Goody Parsons that she was not right."

That was all that the Commissioners asked of Goody Bridgman. It seemed clear to me that she had admitted to listening to gossip and adding to it. I wondered why the Commissioners asked her no other questions. Were they satisfied that she had proven herself a slandering gossip?

I heard the name Margaret Bliss called. I had no idea that Mother had gotten herself involved in any significant way in this. I learned from her testimony that Mother had taken it upon herself to go right to Sarah Bridgman to confront her about her accusations of me. My mother had defended me! My Mother sat like a lioness, a woman of clear and no-nonsense intelligence, free of any inkling of pettiness or vengeance. Her character was instantly recognizable as earnest and honest.

Mother stated, "Sarah Bridgman told me that she did hear that my daughter was suspected to be a witch. She said that she had heard there was some discontent between the blind man at Springfield and Mary Parsons, and that she had done him hurt, that there were some words between them, and that afterwards the child had had a sounding fit."

To any thinking person, Mother's words proved that Sarah Bridgman had outright accused me of being a witch. My mother returned to her seat next to me. I felt thankful that she had taken my side against my accusers.

Hanna Broughton, a well-respected woman, was called. I was uncertain of her feelings, but thought it likely that she sided with Sarah Bridgman, in-as-much as she had been such a help to her during the sickness and death of Sarah's last child.

Hanna Broughton said, "Sarah Bridgman, the wife of James Bridgman, said to me that Mr. Pynchon had said that if it were true what he had heard about Goody Parsons, than she could not be right. Sarah told me that if Goody Parsons is such a one as that, a witch, then she desired God to keep her and hers from having anything to do with her. I decided then to go about without having anything to do with Goody Parsons myself. I affirm by oath that my statements are true."

So, I thought, Hanna Broughton just showed the Commissioners that Sarah Bridgeman's gossip has hurt me, and that Bridgman has also involved Mr. Pynchon in her slandering.

No one else was called that day at Northampton. The two Commissioners spoke inaudibly among themselves while the crowd waited. After a good bit of time had passed, the Commissioners stated that they would seek further testimony on the matter as they learned of it. I gathered myself up, smoothed my skirts, took the arm of my husband, and went straight away home, looking neither to the left nor to the right. I thought the matter was over in Northampton. It seemed to me that Joseph's case for Sarah Bridgman's slandering of me had been proven.

The trial before the Commissioners at Springfield was held on August 11 at the meetinghouse before Commissioner Elizur Holyoke. John Pynchon had withdrawn from hearing the case for the time being. My entire adult family was in attendance. Even though Sarah Bridgman had many supporters in Springfield, after what I had heard at Northampton, I felt confident that my reputation would be cleared. I held my head high among my family, friends, and former neighbors.

First to be called were the Hannums. Goody Hannum reminded me of a peckish hen as she stood before the Commissioner, all fluffed up in her righteousness.

She said, "I have been warned by some of Windsor and some of Norwottuck to beware how I had to do with Mary, the wife of Joseph Parsons." Goody Hannum went on at length about how I had accused her of shorting the yarn she had sold me, and how her daughter had become sickly and unhealthy when she refused to let the daughter come into my service. She clearly held the notion that I had put a charm on her yarn, and then upon her daughter.

After listening to every last detail about how offended Goody Hannum was by me, Mr. Holyoke thanked Goody Hannum for her time. He next called William Hannum.

"What say you of any suspicion you may have as to the validity of the claim by Sarah Bridgman that Mary Parsons be engaged in witchcraft?" said Mr. Holyoke.

William Hannum expounded upon his feelings against me. "I have had some jealousies against this Mary Parsons, on these grounds: first this Mary came to my house about the yarn and we had a falling out about it. Some discontented words passed on both sides. That evening, March last, all my cattle were well. The next morning, one cow lay in my yard, ready to die. I considered this as I endeavored to get her up. At length I got her to stand, but she languished away and died about a fortnight after."

He went on about everything he had tried to save the cow, and how young and lusty she should have been if not for me. Goodman Hannum also testified about the time I caught him jesting with neighbors about who should "ride" me. He said that I had unreasonably "chided" him. He went on a tirade about how I had taken revenge upon him by making his sow with four young pigs go missing and how when he found the animal it was in the swamp staring at the ground. He blamed me for the death of his "lusty and well fleshed swine."

He went on to relate the incident when I scolded him for whipping my brother's oxen. Goodman Hannum held his palms upward and whined. "Three days after, I was going to Windsor with my oxen and cart. About four mile from our town, as I was going, whether my ox hung out his tongue or whether he went to eat, its tongue fell out. A rattlesnake bit him by the tongue and there he died. These things do something run in my mind that I cannot have my mind from this woman, that is she be not right this way, she may be a cause of these things, though I desire to look at the over ruling hand of God in all."

These were the very words that Joseph had reported to me! The words that had stung me so much hung in the room for all to hear. I stiffened with outrage.

The name of Sarah Bridgman was called. When she stood, I noticed that she seemed stronger and more resolute than when she had testified in Northampton. My heart dropped in heaviness. She was a woman trapped in her fears and disappointment. She needed someone to blame.

Mr. Holyoke had her swear her oath that her testimony would be true. He asked her to describe what had happened that had made her fear that her children had been bewitched. With that question, Mr. Holyoke gave Sarah Bridgman free rein to say anything she wanted about me right there in the meeting as part of the proceedings. How could someone who was being accused of speaking ill against another be encouraged to do so in public as if it were lawful testimony? It was as if she was no longer the one on trial. Mr. Holyoke's questions had changed the nature of the case. He was not asking whether or not Sarah Bridgman had accused me of being a witch. He was asking if I was a witch. Joseph was glaring. I dreaded hearing what she was about to say.

She started her story in a voice soft and timid, in the way of children speaking that women may do when they must talk in front of men. She testified to the same vague tale she had spread about me, which started with the "great blow on the door" story. She told how her daughter had answered the door only to find no one there but two women passing by "with white clothes on their heads." She admitted that from this event she "then concluded" that her child would die. Sarah did not say what made her believe that I had anything to do with that vision of "wickedness." She did repeat that I supposedly had taken the form of a bird and given her son a blow on the head, causing his knee to go out of joint. She was agitated when she described how he had cried out that I was trying to pull off his knee. Sarah described in detail the claim that her son had cried out that he saw me with a black mouse at his bedside. She imitated a child's voice screaming, "There she sits on the shelf."

She kept her eyes fixed on her fingers in her lap. Occasionally she looked up at her husband, James Bridgman. He nodded at her to continue. After each time he did so he would turn his head to look as me. I returned his gaze until he averted his eyes. When he rose to testify, he confirmed wife's story almost word for word. In a voice strong and angry, he described the horror of his child's injury and fears.

Mr. Holyoke called upon Goodman Branch to arise and state the reasons why he had come to testify. Goodman Branch and Bridgman passed each other. I noticed that Bridgman flashed his friend a look of victory. I was not sure what Branch would say. I listened carefully.

"I lived at the Long Meadow. Once, during the time while Joseph Parsons lived there, he told me that wherever he laid the key, his wife could find it. She would go out in the night and that when she went out, a woman went out with her and came in with her. Says Joseph Parsons to me, 'God preserves her with His Angels.' Furthermore, George Colton told me that he followed Mary Parsons in her fits. He said he followed her through the water where he was up to the knees and she was not wet. This thing I told to Old Mr. Pynchon when he was here. He wondered at it, but said he could not tell what to say."

I thought it not right that Mr. Holyoke would let Goodman Branch speak about what Mr. Pynchon might have said, because he was not here to confirm that it was so. This was not supposed to be a witch trial of me, but it was turning that way. I sat on and listened, it was all I could do. The trial became a pouring out of slander, unchecked by law or reason.

Lies and truth all melded into one as the words of those who rose against me to speak that day were scratched upon the paper. The ink looked dark and dangerous. The impersonal hand that held the quill dipped the tip into the inkwell. Thin curlicues of accusation against me filled page upon page. My thoughts about my own life and everything I believed in did not seem to be as real or tangible as those deepening stains written about me on the paper. I despaired at the nature of people.

My brother-in law, Benjamin, made a very convincing statement that he had seen signs of mental unsoundness in me. He said, "My sister Parsons had fits like the Moxon children. She would sometimes tear her clothes, beat herself on ye breast, and beat those that held her so strongly that we could hardly hold her. Sometimes in her fits she would run away, and sometimes she would fall down like one dead."

George Colton testified his agreement that I "was seen to act very strangely, in the same way as the children of Mr. Moxon, whom I verily believe were possessed with the Devil." Then, while still under oath, Colton changed the story he had been telling everyone and denied that he had ever told Goodman Branch that he followed me through the water!

Sarah Bridgman must have been thinking that the proceedings were going well in her favor. Twice during the proceedings, she asked that the matter be left to referees rather than to continue the case. Both times Joseph and I refused. I answered each time, "What ye court would give, I will hold to."

The sitting of the court in Springfield ended with Mr. Holyoke stating that he would take some time to consider what he had heard before giving his opinion about the evidence to the Magistrate, Mr. Burt.

On August 15, the Commissioners of Northampton called for another hearing on new matters that had been made aware to them. This hearing turned out to be a complaint against Sarah Bridgman. The Commissioners wanted to record that they had desired to speak with the Bridgman boy about his injured knee, and that Sarah had refused to let him come before them.

I went to the meetinghouse in Northampton on August 16 to hear my friend Anne Bartlett testify. As I walked to the meetinghouse, I encountered people streaming up the rise towards the door of the building. I gave no opening for exchange of pleasantries. I acknowledged people with a nod only as I saw fit. I sat at my bench straight away and waited for the proceedings to begin.

Anne was rigid faced and poker straight as she gave her oath before the Commissioners. The Commissioners asked Anne about her knowledge of the nature of the illness that had overtaken the Bridgman infant. Speaking of it seemed painful to Anne.

"The child of Sarah Bridgman, when she last lay in, was sick as soon as it was born, in so much that it did groan something much. When I went to Sarah to inquire how her child did, she told me that her child had the looseness still which it had at the first. She told me that she feared if it continued it would be the death of her child."

Sarah Bridgman could be heard sniffling and swallowing tears. Two more Northampton women who had helped Sarah Bridgman with her baby testified that the infant had come into the world too weak and sickly to live on its own. Despite my problems with the child's mother, I could not help but be gripped by the sadness of her baby's short and failed struggle for life. It was a sorrowful thing, but no one gave evidence of any malicious force at work in the baby's death. Any sympathy I might have had for Sarah was extinguished by the next testimony.

William Houlton was called up. He was asked what if anything Sarah Bridgman had told him regarding my relationship to the child's death. He said, "Sarah Bridgman told me she had such jealousies and suspicion of Mary Parsons that she could not be satisfied unless Mary were searched three times for signs of the witch's teats."

The list of names of people willing to speak for and against me only continued to grow. As many as three men testified on oath about William Hannum's cow that had dropped dead in the yard after he had words with me about his wife's shorting me on the yarn she had spun. In their opinion, the cow died of natural causes.

The Commissioners next wanted hear more about the death of William Hannum's formerly lusty ox. Speaking to that were three more men. Each stated that they were present when the ox of William Hannum was stung by the rattlesnake. Each man avowed that they did not notice anything "but what might come to pass in an ordinary way."

By way of new evidence regarding the nature of the Hannum's claims against me, both my brother John and my Mother rose when called to make their oath that William Hannum and his wife had come to each of them on the twelfth of August last to say that they "had nothing against Mary Parsons."

Most amazingly, when Goodman and Goody Hannum were called up again by the Commissioners to see how they answered to this testimony, they each admitted, "James Bridgman hired us to go down to Springfield to give our testimony against Mary Parsons. Otherwise we would not have gone, but he is very important with us."

Joseph nudged me with his elbow. On the other side of me, Mother squeezed my hand. Both kept their eyes on the Commissioners faces. It was difficult to contain myself from uttering a telltale sound. I was consumed with wonderment about whether the Hannums were experiencing sudden "lusty" remorse or "ordinary" convenient remorse?

On September 19, one testimony was given before John Pynchon at Springfield. I did not go. Simon Beamon testified about the time I had the fit in church and he had carried me home. His story was well known and I did not see how it shed any light on whether I should be slandered as a witch.

On September 27, John Pynchon heard two testimonies at Springfield. Neither Joseph nor I went. Had we traveled back and forth to every proceeding, it would have been at the expense of everything else in our lives. Mother was there and told us later what happened. She said John Matthews, the barrel-maker, was brought in to tell what he had seen at the time when Joseph had locked me in the cellar. He testified that I had confided in him that spirits were troubling me. Richard Sykes told yet another fit story about me. Goodman Sykes told about a time I had run into the meadow and fallen down. He and George Colton had carried me home. He said, "We brought her in and laid her on ye bed and she would look fearfully sometimes as if she saw something, and then bow down her head as others did on their fits about that time."

The trial Joseph brought against Sarah Bridgman dragged on through September 30. John Pynchon himself made the final statement that day. He rose to speak before the few stalwart souls who still assembled to witness all the testimonies over this many weeks. John Pynchon testified on oath that he had never said that I "could not be right." I felt good about him denying that he had made a statement that had so severely damaged my trust in him.

Finally, all the testimonies had been heard in Northampton and in Springfield, in all the places where the parties involved lived. The sum of evidence was to be presented to the Magistrate of the Court of Springfield. Nothing more would be heard for weeks until the matter was deliberated by the Henry Burt, Magistrate at Springfield.

Waiting was unpleasant. It was as if there was the stink of a hidden dead mouse surrounding my life. I could only wait for the rot to go away. There was nothing more that could be done but to pass each day wondering when the decision would be made about the disposition of the slander trial. I wanted to feel clean, for all things around me to be wholesome and simple. The trial had come to be more about me than about my being wronged by slander. It felt as if nearly everyone around me held an opinion about my reputation. Fifteen of my neighbors had testified in the trial. Seven families from Springfield had seen fit to involve themselves. Twenty-four people in all had spoken before the commissioners. Thirteen had risen to stand for me, and eleven against me. Five of those for Goody Bridgman later regretted their testimony and rose to recant. In the end, there were eighteen supporting me, and five supporting her. If numbers could be trusted, my redemption before the community would come at last, if there were any fairness in the world.

On Sept. 9, 1656, Joseph rushed into the house, saying that he had just been told that there was a new posting on the meetinghouse having to do with the trial. Together we went to see it. An official paper was flapping in the light breeze. Joseph put his hand on it to hold it down as he read it to me.

> To the Constable of Northampton,
> By virtue hereof, you are required to attach the body of Sarah Bridgman, wife of James Bridgman of Northampton and to take Bond of her to the value of an 100 pounds with sufficient surety or sureties for her personall appearance at the next County Court held at Cambridge on the 7th of October next ensuing the date here of, then and there to answer at the complaint of Joseph Parsons for Slandering his wife Mary Parsons and to make a true return there of under your hand. Hereof fail you not.
> Springfield, this 8 of September, 1656, by the Court, Henry Burt

Turning to me, Joseph said, with firmness, "We are vindicated. You can put all this behind you. Sarah Bridgman will be arrested, unless she gives bond. She will go on trial now for wrongs she has done against you."

Joseph thought his case against her would go better if I did not go to the court at Cambridge. He said, "If you go, the judges will be distracted by the rumors of witchcraft about you, which will take away the focus on the crime of slander by Goody Bridgman. When any man brings charges against a woman, it makes a woman look bad. The judges are more likely to sympathize with me, a freeman like them, but not so much if they have to deal with a woman, if you were to stand by my side."

Of course, Joseph was right about the politics of women appearing at court. I would have liked to go with Joseph to witness when Goody Bridgman received justice for what she had done to me, but I did not go to Cambridge. In the end, neither did Goody Bridgman. The Constable, Alexander Edward filed a response to the Warrant with the court stating that he had committed Sarah Bridgman to safe custody in Northampton, "she being weak and with child, is not able to appear at this court without hazard to her life." Neither she nor I would be present to witness the trial against her for what she had done.

As I waited for the last court proceedings, I sat at my spinning wheel and occupied my time by spinning my own yarn. The fibers passed through my fingers pleasantly, soothing me with the notion that here was one place where everything was controllable and right. The General Court had ordered all women, girls and boys not otherwise occupied to spin as a remedy to the great lack of clothing in the colony. Under the law, each family was enjoined to assign one or more spinners to spin 3 pounds per week of cotton, wooling, flax, or hemp for thirty weeks a year. The Selectmen of each town were to fine any family that fell short. I found that spinning under edict of the law somehow satisfied a desperate urgency to prove my correctness. I could have assigned my girls to the task, or hired someone. After all that had happened, I preferred to do it myself.

On October 7, 1656, the final decision was made in Cambridge. When Joseph returned to report what had occurred, the verdict was already posted at the meetinghouse.

> *The court having read the attachments and perused the evidences respectively presented on both sides which are on file with the records of this court do find that the defendant hath without just ground raised a great scandal and reproach upon the plaintiff's wife: and do therefore order that the defendant shall make acknowledgment before the inhabitants of the place where the said parties dwell; viz. Northampton and also at Springfield at some public meeting at each place by*

order of Mr. Pynchon or Mr. Holyoke or either of then and in such words and manner as shall be suitable satisfaction for such an offence and the same to be testified under the hands of the said Mr. Pynchon and Mr. Holyoke, within 60 days next ensuing, and in case of default having notice of the time at each place the said defendant viz. James Bridgman shall pay damages to the plaintiff ten pounds sterling: Also this court doth order that the defendant shall pay to the plaintiff his cost of court viz. seven pounds one shilling and eight pence. Oct. 7. 1656.

Joseph said that on the way back to Northampton from Boston, he had been thinking. At the risk of appearing vindictive and further dividing the sentiments of the community, he had decided that it would be better not to go to Mr. Pynchon or Mr. Holyoke to demand the damages owed him from the Bridgmans. Neither did he think that we should prompt Goody Bridgman to make a public apology if she did not do so herself. We knew that her pregnancy, which had kept her from being presented at court, had failed. We agreed it would not be well for us to break her back with the consequences of the verdict. All I wanted was the gossip to stop.

That evening I walked alone and climbed the hill over the town to look down upon the meadow and all its inhabitants. In many of the houses, there were those who despised me. I remembered when the land was just being opened, when settlers and Indians alike responded to a new spring's warmth by preparing gardens in the rich soil. We had so much hope then.

I cried out unexpectedly in sorrow. I waited to be truly visited by Your mercy, to feel lightened in my spirit. I did not feel it. I wanted the first colors of fall that faintly lit the trees in advance of the coming brilliant yellows, oranges, reds, and russets, to be a sign of Your Grace. I did not see it. I wanted to shout out my mother's words, "The Holy Spirit illumines the heart," but I could not. Instead, I noticed that across the valley, the hills were rimmed in shadow. I saw beauty but no promise for peace. I felt grieved in a way that could not be lifted. I raised the prayer of a woman waiting in pain.

For I have heard the slander of many. Fear was on every side: while they took counsel together against me, they devised to take away my life. But I trusted in Thee, O Lord: I said You art my God. My times are in Thy hand: deliver me from the hand of mine enemies, and from them that persecute me. Make Thy face to shine upon Thy servant; save me for Thy mercies' sake. Psalm 31:14-17

Chapter 26

How Many Are the Days of Your Servant?

Northampton to Boston, 1656-1673

How many are the days of they servant?
When wilt You execute judgment on them that persecute me.
Psalm 119:84.

After the slander trial, I continued to look for the way to Your grace. It began to seem to me that whenever I asked for a sign to show the way to Your mercy, You would remember me by providing another son. Your answers were often so mysterious, the meanings difficult to understand.

Children continued to come to us, not always with ease. Our sixth son, Jonathan, was born to us June 1657. I came to understand that I had been with child when I stood upon the hillside waiting to be lightened by Your hand.

Barely ten months after Jonathan, a surprise baby came; one that I had only just begun to suspect was growing within me. The tiny boy slipped into the world with hardly a signal that his time had come. He was in my arms before the midwife could be summoned. We called the frail babe David, after the King and poet of the psalms, hoping a mighty name would help him grow. Thereafter, You opened Your hand to me gently, with girls. I was delivered of a healthy daughter, Mary, born in June of 1661. Hannah came in Aug of 1663, Abigail in Sept. of 1666. We lost twins on the same day they were born, a boy and a girl. We named them, Esther and Benjamin, and then buried them in sorrow. In December of 1672, a child of our late age was delivered—a girl, Hester. I bore thirteen children and raised nine. Children filled my life.

I deliberately stayed out of town doings. Joseph continued to have his hand in everything. I knew from what he told me that the town remained divided by the rifts created when I was slandered. Nearly everyone had taken sides. Joseph said that, consequently, every decision that had to be made was colored by feelings between neighbors and friends.

Not even division and quarreling could stop my Joseph. Through all the trouble, Joseph held on to his status as a man of good standing. One night he came home from attending a Selectman's meeting to tell me he had been appointed Clerk of the Train Band. As the Clerk of the Band, he would keep the records of the town militia. He was to list the men who assembled at muster as well as those who failed to report, to inspect that each man supplied his own required arms and ammunition, and to record and report any defects to the court. The town militia in Northampton was so small that there were no commissioned officers. The Clerk of the Train Band was the only man serving upon the authority of the court. Joseph was pleased with this position.

"On the training field, men are expected to be disciplined. I can abide by that much better than I can with what is happening elsewhere, at meetings."

Town Meeting elected Joseph to the office of Selectman in March of 1659. He felt it his duty to serve, even though, at the time, he was trading strongly in beaver pelts and other goods with Mr. Pynchon of Springfield, and with John Webb of Northampton. Also, he and William Clarke, Alexander Edwards, and Samuel Wright Senior had begun planning together to build a gristmill on a piece of land the town let them use for that purpose. It was located along the north side of the small river that ran through town. The town had a great need for a way to grind our corn. Because the nearest gristmill was in Springfield, most grinding of the grist was done in each home, a hard and laborious chore. Building a mill required men who knew the trade. Joseph hired an experienced millwright to oversee the project.

After two years in construction, every woman who ever ground corn rejoiced when the new dam at the mill site began to hold water. Next to the dam, the millwright and his men dug a narrow chute designed to squeeze the slowly meandering stream into a powerful surge. Its walls were straight and tall, built of heavy stacked boulders. A large waterwheel was set in place. When it became known that the corn mill was ready to run, almost the entire town gathered to watch. I brought the children. The millwright and his men checked the waterwheel. Once they were satisfied that the waterwheel spun on its axle without wobble, they began discussing raising the boards that blocked the chute. The men assembled at the top of the dam. Carefully they lifted up the topmost board. Water poured out of the pond into the chute with a roar. As it spilled over the paddles of the waterwheel, the waterwheel began to turn. A cheer went up. Children ran up and down the bank laughing in the excitement. Leather belts attached to the axle of the waterwheel began straining against wood. Gears began to engage. A low steady rumble told us that the heavy grinding stones were gnashing against each other. We saw Robert Hayward, our first miller, grinning at us through the doorway of the new mill. That day, corn was ground to satisfactory grist. Everyone there took some home. Over the following days, the smell of cooked corn rose across the town.

As one of the owners of the gristmill, Joseph commented proudly on the sweet aroma. "That must be the smell of a secular communion," he laughed, "because the love of food is the only thing we can all agree upon to share."

Within a few years, Joseph grew frustrated with the mill because it was not always reliable. Weather affected its running too much. In dry seasons, there was not enough water fall to run the wheel. Other times there was too much water. After large rainstorms, or in the spring when the river was in freshet, the current endangered the waterwheel. Joseph sold his share of the partnership in the mill for a good profit.

It was no surprise to me when Joseph announced that he had been granted the town license to keep a tavern, to sell wines and strong liquors. It was 1661. Joseph had long planned to own this business. Once he had the sole proprietorship for the town ordinary, he ran it out of the portion of the house he had built for just that purpose. From the first, I never liked this business. The temptations caused by strong drink made it difficult to maintain the good rule of order that was required to maintain the license. Often times there were loud voices that I could hear through the walls and laugher into the night.

In March of 1664, Hannah Roote and Goodwife Salmon took my Joseph to court. They accused him of treating them with lascivious carriage. The court admonished Joseph but he was not fined. The incident did not take place at the tavern, but I believe that the tavern was the cause of my husband's lapse in good judgment in his speech towards them. Joseph disagreed. He felt that the women deserved to be reprimanded for what they had said to him.

I could not help saying, "I am surprised at you, Husband, for acting in such a way. You preach the merits of a restrained tongue. Most think of you as a man of humor. It would have been more like you to make jest of those two."

Joseph responded, "I did make jest of them, and they took offense. You know I have no use for women who create tumult. Those women attempted to influence me in a way I found disagreeable and disrespectful. I reproached them, as any reasonable man would. The court has treated the matter as trivial. Wife, I would suggest that you do the same. Do not cast your questioning eye upon me for this."

Lord, such are the ways of men. In September of that same year, Joseph and Robert Bartlett got into such a serious fight that they each were called before the court. The fight was over taxes. Goodman Bartlett, in his service as the Town Constable, had come to Joseph to collect taxes for the town. He and Joseph got into an argument over the rate. Bartlett tried to take away Joseph's oxen and a sack of grain to pay the levy. Joseph resisted, and both ended up giving each other a good bloodying. Joseph and Robert were both fined for the complaints against them—Joseph for opposing and resisting the Constable. Joseph apologized to the court, and managed to get his fine abated.

I thought Joseph was right for resisting unfair taxes. My father had done the same. Also, this was not the first time Bartlett had been complained of for being unduly physical with people. He had used a stick against Thomas Roote's wife, and he had pushed himself upon a young woman when he went to help her with her sheep in the swamp. He had been excommunicated from the church but then he was reinstated. We drew apart from the Bartletts after what happened, although Joseph and Bartlett continued to work together on town business.

The license to keep the tavern was eventually turned over to Henry Woodward in 1665. I was most grateful. Joseph formerly been active in building the church and settling in the new minister. He now recommitted himself to church activities. He saw to it that our younger children; Samuel, Ebenezer, Jonathan, David, Mary, Hannah and Abigail were baptized. Joseph Jr., John, and I attended church but we were not baptized. I did not become a member. It was probably understood by everyone that, although my husband's presence was greatly appreciated, mine was much less so. It is true that the new minister, The Reverend Eleazer Mather, tempered the mood of the congregation by encouraging repentance and the seeking of forgiveness. I listened to his sermons as carefully as anyone did. I thought that The Holy Spirit still had many souls to move if penitence were ever to pervade this meadow.

A time of great peace came upon us. At the October 7 session of the General Court in 1668, Joseph was appointed Coronet of the Troop of Horses of Hampshire County. Of all Joseph's accomplishments in Northampton, this was the one of which he was most proud. As second officer under the command of his friend, Major John Pynchon, his new duty was to serve as color-bearer for the militia. I went to the training field to watch the men parading and training. Joseph was mounted on his best horse, carrying the flag of his troop ahead of Major Pynchon. Joseph was in his glory. Standing alone under the trees, I remembered what had happened to my father's best horses. I reminded myself of the necessity to live in caution.

Years passed. In 1674, with the full flush of the August summer sun upon us, I had no inkling of danger. There were beans and corn to pick in the gardens. Days were long and productive, the nights warm and soft. We had lost our son David, but all our surviving children were thriving. My husband was successful at everything he did. We had never been more comfortable.

When I heard that Mary Bridgman Bartlett had died suddenly, I only thought of the condolences I should offer to her family. The gossip that she might have died of unnatural means caused me no alarm. I would have never thought that what happened next might have anything to do with me.

It was Joseph Jr., my oldest son, who came knocking to warn me of danger.

"Mother, they say it was you who killed Mary Bartlett."

I just stopped and stared at him, stunned with disbelief.

"Is it about being a witch?" I asked.

He did not answer me. He only nodded his head.

I tried to go back to my work. A sound of roaring wind filled my ears. I felt as if I might tip over. I watched my hands shucking the first ears of corn. Corn made sense. Shucking corn made sense. I went on doing what I had to do, as if the rhythm of my fingers could make things right. Slowly I had to accept what was. The madness around me had not gone away, not with work, not with prayer.

Within a few weeks, it became clear that there would be no end to the wild gossip. Samuel Bartlett, and his father-in-law, James Bridgman were certain that, by some supernatural means, I had snuffed out the life of their wife and daughter. They were also accusing John. They thought my son a witch.

At the end of September, Joseph took me to the Hampshire County Court at Springfield, where I presented myself before the Magistrates. Thinking that I would probably be called later, I wanted to come before the court in dignity. The Magistrates were respectful as they read the evidence they had been given against me. I did not let the words I heard circle in my head like vultures. I could not let the insanity of others cloud my reason. I was single minded about clearing myself. I willed it to be so. Lord, this is difficult to speak of to You. I do not like to recall it, but I must, or else You might not know how I held fast to You through this time.

It is inconsequential to my memory what the weather was like that day I went to court in Springfield. I do not remember what I wore. I kept my mind to You as I declared my innocence of such a hideous crime. The Magistrates considered my words and said that they must take up the matter for further discussion in November. They said they would call me "to make further answer." I was dismissed.

On our way back home, Joseph stopped the horse cart. I was listless, with no desire to move. He pulled me down from the cart. He led the horse to drink from a small stream that trickled into the river. He dipped a cloth into the water and gently wet my temples.

"Mary, they will not prevail. You must always look strong, even when no one can see you. If you look strong, you will feel strong. I will help you as I have before. You must never lose heart," he said firmly, "or they will have you."

"Yes, Coronet. You speak like a militiaman."

"I am a militiaman. I do it because I must, to protect my family. I speak as your husband."

He sat beside me and put his arm around me. I leaned my head against his chest and watched the broad river flow through the narrow place in the mountains. Northampton was miles away, upstream from the curving ox bow. I enjoyed the warm feeling of being beside Joseph, and sopped up all the sweetness of his embrace. That was the only time we ever made love outside in the daylight. It was quick, with our clothes on. We were laughing at ourselves.

The comforts a man can give are so immediately satisfying, but I knew that I could reveal my inner thoughts only to You. You accept my weakness and You have given me my strengths. There in my husband's arms, I resolved that You must be my sole confidant in the battle that lay before me.

I went home, went inside, closed the door, and waited. Joseph and my children let me remain there. I did not want to see anyone except my family. I trusted no one else. People had betrayed me, again.

The snows of winter came. Whiteness covered the ground deeply. I appreciated the cold, pure insulating distance between me and the grievous things that abounded within the minds of those who had set themselves to be my enemies.

On January 5, 1675, I appeared before the Magistrates of the Court. There was a long wait as the Magistrates reviewed the dispositions they had taken in November. Samuel Bartlett was present. He ignored me. Finally the Magistrate were ready. They called him first. He asked that he be allowed to speak away from my hearing. I was escorted out of the meetinghouse. When I was called back, I straightened my back and walked toward the Magistrates with as much dignity as I could possess. I did not wish to be caused to wear upon my face any look that might appear to show guilt or threat. The Magistrates read many and various charges of witchcraft against me and asked how I would answer.

To each accusation I answered, "I am innocent. I am clear of such a crime. The righteous God knows my innocence. To Him I leave my cause."

I was satisfied with how I addressed the Magistrates. Their faces gave no clues as to their thinking as they listened to me. I had every reason to hope in the rationality of these most respected men.

I was the last to be heard. The Magistrates rose and retired to some private place to confer. My family and I waited for them to return. After some time, a court official announced to all to be silent. The Magistrates filed back into the room. They first took up the charges against my son. The Magistrates declared that in the matter of the witchcraft charges against John Parsons, they found no weight in the evidence against him whereby he should be prosecuted on suspicion of witchcraft and they dismissed him from such charges. This was a huge relief, a good sign. My son was twenty years old, a man of whom I was very proud. This was a just verdict. I expected the same. Instead, the Magistrates of the Court of Hampshire County declared that the case before them against me was outside of their jurisdiction and belonged to the Court of Assistants in Boston.

In consideration of the lateness of the season, the remoteness of the court at Boston, and "the difficulties, if not the incapabilities of persons there to appear" the Magistrates went on to make it known that they would continue their duty of inquiry into the case. They paused, and then said that it was their intention to appoint a committee of soberized women to conduct a body search upon me to see whether any marks of witchcraft might appear, with instructions for the committee to report to the court with their findings. Joseph was ordered to pay bond for my appearance, if required, before the Governor or Magistrates or Court of Assistants. What Sarah Bridgman had wanted so long ago came out of the past and was enacted, the indignity of a search of my naked body for marks of the Devil.

This, Lord, is how I came to be presented at the Court of Assistants in Boston, and how I came to be indicted for witchcraft by the grand jury. We had to travel all the way to Boston in early March to appear before the court.

I never expected to be taken directly from court to jail. Three months I have waited in the dark, fighting to preserve my mind against wickedness. How it will end, I do not know. Only You know my fate.

I have passed these ten weeks of my life in the darkness. I know the answer to the question I once wished to ask my father when we were ten weeks aboard the ship. I had wondered if the terrible crossing was like being in jail. Now I know the difference. When I was confined in the hold of that miserable ship, winds of hope filled the sails and pushed us toward an imagined paradise. The ministers prayed over us as saints, preparing us for delivery to our divine destiny. Here there is no ministry of mercy, only the rigors of judgment. If judged a witch, I will be hung by the neck from the gallows with a bag over my head. The congregants of the churches will gather to jeer and torment. The ministers will watch, summoning a lesson from my death to use in their next sermon. All the men who govern the colony under the eye of the pulpit will take credit for their vigilance and good works in protecting their communities from the likes of me. I have no anger towards any of them or anyone any more.

I am ready to face Your verdict. I am not ready to die, but if that is to be Your judgment, I will accept it. I have known love. That love fills me; it is all that matters. I think of my father and mother, my brothers and sisters, of my husband Joseph, and my children. Here in the darkness, I have offered the measure of my days to You. I have been caused to see a beauty in living that I did not recognize before. I am humbled by how much has been given to me.

I know what I am to do when I appear before the court. I am to find my family and friends with my eyes and let them see by my attitude that their love has been enough to sustain me. I am to pay attention to their love only, and turn a deaf ear to accusations. Their love must be all that matters today. I must stand quietly, surrounded and in awe of their fidelity. I know this is Your will, Your blessing. You revealed this to me in a moment last night. I have at last felt the Holy Spirit illumine my heart. Such peace came over me upon this realization. It has taken a lot for me to learn how to listen. I wish that I could tell my Mother.

I have completed my last prayer and am ready for judgment. This is May 13, 1675. The court is to convene at 10:00 o'clock. I have no idea what time it is, but the jailers have warned me to get ready, that soon the officers of the court will come for me. Joseph prevailed upon my jailors to move me to this private cell. A bucket of cold water was brought for me to wash my face and body. As much as possible, I have tried to remove the foul smell of prison from my person. I know a strong odor must still cling to me. I hope that the jury and the judges will not detect the smell of grief and remorse that fills this place. I am grateful that fresh straw that has been spread around me. Standing in the center of it, I am able to keep my shoes clean. I had forgotten that I owned these shoes. They used to be a little tight, but I must have lost weight because now they are loose. I will have to be careful not to trip when I walk into court. At least I have a fresh cap to cover my stiff and grimy hair. All my clothing feels clean. I cannot see what colors my skirt and bodice might be. I trust that my mother carefully chose the clothes that were brought to me by Joseph, my husband.

I hear footsteps. The men are coming to take me. There is the clink of the key in the lock. The heavy door groans and opens. A shaft of light overspreads me. A man says my name. Lord, preserve my soul and grant me mercy. I go to judgment.

Chapter 27

The Seeds of Eighteen Years

Boston, May 14, 1675

I rouse in a soft bed, which confuses me. Fully awake with a start, I find myself floating upon the softness of a perfumed mattress. Sunshine plays across my body. I realize that the trial is finished. I am safe.

Yesterday I stood alone before the Judges of the Court to defend myself against the charges of witchcraft. For all those months in jail I had prepared myself for what I would say when the time came. When my name was called, I rose. I took my vow to speak honestly, and then I simply pleaded innocent. An imposing line of gentlemen sat above me to hear the case. They were the men representing the interests of the church and of the government: the Governor, the Deputy Governor, and a dozen Magistrates, including John Pynchon himself. They had selected twelve ordinary men to fill the benches of the jury. It was to the men of the jury to whom I directed my statement of innocence.

Unlike Anne Hutchinson, who had spoken with futile eloquence before the ministers and judges, my words were few. I said much the same to that jury of twelve men as I had said before to the Court at Springfield. I knew my strength lay in humility and obedience to You. I willed the part of myself that had become Godded to draw close under Your wing. I vowed in faith that "What ye court would give me I would stand to." I wonder if Major John Pynchon, who also sat on the first case as a Magistrate, remembered my having said those words before.

In the end, after all the waiting, the charges against me were read one more time. Then I heard the judges dismiss me of any crime. The words were no sooner said than Joseph took me by the arm, led me through all the people, out of the building, and into his carriage. It all suddenly happened very fast, it seemed to me.

That was yesterday. This morning I am as safe under my husband's roof as a woman can be. This morning is an ordinary morning like most people would have. The ordinariness of it is astonishing and frightening, because at the corners of my thoughts are the faces of women still jailed, waiting and fearing the judgments against them, as I did.

I have just woken from having an odd and terrible dream. It was about a dangerous garden. Bad weeds were erupting between vegetables and flowers, turning orderly rows into thickets of thorns and twisting vines. Choking clouds of seeds spewed forth, blinding my eyes with tears. Seeds blew into the faces of my children, and they recoiled. Joey and precious Benjamin, who died in his crib; and John, and Samuel were being pelted with seeds that sprouted as soon as they are touched. Too exposed to save themselves, they tried to protect their brothers, Ebenezer and Jonathan. I heard David, who died young, crying but I could not help him. The seeds grew madly into an entangling wild ground vine that spread poison ivy-like leaves, reaching towards my eighth, a girl named Mary; then to Hannah and Abigail. The twins, a boy, and a girl: Esther and Benjamin, who died as they were being born, were being entwined by the mass of greenery. I ran with my thirteenth child, baby Hester, probably my last, in my arms. I woke from the dream believing I was running, running as I have so many times in my fits. Something I could not see was pursuing me in the garden. There was no escape. The seeds were growing too fast among the children. Joseph was there, but he could not stop the seeds as they burst. Weeds of dreaming tangle in my mind. It was just a bad dream, another bad dream. It was about the children. It was always about the children. I was the Eve in the garden, tainted by the terrible sin of being a woman, a spreading sin that reached for the children to infect them with its venom. My boys do not know yet that one day they will be given the respect granted to free men. My girls do not know yet that they must become silenced women.

Looking at my hand lying on the pillow, I see it is so clean. The dirt of the jail that filled my nails, my skin, my hair, has been washed away. Last night my daughters laughed as they soaked me in a tub of hot soapy water. They made bubble crowns in my hair. Only yesterday I was in the courtroom hearing all the same old testimony against me again; the stories of the fits, the running, the falling down. The strangeness that people saw in me years ago was all told again, as if to prove that the unusual death of my neighbor was because of the uncanny signs of the Devil that my accusers say they see in me to this day.

The Devil has never gotten me. His devious fingers may have tried to reach out to touch me. It does not matter now. I have done the best I can. I have survived. Here am I. Hah! Here I am.

My family is letting me sleep in. My toes stroke the soft sheets. I remain quiet. I do not want to let anyone know that I am awake. I struggle to enter this new day. I am not the woman I once thought I was. When I rise, I will go to my youngest child and hold her close. What I should do next will be made plain.

No one is likely to disturb my rest for a while. My husband is out, I remember. Joseph said that today he would be closing the deal on a large warehouse at the Boston wharf. He also told me he intends to speak to Mr. Pynchon about my acquittal and the filing of the records of the court. It upsets Joseph that testimony from the slander trial against Goody Bridgman so many years ago was brought out and heard again at my trial. Given that Goody Bridgman was found guilty of slander, he feels that all her testimony and that of all her supporters should have been considered slanderous forever more. Joseph told me that it is his intention to do something finally about the court records before another day goes by.

I think that I should feel happy. In a way, I am sad. I am sad for the family of the woman I stood accused of killing. Poor unfortunate Mary Bridgman Bartlett was only twenty-two when she died. She was the little daughter Sarah Bridgman said supposedly beheld me as a mysterious women in white, the bringer of the curse of death upon the Bridgman's infant boy. Sarah's Mary was a pretty little girl. Two sisters who had been born after her had died as babies, but she grew up and married Samuel Bartlett, the son of Robert and Anne Bartlett, our dear friends. It should have been good, but they were married for only two years before she was so suddenly taken. It is heartbreaking to me that, in his grief, Samuel turned on me as the cause. It is as if Sarah Bridgman's long dead finger still points at me from the grave, accusing me for the deaths of four of her children.

Joseph and I had watched Samuel grow up. He sat at our table many times, almost as one of our own. It hurt me to see him standing with his father-in-law as my primary accuser. What stories they must have told him to make him believe me capable of wanting his delicate bride dead. In the end, I know that the Bridgman and the Bartlett families left the court believing that Mary Bridgman Bartlett's death remained unrevenged. My acquittal by the Court of Assistants at Boston for witchcraft does not mean that suspicions about me have been discharged; only the case has been discharged. When the Bridgmans and the Bartletts go home, nothing will have changed. I am sad for them, and sad for my family. I am innocent, but I have not been redeemed. The trial is over, but the lingering taste of bitterness remains in my mouth. My family will return to their lives with no assurity of relief. They have seen, heard, and witnessed everything that has caused my life to be what it is.

I think of my dreams. Faces of women come to mind. I wonder if it was the dreams that come after babies are born that drove the other Mary Parsons, the witch at Springfield, to kill her infant. I wonder if it was dreams that drove Sarah Bridgman to see demons as her babies withered away and died. How alike to them am I?

It is time to put all that behind me. All the accusations against me are just writings upon paper. Paper is fragile. If it falls to the ground, it melts away. Paper is weak. I am strong.

I will lie here a little longer, in this clean, soft bed with its thin white surrounding drapes filtering the sun and protecting me from the day. Joseph has put a vase full of yellow daffodils on the table beside my bed. The fragrance of the flowers caresses me with their triumphant scent. Finally. As I gaze at the blossoms, they seem to transform into butterflies rising.

Chapter 28

The Compass

Springfield, MA, Late Summer, 1711

It is a long time since the days in Northampton and Boston. My husband and I gave up trying to create an earthly paradise, and moved back to Springfield. We made a good home here, then my Joseph died. Among his things I found the small fur that he had held out to me when we first met. All these years he had saved it, unbeknown to me. I still stroke it and remember the thrill of feeling the warmth of the cup of his hand beneath it. I know he cared for me. A year after Joseph went, my ancient mother followed him. It seems like yesterday. I am alone in this house now. It is my choice.

My sons insist that I should let family live here in this house, but I will not have it. I have a hired girl who comes and helps, that is enough. I cannot think of her name. Toby, her name is Toby. She is good except that she puts my things away where I cannot find them. She is always losing my things. More and more I can never find anything. My children think that I am absent minded. They do not trust me to spend nights alone. That is really none of their business. In the past, it troubled them when I could not sleep through the night. These days I often get up in the night and walk around the house to ease my restless legs. When I can manage it, I go out to be in my garden. Being alone, I can finally do what I want without bothering anyone. I am happy here in Springfield in this old house. When I am by myself, I do not feel that much differently than when I was a girl. True, I have become slower, much slower, and I must always be mindful where I place my feet. My sense of balance is tenuous, but when I was a girl, the agility I had was restricted by so many worries. Now I care less what people think. I am much better at being an old woman than I ever was at being a girl. I am surprised at how old I have become.

I do nap a lot in the day. Often my children wake me. They have their own lives but they visit regularly. They flutter around me dutifully. They treat me as if I am a child. I hear them talking about me when they think I do not hear. They must think me deaf. I know they think my mind is going. They talk about what must be done to keep me safe. They discuss who should take me in. I find it very annoying for them to be making decisions about me, but I need my children and it is right that they should help their mother.

It is my great-grandchildren whom I enjoy completely. I do love to watch them. They change so fast that I am forever calling them by the wrong names. It is of no matter. They understand what I am saying. They forgive me everything. I tell them about their Great Great Grandmother, Margaret Bliss, who learned from her teacher, Anne Hutchinson, that You can fill hearts with grace, the boys the same as the girls. I now believe You love what You have made all the same. I try to teach my great-grandchildren to know what is kept secret, that "The Holy Spirit illumines the heart."

There has been one small twist. One of my granddaughters has recently married the grandson of James and Sarah Bridgman. I did not go to witness the event. I begged the frailties of an old woman. The bride brought her new husband to visit me later, which was only proper. Imagine, my own granddaughter, Mary, is betrothed by a Bridgman; and the boy's name is Ebenezer, just like my son who was killed by Indians. I have to think that there must be some symbol in this union, some sign to me, but I am past wondering what it might be. The marriage gives me a measure of satisfaction, I suppose.

This is my life. I have no wants. My family brings anything I need to me. I am relieved of having to go out into the community. I am not afraid but, for me, it is well to live quietly and privately, away from prying eyes. I just like to go into my garden. I am happy that my family supports me in this.

The other day I did make an exception. I made an exhilarating decision to change something that has bothered me for a long while. Certain of my conviction, I instructed Toby to bring the stonemason to the house. When he came to my door as bidden, I asked him for advice.

My problem had to do with the large stone step outside the front door, about which I have very strong feelings. The step is a constant reminder of my husband. When Joseph and I moved back to Springfield, one of the first things Joseph did was to have a large stone step laid before the front door of our new home. In all the years that we had lived in Springfield when we were young, we made do without a proper doorstep because of the scarcity of local rock. Joseph believed that a door stone marks a house as being respectable and solid, which is why he hired a man to go find a large flat stone, haul it here, and set in place. The stone the man brought was remarkably large and very flat across its top, although a bit rounded and irregular on the bottom. Joseph thought so much of that stone step that he had his man chisel a compass deeply into its surface. Despite its being a fine stone, it never settled properly. No matter how it was shimmed, it always tended to rock slightly. I told the stonemason that, on account of my age, I should not have to put up with the unsteadiness of the stone a day longer. After all, think how much easier it would be to walk to the garden if I did not have to worry about being tipped over by my own doorstone.

The stonemason agreed to reset the stone. The next day he came back with a young helper. They started to dig around the stone. It was not long before he asked to speak to me. He explained that there was a problem. The shape of the stone was such that it could not set squarely with the sill. He advised that the stone be turned a bit, although he warned that shifting the stone would change the directions of the compass. I studied the stone, pondering what to do. I did not need the stone for its dignity. I needed it to get out the door. In the end, I chose to have the stone made stable by whatever means the stonemason thought best. True to his word, once the stone was rotated, it was at last firm and solid under foot. We all stood on it together and the men twisted and jumped upon it to show me that it was unmovable. I was pleased with it and paid them well for the job. Before they left there was something the young helper said that hinted at a bit of unpleasantness. I decided to let it pass.

He looked at me with a frank and gap-toothed smile and said, "Goody Parsons, I have heard a lot about you, but I think you seem very nice."

I assume he meant to be polite but the words smacked of gossip that never dies. I looked into his eyes to find his meaning. I saw only ignorant innocence. I fixed him with a cautioning stare and admitted gruffly, "Not always am I."

The boy's face fell. His smile closed and the tip of his tongue darted out to lick his lips nervously. He stepped behind his employer, who was glaring at him. They quickly left with their pay. I stood upon the stone as I had a thousand times and let the satisfaction of it come up through my feet.

My sons disapprove of the shifted stone. They say that the compass being askew will annoy people. They insist that I have it put back the way their father had it. I will not. What makes my boys think that anyone looks to me to point out the way? Once I believed it was my duty to tell where the right path lay. If I have learned anything, it is that advice is mostly unwelcome. No, I do not offer directions unbidden.

The compass at my door, with its hands shifted, is for me. It serves as testimony that my life's travels are more than points to the north, south, east, or west. The old compass never pointed to where I long to be, which is right here. At night, standing on the cool stone, I feel Joseph again by my side. When I join my husband, which I believe will be soon, I will go towards You as I am. You wilt take care of my soul. My children will take care of my body. They already have my mind, whether or not they know it. One day they will redeem what I leave behind according to their own making. Perhaps they will repair what one woman alone could not. The beckoning glow of peace summons me to the arms of my love. The faint melody of a murmuring psalm drifts upward toward the high moon.

Beautiful!

The End

Historical Epilogue

As Mary waited in jail in the spring of 1675, the opening events of the King Phillip's War were unfolding. King Phillip was the chief sachem of the Wampanoag tribe, the head of a powerful nation that had joined with several other tribes, including the Nipmucks and Narragansetts, in resistance against the appetites and hostilities of the colonial expansion. By July of that year, the settlements at Dartmouth, Taunton, and Middleborough had been attacked, houses burned and settlers slain. The uprising would envelope New England in the fierce battle for competing interests for over three years. Every town in Hampshire County, with the exception of Hadley and Westfield, would be at least partially destroyed.

On September 2, 1675, militiaman Ebenezer, the Parson's first son born in Northampton, was killed at age twenty-one in battle with the Nipmucks and Wampanoags at Northfield. where he was serving as a militiaman. Among the seven others killed was his family friend, Samuel Wright. There were those who said that the death of Ebenezer was proof of God's desire to punish his mother.

Joseph Parsons held the "patent' on the development and settlement of Northfield at the time. Palisades were built around Northampton in the fall of 1675. On March 14 of 1776, the town was attacked in the night. The palisade walls were breached. Killed were Robert Bartlett, Thomas Holton, a young girl named Mary Earle, and two of the soldiers garrisoned there under Captain Turner. (Captain Turner would later become famous for the massacre at Turners Falls.) Robert Bartlett was buried in front of his door where he fell at the lower end of town at what is now Pleasant Street.

Joseph and Mary Parsons were living in Boston at the time of the attack upon Northampton. They would not return to Northampton until 1678. Shortly after their arrival, a Northampton neighbor, John Stebbins, an in-law of the Bridgemans and Bartletts, died mysteriously. Samuel Bartlett again accused Mary Parsons of witchcraft. For the second time, she presented herself at court in Boston. No action seems to have been taken.

It is no wonder that soon after, sometime around 1679 or 1680, Coronet Joseph Parsons and his wife left the homes they owned in Northampton and Boston to settle in Springfield. On Oct. 9, 1683, at the age of 65, Coronet Joseph Parsons died there. He left a remarkably large estate including extensive landholdings and businesses, the products of his lifetime as a clever and hard-working entrepreneur.

Mary Bliss Parsons survived her husband, Joseph, by almost nineteen years. Mary's mother, the remarkable Margaret Bliss, died in 1684. The shadow of witchcraft was never lifted from Mary Bliss Parsons during her lifetime. The Parsons family continued to endure unkind words and suspicions.

Long life was considered proof of God's favors in those days. It is therefore ironic that Mary Bliss Parsons died at an advanced age. Her exact age is unknown, but she was deeply into her eighties when she died at her home in Springfield on January 29, 1712 under the care of her family. Her two eldest sons, Captain Joseph Parsons Esq., and Captain John Parsons, were administering her property and finances at the time. Five of the 13 children she bore survived her: Joseph, John, Samuel, Hannah and Esther. She was probably buried alongside her husband and mother at the burying ground near the Connecticut River at the end of Elm Street in Springfield. A rail bed was laid through that cemetery in 1848. All the early settlers' graves that could be found were dug up and moved to the present Springfield Cemetery. The soils and remains were buried in a common grave near the entrance at Pine Street. Mary Bliss Parsons lies with her husband, her mother, and her contemporaries at that site, marked by a single stone.

> *The stories of the ancestors are handed down,*
> *polished in each retelling by the descendants.*
> *Fact and fiction whispers to the magic of our blood...*

Bibliography

Bliss, Aaron Tyler. *Genealogy of the Bliss Family in America.* Midland, Michigan, 1982.

Bradford, William. *Bradford's History of "Plimoth Plantation".* PDF version: http://tinyurl.com/km5r8mg

Burt, Henry M. *Cornet Joseph Parsons; One of the Founders of Springfield and Northampton, Massachusetts, (Springfield, 1636, Northampton, 1655). An Historical Sketch From Original Sources, Viz., Town, County, Court, and Private Records.* Garden City, Long Island, NY: Albert Ross Parsons, 1898.

Burt, Henry M. *The First Century in the History of Springfield: the Official Records from 1636 To 1736 with an Historical Review and Biographical Mention of the Founders by Biography of Margaret Bliss.* 531–532.

Clapp, Ebenezer, ed. *History of Dorchester.* Dorchester Antiquarian and Historical Society.

Colonial Records of Connecticut. 55:28. Connecticut State Library, Hartford.

Connecticut Colonial Probate Records III. County Court 1663-1677.

Connecticut Historical Society, *Collections,* 14:256-258. Hartford.

Cowing, C. B. *The Saving Remnant, Religion and the Settling of New England.* Urbana and Chicago: University of Illinois Press, 1995.

Crawford, D. *Four Women in a Violent Time.* New York: Crown Publishers, Inc., 1970.

Demos J. P. *Entertaining Satan, Witchcraft and the Culture of Early New England.* Oxford University Press,1982.

Encyclopedia Britannica. *The Annals of America.* Vol. I, Discovering a New World. Chicago, 1976, p. 157.

Essex County Court Papers: Original Depositions and Other Materials from the Proceedings of the Quarterly Courts of Essex County, MA. Essex County Court House, Salem.

Fischer, D. H. *Albion's Seed, Four British Folkways in America.* New York, Oxford: University Press, 1989.

Geneva Bible. 1560.

Greenfield, Moses. *The Book of Tehillim with English Translation,* copyright 1985.

Hodgson, Godfrey. *A Great and Godly Adventure.* Public Affairs: New York, 2006. http://mayflowerhistory.com/cooking.

Kamensky, J. *Governing the Tongue the Politics of Speech in Early New England.* New York, Oxford: Oxford University Press,1997.

Karlsen, C.F. *The Devil in the Shape of a Woman, Witchcraft in Colonial New England.* New York: Vintage Books, (1987).

Middlesex Court Files: Original Depositions and Other Materials from the Proceedings of The Quarterly Courts of Middlesex County, Mass. Middlesex County Courthouse, East Cambridge, Mass.

Morgan, E.S. *The Puritan Dilemma the Story of John Winthrop,* Boston. Toronto: Little, Brown and Company,1958.

Old Hampshire Co. Deeds, AB: 19-20. At Hamden County Registry of Deeds, Springfield, Mass.

Parsons, G. J. *The Parsons Family, Descendants of Coronet Joseph Parsons(c.1618-1683 Springfield, Mass., 1636; Northampton, Mass., 1654 Through His Grandson Jonathan Parsons (1693-1782 of Northampton, Mass.; Suffield, Conn.; Sandisfield, Mass.; and Dorset, Vermont.* Baltimore: Gateway Press, Inc. 1984.

Probate Records of Thomas Bliss, Volume 2, page 17, 28. FHL film 0004572.

Pynchon Account Books. Manuscript volume in the Judd Manuscripts at Forbes Library, Northampton.

Records of Massachusetts, vol. 4, part 1, p. 136. Retrieved from http://ccbit.cs.umass.edu/parsons/hnmockup/home.html

Records of the Particular Court of Connecticut, 1639-1663. Hartford, 1928. Reprint Bowie, Md., 1987.

Savage, J. A Genealogical Dictionary of the First settlers of New England, before 1692, Volume #1. http://puritanism.online.fr/puritanism/Savage/SavageVol1.txt

Talcott, M.K. *The Original Proprietors*, Hartford: From material published in 1886. Edited by Trumbull, J. H., The Society of the Descendants of the Founders of Hartford.

Trial transcripts at Springfield and Northampton retrieved from http://ccbit.cs.umass.edu/parsons/hnmockup/home.html

Trumbull, J. R. *History of Northampton Massachusetts from its Settlement in 1654*, Vol. 1. Northampton, MA: Press of Gazette Printing Company, 1898.

Wessels, T. *Reading the Forested Landscape, a Natural History of New England.* Etchings and illustrations by Cohen, B.D., Woodstock, Vermont: The Countryman Press, 1997.

Wright, Harry Andrew, protractor. 1940 *Map of Longmeadow: "Land Grants of 1645 in Longmeadow, Massachusetts, Being All of the First Grants There.* Springfield, Mass., 1997.

Descendants of Coronet Joseph and Mary Bliss Parsons

1) Mary Bliss1628 - 1711/12
+Joseph Parsons 1620 – 1683

2) John Parsons 1650 - 1728   2) Mary Parsons 1661 - 1711
+Sarah Clarke 1658/59 - 1735   + Joseph Ashley 1652 -1698

3) William Parsons 1690 – 1768   3) Mary Ashley 1692/93 - 1757
+Mary Ashley 1692/93 – 1757   +William Parsons 1690 – 1768

4) Samuel Parsons 1733 - 1812
+Lucy Pomeroy 1738/39 – 1782

5) Mary Parsons 1769 - 1826
+ Zephaniah Hull Judson 1770 – 1834

6) George Judson 1800 - 1868
+Anna Minerva Hurd 1817 – 1885

7) Fannie Amanda Judson 1862 - 1948
+Jacob Behe(e) 1838 – 1921

8) Elmer Judson Behee 1892 - 1939
+ Edna Viola Sullivan 1893 – 1974

9) Wells Elmer Behee 1925 - 2011
+ Mary Evelyn Newhall 1926 – 2011

10) Kathy-Ann Behee Becker 1950 -
+ Myron J. Becker 1944 –

CPSIA information can be obtained at www.ICGtesting.com
Printed in the USA
BVOW08s1044070515

399216BV00002B/554/P